THE
WILD
ONE

THE
WILD
ONE

A Novel

COLLEEN
McKEEGAN

HARPER

An Imprint of HarperCollinsPublishers

Library of Congress Cataloging-in-Publication Data has been applied for.

ISBN 978-0-06-306180-4

22 23 24 25 26   LSC   10 9 8 7 6 5 4 3 2 1

To Pat,

for being one of the good ones and helping me raise two more.

She felt as if a mist had been lifted from her eyes, enabling her to look upon and comprehend the significance of life, that monster made up of beauty and brutality.

—Kate Chopin, *The Awakening*

THE
WILD
ONE

NOW

. . .

The three of us hadn't been together, in real life, since that first summer. That was by design, at least on my part. I didn't want to talk about the thing that bonded us, the thing we swore as girls to never tell anyone. Not the police, who were happy enough to say it was the alcohol abuse that caused a seizure, which led to the fall, which led to his death. Not our family, or friends, or the expensive lawyers my parents hired to represent me and Catherine, or the one Meg's aunt hired to represent her. It was easy to write off a man like him, so everyone did. They weren't wrong, not exactly, but they missed a few key details. Namely the trigger, which Catherine took care of for me. We hardly knew Meg, and Catherine, after the way I treated her, should have prayed for my downfall. But we all played a part in what happened that summer, and so we shared the burden of silence. For years, the three of us were the only ones who knew that I'm the one who killed him. And now I'm back in the same woods where it began, once again helpless beneath towering oaks and elms and pines.

They whisper to each other like they, too, want to unleash the truth.

It was Meg's idea to meet here. She's still local, working as a waitress at the casino resort about twenty miles down the road. So much of this place is a wasteland, but the slots still draw a regular stream of tourists, and with them Meg's income. We talked on the phone last week, our first and only call, their voices at once strange and familiar, and she told us she needed the tips from her Saturday-brunch and Sunday-afternoon shifts to cover her rent. Catherine and I are both grad students, she in Boston and me in New York, so we agreed: we'd road-trip to the Poconos, to the place where he died. A funeral for our past, Meg said, her voice grainy on the other end of the line.

I wasn't really sure what to bring to a funeral that should have happened over a decade ago. I shoved a fifth of vodka and a few cans of Diet Coke inside my tote bag, in the likely case that things got awkward. When I dressed in the frigid air-conditioning of my bedroom that morning, a black sleeveless maxi dress seemed like an appropriate outfit choice, but I regret the decision as the sun bears down on the dark fabric. Sweat slides along my spine, pooling where my skin meets my underwear, a reminder that the shade in these particular woods offers no protection. I unfold the blanket I packed, the fleece one we huddled under as kids hours after we watched his head split open, the only thing I kept from that summer. Still glued to one corner, the faded tag reads *Amanda Brooks*. At the time, I convinced myself I kept the blanket because it was my mom's, a hand-me-down from her stint at camp. In this light, the early-June sky as merciless as it was in 2003, I worry it's a trophy, a twisted souvenir to always remind me of the evil that lurks beneath the neatly polished façade I've carefully built. I brought nothing else to sit on, though, so I toss the blanket messily against the forest floor, rocks and sticks poking their craggy shapes into my tailbone as I'm cross-legged and waiting. We'd kept our secret for more than ten years. Until I didn't—and I learned why we promised to never tell. One cryptic email later, our friendship, if you could call it that, was reignited.

My phone buzzes, another barrage of texts from Jackson.

can we talk?
why won't u just fuckin answer

I turn the screen dark. When I used to see his name plastered across my phone, my stomach would somersault. It reminded me of the comfortable weight of him, his arms wrapped around me, his fingers laced through mine. Flashes of our early days together. Memories I thought I'd never want to forget. Unlike the ones that happened in these woods. The ones I shared with him, breaking the pact I made with Catherine and Meg. Now his texts make me jump, each vibration a screaming warning to quiet the chaos I've unleashed, this flailing man desperate to keep what he views as his most prized possession. Me.

So that's why I'm here, hoping Catherine and Meg can once again help me clean up a mess of my own making. I spin the over-sized pearl on my left ear around in its piercing, a tic. I thought pearl earrings would give me a sense of control, the quiet reserve of a person who wears such preppy accessories. As the minutes click by, I grow increasingly unsure if Meg and Catherine will show, that this crazy reunion I triggered will actually happen. Our past binds us, a steel chain with no bolt to cut. Is that enough, or will the fear of our combined power, the dangerous force we can become when the ingredients are just right, keep them away?

I look up, amazed that the leafy rooftop isn't a permanent shade of crimson. But like my memories, blood fades with time.

— 2 —

THEN

· · ·

I was a few months past twelve when my parents shared the news that I would be spending eight weeks at a summer camp in middle-of-nowhere, Pennsylvania.

My mom had gone to Camp Catalpa when she was my age. Her eyes got dreamy when she told stories about her summers there: the open-air cabins, the overnight hikes, the color wars, the lasting friendships. Two glasses of wine deep, my dad would egg her on. "Tell us about the time you won the 'Best Camper' bowl," he said, his mouth twisted with mischief while pure joy filled my mom's face. She huffed in annoyance when, after a few breathless minutes retelling a story we had heard approximately one zillion times, she understood his tone as mocking. But she couldn't help it; she was totally and completely a camp person, that unique breed of human that's everywhere once you know the code words. They keep their love of camp a secret until some little anecdote makes its way into conversation—"When I was at summer camp," it begins, and their gaze is suddenly met with another knowing look: *You went to camp? Me too! Where did you go?* I get it: Who wouldn't want to reminisce for a moment that they're back living in the wildly freeing constraints of the woods with their whole future in front of them and not trudging through the gray, depressing fog that is adulthood? For these people, camp is a part of their identity: my mom spends her days glued to Excel spreadsheets, working with a numbing series of numbers, but she loves rainbow string friendship bracelets, prefers fresh over salt water, knows the words to an impressive number of campfire songs, and, if it weren't for her job, she'd love to move us to the woods of Pennsylvania, our days filled with hiking and canoeing and catching fireflies. She's a camp person—nostalgic, romantic, and peppy about the tritest of activities.

Back then, I was not a camp person. Or at least I didn't want to be. All I knew was the city; we lived in Manhattan my entire life, on the twenty-fourth floor in a gleaming Sutton Place apartment, on a block full of identical buildings. My wilderness was the perfectly manicured greens of Central Park. I was as confident roaming the city's sidewalks as any Outward Bound kid on a mountain. But the great outdoors? The great outdoors was *not* my friend. The summer when I was ten, my grandma rented a lake house on Lake Wallenpaupack in the Poconos. My mom planned a day hike for us at Promised Land State Park, where she sprinted up trails, dodging the rock formations in her way. I tripped over every bump imaginable, fresh stripes of red decorating each knee. And the bugs, oh my god. They were obsessed with me, gnawing at the places on my body that seemed inconvenient to scratch: the fleshy area between my foot and my ankle bone, behind my knees, right under my butt cheeks. By the end of the week, I looked like I had rolled in poison ivy. Plus I hated the lake water, discomforted by its murky depths and the patches of cold and warm, their proximity always jarring. My dad couldn't stop laughing. "Mandy bear," he said, "you're a Brooks, through and through." My dad got me. Born and raised in the city, he was equally confused by the allure of a summer filled with bad plumbing and mosquito bites. We had both shrugged off my mom's urging that I go to camp; my dad seemed bored by the conversation, pegging it as an exercise for adults who wanted a significant break from parenting. Until that summer, when he caved.

I knew why they wanted to send me away. Sixth grade had been harder than fifth. Pre-algebra hit me like a two-ton truck, causing me to question my intelligence as I pored over problem after problem, night after night. But the biggest blow was that my best friend, Grace Cunningham, had moved to California that fall. We were both cute enough to be popular, but the games required to maintain that sort of status didn't interest Grace, so they didn't interest me. Being around her, sharing her air, was seductively powerful, like I gained her confidence through osmosis. We had each other and that was enough. Until her dad got a job out west. I was suddenly without my sidekick, my safety blanket. I had to find new ways to survive middle school.

Rachel Robbins was our grade's queen bee, the type of girl who seemed to experience everything first: boyfriends, boobs, highlights, braceless teeth. She wasn't mean, per se, but she had a magnetism that drew people close, an ability to amass a legion of minions without ever giving a direct command. We all wanted her to like us, never fully understanding why. Even when Grace was still around, a small part of me wanted to be in Rachel's crew. Grace's friendship kept me from succumbing to that craving, but who knows how long I would have lasted, even if Grace hadn't moved away. I was on the cusp of being a teen and filled with a desire for more.

I was painfully lonely those early weeks after Grace left. Losing Grace felt like the end of the world, my first major heartbreak. Getting up in the morning seemed impossible, my mind fighting with my body to execute the simplest tasks. At school, I kept my head down. I went to class, ate lunch at the table where I used to sit with Grace, and politely smiled when teachers asked me how she was doing at her new school. That is, until Rachel decided to befriend me. In the years after, Rachel would randomly reminisce about plucking me from obscurity, anointing me into the cool crowd, how her only reason was that I seemed smart and pretty and boys liked me. That was it, she laughed, adding that we were so simple then, as if anything about the friendships of preteen girls is simple.

I was walking to school in a particularly sullen mood on a frigid January morning when Rachel swooped in. It had been ten days since Grace had answered my last email, her tendency to focus on the present, to pursue her happiness with single-minded obsession, already eclipsing our years of friendship. I was spiraling.

"Hey, Amanda," she said from behind, giving my backpack a little nudge. "It sucks Grace is gone, huh?"

She sounded genuine, her dark eyes sparkling against her wind-flushed skin. Rachel's voice was much deeper than most of the girls' in our class, mine included. I always loved when it was her turn to read aloud in English, the words of *A Wrinkle in Time* or *Little Women* a raspy vibration when they rolled off her tongue. I nodded. "Yeah. It sucks."

"I know you guys never liked me that much—"

"That's not true!" I interrupted. It was only once Grace moved that I realized we had given off an air of superiority. We had each other, and that was enough, and our self-sufficiency read as snobbishness. Without Grace, I was alone. I didn't know how to find a new friend group. I still sat at the lunch table she had picked for us last year with her basketball teammates. The other girls' obsession with athletics never really bothered me when Grace was around. She was fluent in their language and often translated for me. Sans Grace, I found them *so* boring, their interests beyond simplistic. All they did was talk about Teresa Weatherspoon and Becky Hammon. I knew the girls at Rachel's table talked about traveling abroad with their parents, weekend getaways in the Hudson Valley and the Hamptons, watching R-rated movies at one another's apartments. And boys. They actually talked to boys, and not just in a "Hi, how are you?" kind of way. But I was terrified of them—of Rachel, really—every interaction filled with land mines, so scared that whatever words left my mouth would be deemed hopelessly uncool. They were not a group you approached without an invitation.

"It's fine," Rachel said. "But you should sit at our lunch table. You'd like it, I swear." She smiled again, her shiny teeth and the offer behind them like a sip of ice water after a long run. Immediately, something clicked with us. I knew I would follow her, blindly so, which made it all the more entrancing when, with Rachel's blessing, I was quickly welcomed into her world: study sessions after school, sleepovers, brunch and Broadway shows with her family. I even invited Rachel and the Ashleys, Rachel's best friends since first grade, on a weekend trip to ski with me and my parents in Vermont. I loved the life so much, the activity and acceptance and feeling of floating on a sparkly unicorn throne, but instead of being happy, basking in this easily obtained popularity, I grew insecure, an underlying dread that this new world could vanish, leaving me once again alone. It was a toxic venom, seeping into every conversation with the girls as I said what they wanted to hear, only releasing at home, snapping at my parents when they asked me to do anything. Looking back, everything began when I joined that lunch table, the catalyst of a series of truly unfortunate events, choices, decisions. A push in a direction I never should have gone in.

It was tame enough until late April. Our crew had been squeezing ten to a lunch table, rather than the permitted eight. Sometimes we broke into two groups of five, a stressful dance that always made me sweat with anxiety. No one wanted to be at a table without Rachel, and she was getting impatient with the unfairness of our not being able to sit together. "Girls, you know you're breaking the rules," said Mrs. Kerry, the world's coldest lunch aide, warning us that detention was the next step. She'd check again in five minutes, she added.

"Hmm." Rachel surveyed the table, as if she were deciding who to kick out. Her eyes stalled on me, my body unsure if it was about to spew vomit or tears. Heart racing, my hands shaking under the table, I took a deep breath. Instead, she handed the decision to me. "What do you think, Amanda?"

Maybe it didn't register that I was safe, or that I was suddenly in the position of power, because I launched into the only defense that made sense to me in that moment—an unkind one. "I vote to kick out Haley and Brittany." My delivery was calm, despite my panic. There was still a nervousness that if I said the wrong thing, it would put a target on my back instead of others', and I'd be kicked out of the table, which would absolutely ruin an already terrible year. It couldn't—seriously couldn't—happen. And, honestly, I didn't care that much about Haley and Brittany. They rarely got invited to the other girls' birthday parties.

"Interesting." Rachel drummed her fingers on the table, looking at Haley, then Brittany. Both were pale, with wet eyes. "Why should I do that?" She had—still has—a knack for delegating confrontation.

"Brittany never shares her lunch, and Haley doesn't shave her legs." Again, the words came out so effortlessly they even took me by surprise. I had always thought Brittany was weirdly protective of her lunch, and the hair poking through Haley's school socks was disgusting. We had all talked about their quirks behind their backs. The other girls nodded their heads in agreement, a few with big eyes like they, too, couldn't believe I had actually shared these secret thoughts out loud. I rationalized that my comments weren't *that* bad. I was doing them a favor; sharing is one of the best parts of friendship, and if the hair on your legs poked through your school uniform's knee socks, you were asking to be a target. Buying a razor was *not* difficult.

Rachel looked impressed. She raised her eyebrows and gave me a smile. "You heard the lady," she said to Haley and Brittany. "You're cast from the island today. This whole lunch table rule is so lame. We'll figure out something tomorrow. But for today, maybe sit over there?" She pointed to a free table on the other side of the cafeteria. Haley and Brittany didn't fight back; they walked away, heads down. "Good choice, Brooks," Rachel said, her Cheshire smile wide. "I'm glad you didn't say we should split into five and five again. God, I would have freaked. You're so good at this stuff." Belonging is a powerful thing, its warm comfort stronger than any guilt. I smiled back.

Haley's mom called my mom that night. Haley had come home crying and named me the cause. I argued that it wasn't my fault, it was the system. I was merely a survivor of a structure that caused cliques, that didn't let us eat in harmony. My mom tried to force me to call Haley to apologize. "You can't just tell girls that their legs are hairy, honey. That isn't appropriate or nice behavior. Do you understand?" she asked, her patience thin. "But they are, Mom," I answered. "Why don't you call her mom and tell her to buy Haley a razor? I didn't do anything wrong." My mom glared at me, her hazel eyes dark with disappointment. I was sent to my room with such quiet force it frightened me. Not because I was worried I had hurt Haley's feelings, but because I was scared of what my parents would do. I had managed to find a toehold in this group of friends, and I was desperate to keep it. Even a week apart from them would be enough for new alliances and habits to form, ones that didn't include me. My parents whispered behind their closed bedroom door—and the next day, they told me they'd made a few calls and I'd be going to Camp Catalpa that summer.

I ran toward my bedroom and slammed the door. A pink fire lit beneath my cheeks, fueled by a storm of indignation. "This is going to be the worst summer ever!" I screamed. My parents were leaving me alone in the wilderness, like some scavenging Neanderthal. So clueless, parents, their solutions earnest but oft misguided. I didn't want to go to my mom's stupid camp. Especially not that summer. My parents seemed to think an all-girls camp in the middle of nowhere, this bubble of childhood innocence, would pause, or at the very least slow down, my transformation to adulthood. But I had already figured out what surviving my teenage years would take, and being good wasn't going to get me anywhere.

"Honey, please calm down." My mom tapped the door lightly and rattled the doorknob.

I felt like my life was over, in the way that only a twelve-year-old girl who has just been told that her social life is being taken away could. I would miss out on everything worthwhile that summer: weekends in the Hamptons, sleepovers and birthday parties, maybe even kisses (first, in my case). Drew Campbell had been talking about his thirteenth-birthday party for months. It was going to be my first boy-girl party, a pool party at his aunt's on Long Island, and I was going to miss it because of dumb summer camp. I would come back to school a total outcast. Rachel would replace me with the Ashleys again, their summer memories all shared together. I flung myself on my bed, pulling my legs into my chest as I fought back stinging tears.

That June, my parents packed up our car and the city skyline faded in the rearview as we drove to the Poconos. Highways and turnpikes morphed into shaded roads lined with green. After two hours, we made a right off of one, the Camp Catalpa sign arched over a short dirt path that led to a soccer field. The grass was crunchy and colorless, the result of a month-long drought, torn up from the SUVs with backs filled to the brim, trunks and duffel bags and pillows and mess kits smashed against their windows. Camp Catalpa was smaller than I expected. There was a tennis court on one side of the field, its green asphalt surface running all the way to the line of trees that separated camp from the road, and an archery range on the other, a ramshackle shed with arrows slouching against its door next to the shooting line. There were a bunch of huts and lodges at the center of camp, houses for activities like crafts, photography, campcraft, and the more mundane, like a mail-sorting room and offices. They were named after birds: Quail, Roost, Sparrow. Senior, Intermediate, and Junior Row cabins sat between those huts and the lake, the rows' personalities as different as the campers in their ranks. Senior Row didn't have cabins, really; instead, square platforms topped by heavy mint-green plastic tents housed four campers each. Int Row was the best, a semicircle of sturdy cabins with a bonfire space at the center and a small dock right on the lake. The cabins' windows were glassless, fresh summer air flowing through one opening and out the other, and there were four wood bunk beds inside, the whole place smelling like the cedar closet where my grandma stored her best threads to keep the moths away. Cabin 5, my cabin, was in Junior Row. With only six cabins total, each pair connected by a hallway, Junior Row had an intimate feel. Everything about it was smaller, more compact—like its tenants, ranging from ages six to twelve. (Int Row was for thirteen- and fourteen-year-olds, and seniors were fifteen to seventeen.) The entire camp hugged a rocky shore, Lake Fairmont's gentle waves rolling against the misshapen pebbles with calming consistence. I knew most of this from the brochure, but the crowd of girls, some meek and shy, others loud and confident—return campers, I assumed—piling out of their parents' cars, their sloppily sporty ponytails tied up with green or blue ribbons, brought it to life. Instinctively, I reached for my mom's hand.

My dad popped open the trunk, his weekend uniform, golf shirt with pressed khaki bottoms and loafers, a bad choice. Dust collected on his shoes and the bottom edges of his shorts, turning them a murky brown. My mom was better prepared, her wild curls held together by a plastic claw, a loose spaghetti-strap dress swinging past her knees. I was still mad at her, but the familiarity of my hand in hers grounded me amid the new surroundings. She squeezed and gave my arm a quick tug. "Let's explore," she said, her mind obviously playing a highlight reel of her favorite memories of Catalpa.

"Sure, fine!" my dad said, the veins in his forearms popping as he lugged my trunk from the car. "Leave me here to do the dirty work."

"If you insist," my mom said back, her tone a weird mix of flirty and childish. They had no shame about acting mushy, something I appreciate now but at the time found mortifying. I stayed silent, stubborn. Any utterance would mean my mom had won, that I was somehow enjoying this place. We walked toward the Roost, a small building that housed the camp owner and head counselor offices, as well as an open hangout space that included a Ping-Pong area and two picnic tables. With the exception of the oversized slate step that led into the Roost, it was all wood, like everything else at Catalpa, the pine one of its signature notes. Outside the Roost's main entrance, a colorful sheet of paper tacked to a bulletin board listed the daily agenda. A grid framed the different activity periods for each row, square after square filled with primitive drawings of arrows and bonfires and soccer balls and stick figures holding hands. *SWIM TEST,* the words bold and blue, a scribble of waves underneath, was listed under Junior Row. *Great,* I thought. I hated swimming. I kept a straight face and dragged my feet as we continued on the walkway, the loose dirt dancing around my shoes. I spotted a small rock and gave it a kick to the side of the path. It ricocheted off my foot and went straight toward my mom's heel.

"Ouch!" She whipped around, the underlying anger she felt toward me starting to poke its way through her cheery veneer. "Amanda Elizabeth, can you behave for the next hour? Is that really so difficult?" I shrugged. If I didn't follow her rules, what could she do? I'd be away all summer. Grounding me wasn't an option.

I followed my mom up the three creaky stairs that led to the raised entrance of the Great Hall. Tired accents of green and blue paint splashed the windowsills and door frames.

Inside, the ceiling towered; I could have stacked ten of myself on top of one another and still not reached its peak. Dark wood rafters, carved with tribal insignia with accents of color, criss-crossed above. Rows and rows of benches, each with a different shape, length, and shade of brown, faced the backless stage—the open air, peppered with views of lush trees and a slice of the lake, its background. For a moment, I immersed myself in its grandeur and inhaled. Damp earth, fresh grass, mossy wood hit my nose. I closed my eyes and one of those indescribable feelings that catches you midbreath, a flutter in your chest, pins and needles, rushed over me. The Great Hall was magnificent. My mom droned on about her favorite memories there; I tuned her out, her words like an adult's in a Charlie Brown cartoon. If I had to be at Catalpa for the summer, I wanted to make my own memories. That moment in the Great Hall was my first.

"So, what do you think?" My mom snapped me back to reality. Right, I remembered, I wasn't supposed to like it here. I shrugged again, pivoting and heading for the door.

The path to my cabin was crowded with families, each member weighed down by some oversized duffel bag or packed plastic set of drawers lassoed with duct tape. As we got closer to Junior Row, there was squealing. Girls lunged at each other, arms wide open, all wearing some version of the same outfit: graphic T-shirt, rolled Soffe shorts, and brightly colored Birkenstocks. I looked down at my sandals, a combination of glossy tan leather and wood, a souvenir from my parents' spring trip to Positano. Compared to the other girls' they were painfully impractical, a nagging reminder that I didn't belong. I kept moving forward, refusing to give the girls I passed so much as a friendly smile.

I followed my mom into cabin 5, which was on the left side of the building that housed both 5 and 6. The cabins were connected by a small hallway where two ancient-looking sinks sat below a rusted mirror. I stared at my reflection through the flecks of red. As much as I had protested coming to camp, I had still taken the time to blow out my waves that morning—the last time I could for eight weeks; the outlets in Junior Row couldn't handle the voltage of hair dryers, so they were forbidden—and carefully glossed my lips.

"This is cuter than I remember," my mom said. She climbed the bunk bed, hanging off the side and tracing her fingers along the camp cheers, signatures, and song lyrics graffitied on the walls. I resented her enthusiasm. I stared back at my reflection, put on a second coat of gloss, and smacked my lips together.

"You beat me here!" I heard my dad say as I craned my neck around the corner of the hallway. He was still lugging my trunk, his forehead dappled with perspiration, his gelled hair ruffled from the effort. He was using his fake voice, the one that meant he was feigning excitement. "Mandy girl, top or bottom bunk?"

"Um, bottom." I sat on one of the putrid green mattresses, its hot plastic sticking to my leg. Like the walls, scribbles covered every inch of its surface: *Green Team Girl Forever!; Claire wuz here '00; Sara + Kate: BFFs Forever; We are the Blue Team Girls!!! Stacey, Rachelle, and Mish: Cabin 5 '95.*

"She speaks," my mom said. I glared back.

"Hi!! I'm your counselor, Betsy!" A cheerful teenager, no older than eighteen, interrupted the stare-down. One of the first things I noticed about Betsy was her love of punctuation; every sentence out of her mouth ended with an exclamation point or question mark. "And you must be Amanda?" Her cheeks were tight with enthusiasm and eyes edged with premature crow's-feet from all her smiling. Her earnestness made me uncomfortable, orange juice without pulp, so sugary it gives you a headache.

"Yep. Hi," I said, sticking out my hand. My mom poked my side. "Yes," I repeated, like she had taught me. Yep *is not a word,* she had said. *Always* yes. "It's nice to meet you."

"Aw, we're going to be living together for the next few weeks; I think a hug is appropriate!" Betsy wrapped her arms around my stiff body. She smelled like bug spray and crème brûlée body splash, Bath and Body Works' must-have scent that summer. Her skin was warm, already tan from counselor orientation the previous week.

"Miserable," I mouthed to my dad over Betsy's shoulder, my mom on the other side unable to see my displeasure. He stifled a laugh.

"I saw on the schedule there's a welcome meeting in the Great Hall. When does that start?" I asked while giving Betsy a pat on the back, and, thank god, she loosened her grip.

"Not for another hour—but get excited. It will be awesome!" Betsy clapped as she said *awesome*. In her world, I quickly realized, everything was awesome. "The other girls should be here soon. We have a few returning campers, and a few newbies like you! See?" she said, grabbing my hand and pulling me toward the front door. A blue construction-paper creation I had missed on my way in was taped to it: "5," fat and in bright green, was pasted in the middle, with seven paper turtles circling. They each had a name: Amanda, Catherine, Amy, Larissa, Barrett, Sarah, and Sydney. The first three, including the one with my name, had little top hats; I assumed this meant they were also new to Catalpa. At the bottom of the poster, an oversized brown turtle sat above Betsy's name. "Cute, right?" Betsy asked. I wasn't sure I agreed.

"Mm-hmm," I quietly said, looking at my mom, silently begging her to rescue me, to forgive me and take me home from this saccharine dungeon.

"Hello?" A new face appeared in the doorway. In plain clothes and ratty off-brand sneakers, Catherine Wagner was as unassuming as any twelve-year-old. Her chubby cheeks flared when she smiled, framing a mouth full of braces that caught the sunlight sneaking through the cabin's small glass windows. (Unlike Ints, Juniors couldn't be trusted with barrierless living.) "I'm Catherine," she said with a spazzy wave. Betsy, of course, scooped her into a hug. Catherine's dad trailed her, wearing cargo shorts with muddy boots and a checkered short-sleeved button-down. They had matching glasses—unframed lenses with thin wires looping the top of their noses and clutching the backs of their ears, Catherine's a much lower prescription than his.

"Howdy!" he said, extending a hand toward Betsy, who had moved Catherine from her arms to her armpit nook. "I'm Doug Wagner. We're thrilled Catherine will be in your cabin this summer. Thrilled. This place is a treasure trove of discovery. A treasure trove!"

"It sure is!" Betsy said, with so much enthusiasm I felt embarrassed for her, not realizing she was simply trying to make me and Catherine—gangly tweens with little in common besides parents who seemed to think summer camp would be good for us—comfortable in this foreign place. Betsy let go of Catherine and introduced Catherine's dad to my parents, herding them into a hushed circle, walking them through what to expect from her communication-wise while their kids were her total responsibility. Catherine stood awkwardly next to the group.

"Hi," I said to Catherine. Still stuck to the plastic mattress, I didn't stand up. "I'm Amanda."

"Catherine," she said, walking toward me. The first time we met wasn't accompanied by a cosmic rush, the universe foreshadowing that we would have a huge impact on one another's lives in mere weeks. It was quiet, nervous—two young girls unsure of one another, of the new situation their parents had thrown them into.

"This is where I'm sleeping," I said, splaying my arms with some dramatic flair. "Quite royal, if you ask me."

Catherine stared back, looked at the mattress, then up and around at the other options. She was collecting data, assessing which bed would be best. "That one seems ideal," she said, pointing to my left. "I bet it has better airflow, since it's next to the window." She nodded to herself, an odd gesture of self-satisfaction, then threw her bag on the mattress. It quickly dawned on me that, if Catherine was any indication, I might not like everyone at camp. She reminded me of Lisa Edwards, a girl from school who had screamed in excitement during class last year when we dissected owl pellets. Hers contained whole rodent bones and fur tufts; while most of us tried not to gag, she earned the nickname Mousegirl. Catherine was Catalpa's Mousegirl. I said a quiet prayer to whatever god might be watching over us, begging him to send cooler girls to our cabin. Anyone would be better than Catherine, her nerdiness like a virus I was scared I might catch.

My prayer was answered when the other five cabinmates and their families rolled in shortly after. Barrett Anthony and her mom, both with endless hair that cascaded past their waists, were clad completely in earth tones. Barrett talked a little too loud, like a megaphone was eternally stuck in her throat. Amy Green was a marshmallow of comfort, her soft curves and gentle dimples a welcome invitation to be your friend. Sydney Brenner was all angles, with high cheekbones above a sharp jawline and the bangs of her trendy pixie cut held back by a sparkly spring clip. Larissa Edmonds, who told me to call her Larry, sported a small silver circle charm around her a neck—an honor, I had already learned from my mom (who had eight), bestowed on the very best campers in their various activities; her skin hugged burgeoning muscles, and her frizzy mane was constrained by a hair tie and a pre-wrap headband. Sarah Wilson, though, was the transfixing one. Within seconds, it was clear that she was Sydney's and Larry's leader. I recognized these girls, their energy similar to that of my friends in the city. I hoped I could elbow my way into their tight-knit circle—and then maybe this summer would be livable.

I watched from my bunk as Sarah directed the two to pull their trunks next to hers. Three camp charms hung around her neck. She looked like the quintessential all-American athlete: a sun-streaked blonde whose glowing confidence came from years of never losing. She was one of those girls who seemed to have a gravity about them, pulling you in with their prettiness, trapping you with their bossiness, winning you over with their adoration. The sun didn't just follow Sarah; she directed its every move. She reminded me of Rachel, beaming an envy-inducing radiance I wanted to make mine. I mistakenly assumed she would be softer thanks to a suburban upbringing full of grassy backyards and golden retrievers and Limited Too shopping sprees. I said hi to the group, Sarah's eyes lingering a pause too long as she took me in, but felt myself retreat. I've never been the loudest in a room, even when my mind is screaming for me to take action. It was so much so fast, my environment flipped on its head, my friendships a blank slate. I needed a moment to think. Plus, part of me still hoped that this was a prank—a very wholesome *Scared Straight!* for bratty girls. "Do you want to walk around camp a bit more?" I whispered to my mom and dad, my eyes big as I pleaded for a way to escape.

"It was so nice to meet you all!" my mom politely said to the other parents, each busy unpacking this or stacking that. "And, you girls—well, I know you're about to have the best summer ever." They nodded and mumbled thank-yous as we walked out of the cabin, none of us, including myself, able to foresee the falseness of my mom's statement.

A rocky path nestled against the shoreline and wound from Junior to Senior Row, then back to the soccer field. We walked along it in silence, my mom in front and my dad in back, my own little cocoon of safety. Every once in a while, my dad would ruffle my hair with his hand, or my mom would point to a sailor gliding across the sparkling water in a brightly colored Sunfish. Senior Row was chaos, duvets and quilts spilling off the sides of beds, nearly touching the dusty ground under each tent's platform. The campers didn't care—their parents were already gone, used to the process of dropping their daughters off, and the girls too busy catching up with one another and too excited to be back at camp to think about home or clean bedding. When we got to the soccer field, my throat tightened with the realization that my parents would get in their car and drive back to the city. I wasn't ready to stay at Catalpa all summer. I wasn't ready to be apart from my friends. I wasn't ready to say goodbye to my mom and dad. The rush of change felt overwhelming, too much, too fast. I looked down when I felt the tears welling; I didn't want to be that girl—the homesick one who mopes and cries her entire time at camp. Instead, I put my arm around my mom's waist, a buoy in this sea of new.

"This sucks, Mom."

"You know how I feel about that language, honey," she said before softening and putting her arm around me. "I promise you'll love it," she whispered, and gave me a squeeze. "This really will be the best summer of your life." I nodded and watched them get in their car, my mom waving, then pressing her hand against the window as they pulled away. Eventually I realized the imprint of her fingers against the glass, the frozen moment of our goodbye, would forever symbolize the end of my childhood. The motion was a misty-eyed salute to my rising independence, yes, but also an abrupt shattering of the safe bubble my parents had long provided. Even then, before I knew how wrong that summer would go, watching my parents drive away shook something at my core, a discomforting uneasiness washing over me. I walked back to the cabin, alone.

"Amanda!" Betsy said a touch too high. "You're just in time. Now that you're all here, let's get to know each other. Pull your trunks in a circle, right here," she said, pointing to the center of the cabin. It seemed unnecessary; our trunks were perfectly placed by our respective bunks. I followed suit, but not without a subtle eye roll, making it known I was above this knockoff Baby-Sitters Club meeting. Sarah sat across from me in the circle, our eyes meeting for a second as we both shyly smiled. She wanted to be my friend, too; I could tell, her smirk enough to temper my hatred of the entire situation and, dare I say, actually make it seem like it might not be so bad. Betsy began reviewing her checklist of items to mention: that day's swim test, daily inspection, the buddy system, team selection, dining hall rules, hygiene (apparently one of her previous campers went an entire three weeks without bathing), etc.

"Do you have any questions?" she asked.

Catherine's hand shot up. "Betsy," she said, breathless. "This is less of a question than a statement. Or, perhaps, an announcement. I brought a gift for everyone." Catherine hopped up, her wiry body flailing about as she unhooked her trunk and rummaged around, pulling out textbooks, actual textbooks, as she looked for the gifts.

"So you like to read?" Sarah said, her voice laced with sarcasm. She looked at me after, wanting my approval. I snorted, a small gesture that I was on her side. I knew at that age, there was nothing less cool than being a teacher's pet. Sydney also laughed. Larry nudged Sarah in the ribs. She scrunched her nose, our eyes still locked, her attention all mine, mine all hers. My skin prickled with that familiar surge of adrenaline, the rush that comes with a girl crush. And I, indisputably, had one on Sarah. In seconds I saw my summer turning around, my new best friend hooked to my side, our cheeks rosy from the sun and laughing at inside jokes and wholesome activities like making s'mores over an open fire, a dream sequence I was determined to make my reality.

"Yes," Catherine said, the sarcasm flying miles above her head. She turned around with a pile of paperbacks in hand. The cover featured a brawny mustached man in the middle of the woods. "I brought this super-helpful book on living in the wild. I've used my copy for the past year while exploring the woods around our farm. It's an outdoor bible, really. It will tell you everything you need to know: how to identify poison ivy, the types of berries that are okay to eat, what the different kinds of bark mean, and way more." Catherine put her copy, dog-eared and worn from use, on her trunk and handed out the fresh books to each girl as she talked.

"Just what I wanted!" Sarah said under her breath. I couldn't help but laugh again. Such a weird gift. Betsy shot Sarah a stern look, her attempts to keep the peace toothless even in those early days.

"You do realize you're at a summer camp in the middle of the woods, Sarah, not at a mall," Barrett said. "The directory there is probably the only map you know how to read." She chuckled to herself, like she'd landed the ultimate dis. I sensed a history between them, something tense and full of disdain. More from Barrett's side. Sarah stuck her tongue out. "Thanks," Barrett said, her voice slightly cracking as she ignored Sarah and looked at Catherine. "This is sah-weet."

"Yes! Thank you, Catherine!" Betsy stood up, tossing her copy of the book onto her bed. "So, who's ready to head to the Great Hall and get this summer started?!"

We pushed our trunks back toward our bunks. Catherine's

looked tired, like her sneakers, an obvious hand-me-down. Larry, Sydney, Sarah, and I had the same design, shiny tops and sides framed by even shinier silver trim. For a moment, I sent a quiet thank-you to my mom, who was very adept at the ins and outs of Bunkline's top trends. Theirs were bright shades of green, blue, and pink. Mine was black, topped with a simple white sticker silhouette of New York City that Rachel had given me before I left, telling me not to miss her too much.

"I *love* that!" Sarah said, pointing to my trunk. She had picked the top bunk to my bottom bunk. "I adore New York. Seriously, adore it." It was flattering, Sarah's attention. I wanted her to like me.

"Thanks," I said, trying to keep my eagerness from my voice. I was realizing that at camp the social hierarchy wasn't completely set yet, each year the new campers adding a fresh layer of intrigue. The first day was an equalizer, but things moved fast. I knew I needed to get in with this group now if I wanted it to stick.

"That's *so* cool," Sydney chimed in. "I have stickers, too, see." She pointed to her trunk, the corners bedazzled with gems and a handful of fairy silhouettes. "They're kind of my thing, if you couldn't tell. Remember Britney's fairy drawings in the *Oops* album jacket? That's, like, my dream tattoo, right on my hip." She tugged at the corner of her shorts, a hot shade of pink. Her skin was tan, a bikini line already showing. They all talked fast, like every sentence might be their last. "This is super dorky, but have you read *Ella Enchanted*? I also love the elves in the *Lord of the Rings* books. Have you read those?" she added, a surprise. Camp, I would learn, was full of girls like Sydney, the nerdy or jockish or artsy ones in the popular group at home whose quirks, at camp, were elevated from borderline weird to cool thanks to Catalpa's differing social hierarchies, which had more to do with athleticism and humor and brazenness than who got the most attention from boys.

I shook my head and she looked troubled. "But I saw the first movie?" I added.

"It's not as good," Sydney said. "At least you know what I'm talking about. Larry basically doesn't read," she said, giving Larry a playful push.

"Whoa," Larry said, holding up both her hands. "That is not true. I just don't read geek books like you."

Sarah grabbed my wrist, her overall intensity hot on my arm. "We like each other, I swear," she said, her face close to mine. I'd started to notice she always talked like that, an inch too close for comfort. "Larry and Sydney are my best camp friends. And Larry is my best best friend—we're both from Conestoga." I had no idea where Conestoga was but nodded along as if this made total sense to me. "We met Sydney last year in cabin four and all love soccer—and voilà, we became besties. Though I'm really the glue that holds us together, obviously." Her breath smelled like a combination of overripe fruit and week-old mint. She looked at the two, who were still making fun of each other, then back at me. "Do you like soccer?"

I didn't. I was a tennis girl. "Um, I think it's more of a suburban thing," I said, not really knowing if that was true.

"Wait, you *live* in New York City? I thought you, like, lived near New York. Oh my god, that is *amazing*. Guys," she said, letting go of my hand. "Amanda *lives* in New York *City*. Like actually lives there." I had never been so appreciative of where I was from, something I had never really thought that much about before. Later, in college, I'd come to appreciate the automatic cool points being from the city conferred on me. Suburban girls always seemed to think I spent my days traipsing around the Plaza like Eloise and partying with Leonardo DiCaprio.

"Cabin five ladies!" Betsy interrupted our introductory chit-chat. "Time to go! Go, go, go!" she said, pushing Catherine and Barrett and Amy, who had been talking in a separate corner of the cabin while moving their trunks into place, toward the door.

"So it begins." Sarah jumped to her feet, grabbing Larry's arm and pulling her toward the door. Sydney followed, grabbing mine. When Sarah wove her arm through Larry's, Sydney did the same with me. I felt my heartbeat slow, my nerves stabilize. I had passed some secret test and was in, chosen by this group of Catalpa cool girls. It was a relief. We skipped and giggled the entire way, Sydney talking about her favorite camp song, "White Coral Bells," which, shocker, had a line about fairies. It's funny how girls morph their cliques, how appearances and first impressions can set you on a path you never foresaw, one that seems well trod and comfortable, shimmering fields of cheerful flowers on either side, but is leading you straight off a cliff. Catherine walked ahead, her sneakers turning rattier with each step through the dried-mud paths. The summer air was heavy, only broken up by an occasional breeze rolling off Lake Fairmont's surface. She wiped a few droplets of sweat off her forehead.

"Here," Barrett said, a green spray bottle with a fan-head on top in hand. "This thing is a lifesaver. I learned last year." She didn't wait for permission and spritzed Catherine, the mist coating her face. That's the kind of friendship Catherine needed, one that was forced on her. I'd eventually learn she preferred to skip the courting and small talk that usually launch new friendships, never one for fake niceties and vapid conversation.

At the Great Hall, campers and counselors rushed toward both entrances. Larry and Sarah ran ahead, so Sydney and I followed. Inside, the benches were full, nonstop chatter and more squeals echoing off the wood walls. For a second, I lost the girls and panic took over. I didn't know where to sit, and the feeling that I shouldn't be there, that I didn't want to be there, crept up again.

"Amanda, here!" Sarah, near the front, motioned for me to

come over. "We saved you a seat." She patted a space at the end
of the bench. My heart calmed, and I felt a rush of gratitude for
the attention of these strangers, these girls I had already decided I
needed to make my best friends for the summer. I walked toward
the row and slid next to Sarah.

"What about Barrett and the other new girls? We should try
and make room for them," Larry said.

"Ew, no. Barrett was a total freak last year," Sarah said.

Sydney nodded in agreement, then snorted as she leaned across
Larry and Sarah and looked at me. "Last year we called her Barrett 'Give Me Twenty Minutes' Anthony because she takes forever in the bathroom. Like, actually forever. So gross."

I didn't really find this weird, but I didn't want to be tagged
a freak, too. I nodded, like I also couldn't believe Barrett took
twenty minutes in the bathroom.

"Ew, Sydney. I mean it's true, but that's not the only reason
she's weird. You heard her speak, right, Amanda? Nails on a
chalkboard. And her cankles. They're bad. There are other reasons obviously, you'll learn soon," Sarah said ominously with her
eyebrows lifted. Larry stayed quiet. "Whatever, though. We're at
camp! I'm so excited. I've been, like, counting down the seconds
for camp to start."

They all really had. They started talking about how their
home friends didn't get why they loved camp so much, why they
put Catalpa on a pedestal, but I quickly began to understand
its magic: it's a little like the earliest days of college, when time
both speeds up and slows down; a day feels like a week, a week
a month, a month a year. You spend 24/7 with total strangers,
people you would never cross paths with in regular life, and, like
family members, their personalities wear on you, becoming an
expected and predictable and comforting part of your day. This
bubble is unduplicatable, its apparent safety and happiness and
fun—pure, unadulterated fun—the best cocktail you'll ever sip.

Even now, when I think back to the early days at Catalpa before everything went dark, I mainly remember the good, a bramble of sisters who laughed and cried and fought and made up while they taught one another how to grow up without losing their youth, topping each day off with cheesy sing-alongs under the warm summer moon.

Laura Perkins, the owner of Camp Catalpa, jumped up on-stage and the room slowly hushed. "Welcome, campers! Some of you have traveled quite far to join us this summer." Laura was in her late thirties, with a stocky build and a no-BS attitude. She screamed schoolteacher—she was, in fact, a seventh-grade science teacher during the other nine months of the year—and had inherited the camp from her parents. She herself had been a camper there, and it was obvious she felt most at home during the summer months on the lake. Everyone said it reminded her of her parents. "Both are dead," Sarah whispered. Old age, cancer. "Laura is basically an orphan," she added. Except she had a brother, and he provided the major point of gossip that summer. He had moved into an RV on the public grounds near Catalpa with his daughter, Laura's niece, Meg Perkins. Sarah, who always seemed to know everything happening at camp, later claimed she had already seen them around camp. "White trash—honestly, you wouldn't even know they were related to Laura," she explained with a wave of her hand, then moved on, like even giving those two that little space in her brain had been a waste. I recognized the flicker of interest in her eyes, though; there's little more exciting than the unknown. "Once again, this year's award for longest trip goes to Simone Bialeck, who's joining us from London! Welcome back, Simone—and thanks for traveling all this way to spend another summer at Catalpa." Laura waved a small water bottle above her head, her aging triceps muscle flapping as she tossed it to Simone, who jumped up to catch it. The hall erupted with applause. "A few housekeeping items to get things started. Inspection begins on Wednesday. For new campers, you have today and tomorrow to learn the ins and outs of keeping your cabins tidy. Don't worry, your counselors will help. For old campers: I hope you've been practicing your square corners!" A collective groan escaped the audience. Laura went through her list, detailing lunchtime (noon), where to find your daily assignments (the Roost), the infirmary hours (seven A.M. to eight P.M.), the importance of always having a buddy for every activity, and Blue/Green initiation (Friday night). I tried to keep up, but it was a lot of information to take in—and I didn't understand half of it. At the time, I didn't even know what making a bed with four perfectly square corners meant.

"As you know, Blue/Green initiation can't happen without your captains," Laura continued, the room heavy with anticipation. "In a few days, the Blues and Greens will gather in their respective meeting spots to vote for this summer's captains. New campers—since you're still teamless, we'll have a bonfire during the vote."

"I bet Ali will get Blue Team captain," Larry whispered. "She has to." Sydney and Sarah aggressively nodded.

"Who's Ali?" I asked.

"Only the best Blue Team girl in the history of Blue Team girls," Sarah said. She pointed at a lithe brunette a few rows in front of us. "I want to be her. She's so pretty and nice and good at sports. And her boyfriend Tom is super cute. Well at least he is in her pictures. I stopped by her tent this morning and saw him." She paused, letting us absorb the fact that she was one of Ali's favorite juniors. Most seniors adopted little sisters for the summer, basking in their adorable smiles and doe-eyed adoration. "I hope one day I'll have a boyfriend as hot as him." She stared at the back of Ali's head, a dreamy glaze frosting her eyes. It was satisfying seeing the manifestation of Sarah's insecurities, her want for more, for what Ali had. It turned out we all wanted to be someone else. "Basically, Ali's the sickest LC," Sarah added.

"LC?" I asked, the camp lingo still foreign.

"That means leading camper," she said, her pleasure with becoming my de facto mentor obvious. "And a Blue Team girl, which is all you need to know. Me and Sydney are Blue Team girls. I hope you're one, too. We're way better than the Green Team, and way prettier. When Betsy was a camper, she was a Green Team girl. Enough said." I snuck another peek at Betsy. A few rows behind us, she attentively listened to Laura's every word. Frumpy, sure, but she was far from ugly.

Larry leaned forward and across Sarah, either ignoring or completely missing the slight about her team's looks. "What Sarah means to say is that the Blue Team is full of girly girls who don't know how to play sports. But Ali is a shoo-in. I'm on the Green Team, and we won the cup last year. Emma will probably be our captain. She's the best athlete here, and we plan to win again this year. That's really what matters," she said with a contented smile, the memories of last year's spoils running through her head. Sarah swatted Larry away.

"Ignore her. You want to be a Blue Team girl, trust me." I looked at the three of them, Sarah and Sydney so obviously cooler—and prettier—than Larry, a goofy tomboy, a big Labrador. I wanted to be a Blue Team girl. I had to be one.

After Laura finished going through the rest of the to-dos, several counselors brought out shoeboxes overflowing with green paper books. "Girls, you know the deal!" Laura told the room as the books made their way down each row, girls clutching them like prized treasures. "This is your songbook for the summer. You lose it, you're out of luck. So don't." I leafed through mine, its margins crowded by girls' signatures and doodles from years past. Laura pulled a tuner out of her pocket and blew into it, a solid note reverberating off the wood walls and ringing in each girl's ears. Less than a third of the room opened to the first page, including me. The others, including Larry, Sydney, and Sarah, didn't touch their books. "Hail to Camp Catalpa," Laura sang. The entire room joined in. The volume of the singing crescendoed as we neared the end of the song. Girls clapped, stomped, and jumped up when their team color was mentioned in the lyrics. I stumbled to keep up, mumbling words and nearly getting knocked off the bench when Sarah leaped from her seat to scream "BLUE!" while singing. My cheeks felt warm, a muddled mix of discomfort and embarrassment making me miss home.

"The next one will be easier. Promise," Sarah said at the end of Camp Catalpa's fight song. She pointed to "Pruney," a short song about a family of prunes who were always wrinkled. I laughed, my face returning to its normal color. "We can practice the other song, too. It took me forever—like, actually forever—to learn." She put her right arm around me and her left around Larry, who put her arm around Sydney. I began to feel excited by these total strangers, their welcoming me into their crew so natural, like we were always meant to be best friends. Camp suddenly seemed full of possibility, a world where anything could happen; I forgot about my parents, school, Rachel. Catalpa was my home now—and I was sure Sarah held the keys to all its secret rooms, the ones I hoped would, like my mom said, make this the best summer ever. I grinned like a total idiot, Sarah's grip tight around my shoulders, as we swayed back and forth to the rest of the songs.

Like the morning assemblies, the swim test was a requirement. Every year, no matter their age or if they had passed the previous year, campers put on their blue bathing suits and white swim caps, wrapped themselves in plush beach towels, slid their painted toes into worn plastic sandals, and headed to the H dock, a massive metallic contraption painted white. The lower half of the H was the shallow end, a shameful swamp of banishment for the girls who failed the swim test and had to spend the rest of the summer wearing fluorescent life jackets in knee-deep water while learning to float. The upper half was sweat and joy, work and play, the dark water separated into lanes by sagging rope and the tips of the H, decorated with a slide on the left and a diving board on the right. We sat on the Owl's Perch, a wood patio a few feet above the dock itself.

"Juniors!" A jacked woman in a one-piece and rolled mesh shorts blew a whistle. Her hair was a rat's nest on the top of her head, centered above a visor and holographic glasses. "Juniors," she shouted again, blowing her whistle once more. "Listen up! I'm Julie, the swim counselor. This is Becca, Emily, Ash, and Gregg," she said, going down the row of women standing next to her, all in similar looks with equally aggressive tan lines and biceps. "For those of you who have been here before, welcome back. Lake Fairmont has missed you. For the new campers—who's new? Raise your hands. Okay, for the new campers, welcome to your first major Catalpa rite of passage. The swim test challenges your strength, your determination, and helps us figure out your skill level. Before we dive in, let's go over a few key rules." The test itself was a simple fifteen-minute swim, no touching the edge of the dock or the supportive steel beams crisscrossed below. No taking off your cap, the bright white the only way to spot a sinking camper in the turbid lake water. No messing around, just treading. Almost everyone passed, making it all the more embarrassing for those who didn't. A nervous quiet overtook the newbies in the group, the dark ripples under the H dock like a taunting beast ready to swallow us whole. "The good news?" Julie said after sharing her spiel. "You get a cookie at the end of class." She grabbed a box of Nilla Wafers from the railing behind her, shaking it at the group. A few *woos* escaped, Larry's one of them.

"Oh my god, those are the best cookies in the world," Sydney whispered, the edge of my swim cap tingling against the top of my ear as she spoke. "You'll see." She was staring at them as if they were the only food for miles. In the coming days, I understood their appeal, how a shortbread cookie mushed in our hands wet with lake water could taste so freaking good. It wasn't about the cookie; it was the work that came before it. The burn, the energy expended in silence as our heads turned in and out of the lake with each stroke and breath, the hunger it left in us.

"You ready to swim?" Julie asked, her whistle lolling on her fingers. "Let's do this!" She raised the whistle to her mouth, blew hard, and off we went, a bunch of girls feeling the excitement of the first real activity of camp, no parents, no schoolwork, just a summer of endless opportunity ahead. I even got caught up in the feeling, the counselors' optimism seeping into my pores like the sunscreen we doused ourselves in before swim class.

Looking back, I realize the freedom that came with camp was a total illusion, structured to make you think you were unfettered, able to do whatever you wanted, but really, rules governed your every action. On that first day of camp, I was given more rules to remember than I had been my entire life. There were reasons for the rules, they said. Past mistakes, tragedies, maybe not at this camp, but at others. Rules we learned, later, were truly there for a reason. The buddy system was the most important one at the swim dock. If you didn't have a buddy, you couldn't get in the lake. If you left your buddy alone, your punishment was scraper duty at the cafeteria for a week. On a splintered wood board in the Owl's Perch, one side topped with "OUT" and the other "IN," metal pegs held green chips, each with a girl's name on it. Sydney grabbed hers, then mine, and placed them together on the IN side. We were buddies, as simple as that. I followed her down the steps that led to the H dock, the wood soft from the water. Julie, ever militant, blew her whistle, and the girls who had been at camp before kicked off their shoes and put their towels on a rack near the edge of the lake, already damp from the rippling motorboat wake as wild as it was relentless. The counselors split our group in half, and in single file, we walked out onto both sides of the H dock, its white metal cool against the soles of my feet. We turned ninety degrees once we reached the upper part of the H and faced the water. I curled my toes over the side. The water was dark, the bottom seemingly endless. Julie blew her whistle and everyone jumped, including me, my sinuses drowned, the lake waterfalling down my throat. I coughed, then accidentally swallowed more, the splashes from the group's frantic treading like a scene from *Titanic*.

"Sarah, Lar!" Sydney smacked water at them. "Watch this." She put her hands straight up, fluttered her feet, and spun around like a synchronized swimmer.

"That's nothing," Larry said before dunking her head underwater and flipping three times, her legs an eerie shade of green through the lake water.

Sarah did the same. When she reemerged, she wiped the string of snot dripping from her nose, then asked me, "Want to try?"

"GIRLS!" Julie shouted, her glare directed at us. "Stop messing around. You have five minutes left. If you don't behave, I'll make you do it again!"

I was glad for the reprieve. My arms and legs were already burning. Conserving energy was my only priority, though short, tired breaths were pouring out of my body faster than I could take in oxygen. I had never been a strong swimmer; the few lessons I took each summer had failed to transform me from land to sea creature. I did my best to shrug in the water without losing my arms' cadence, my hands making cups and pushing the water back and forth, back and forth, back and forth. The longer we were in the water, the quieter everyone got, even the most skilled swimmers exhausted, or maybe bored. A few girls

dropped out, mainly the younger ones, their heads hung in disappointment, their cheeks red with shame. *Please don't let that
be me,* I thought. I caught a glimpse of Catherine from the corner of my eye, she and Barrett happily chatting, their heads high
above the waterline, unlike mine, which wanted to sink. Amy
bobbed next to them, quiet and almost tearful. The minutes felt
like torturous hours as one of my toes started to twist, a sign I
should swim to the side and give up. I was about to when Julie
blew her whistle.

"Thank god!" I shouted to no one in particular.

Sarah bopped my head as she sprinted to the side of the dock.
"Smell ya ladies later!" Larry raced after, almost beating her to
the edge of the dock, their bodies shiny as they pulled themselves
out of the water, seals flopping onto a metal dock for a few minutes of refuge from the chilly wet. I was an eel, slimy and limp,
slithering onto land, lying there for a beat, my chest hollow from
exhaustion. A few fuzzies clung to my suit, algae and lakeweed
like spoiled kale against my skin. Sarah, Sydney, and Larry
sprinted toward the shore, leaping from step to step, propelled by
endorphins. Girls stepped over my lifeless body, Amy and Barrett
included. I felt a step behind, like I was running, running, running to catch Sarah but would never get there, a panting hamster
jogging eternally on a wheel.

I peeled my upper body off the deck, leaning on my forearms,
face flushed with exercise. Campers were already toweling off,
high from the excitement of passing the swim test. Perched in the
Owl's Nest above, a girl with a mop of strawberry hair wearing
a tight spaghetti-strap top and rolled plaid boxers leaned on the
railing, looking down at them all, then up at the lake. Despite the
hot air, which was quickly sucking the water off my body with
an impressive efficiency, a chill prickled my skin. I knew every
camper was in their respective activity period. But not her. I tried
to get a better look. I thought she might be Laura's niece, Meg,

the one Sarah seemed to know so much about, fodder for gossip that was sure to strengthen my standing in her world.

"Here." I looked up to my right. Catherine was stopped next to me, her hand reached out, her fingers topped by raisiny tips. "I read once that if you tread slowly, it helps conserve energy," she said.

My head spun, stars twinkling in the corners of my eyes. I looked back toward the Owl's Nest, but the girl was gone. Laura's niece. It definitely had to have been her. I couldn't wait to tell Sarah. "Huh?"

"I saw you were struggling. It's because you were moving your arms too fast. You tire yourself out that way."

Catherine was trying to be nice, I knew, but her approach had interrupted my scouting of Meg, leaving me with less to tell Sarah. Plus, she was blatantly pointing out my weaknesses. I didn't really want to get stuck talking to her, worried Sarah, Sydney, and Larry would see us, relegating me to the loser side of the cabin. The longer I looked at her, at the overly friendly gesture of her extended hand, the way saliva bubbled at the corners of her braces when she talked, the wisps of matted hair spilling out of the back of her rubber swim cap, the more I couldn't stand her.

"Um, okay," I said, not hiding my annoyance, staring harder at the spot in the Owl's Nest where Meg had been seconds before. Still, I grabbed Catherine's hand and started walking with her to land, the irritating reveal that she was such a know-it-all whirling in my head.

April 15, 2014

[Blocked Number]

I'd watch out if I were you. Your
sweet little gf isn't so sweet.

                                    sry think you have the
                                        wrong number

No I don't, Jackson. Watch
her closely and you'll see I'm not
wrong. Don't say I didn't warn you.

                                    what r you talking about

                                        who is this?

— 3 —

NOW

. . .

My eyes are throbbing, like they might explode any minute. The heat isn't helping; why am I always at this place when it's so fucking hot? I massage my temples, hoping to alleviate some of the pressure. I overdid it last night. I've been drinking too much the past few weeks, I know, and the night before, I promised myself I'd be in great shape for this reunion, but I'm twenty-three and living in New York. I lost Rachel, but I still have enough of a circle of friends and loose acquaintances to go out with. They have disposable income and, on weekends, zero responsibilities. I have a past and a terrible relationship to escape. We always overdo it.

It's been hours since my last vodka soda. All I've consumed this morning is a Diet Coke, picked up at a run-down Wendy's during my drive to the Poconos. I finger the cap of the bottle of Tito's in my bag. My phone keeps buzzing—Jackson Jackson Jackson—and my headache is outrageous. I flip my cell upside down, his texts unread.

I met Jackson almost a year ago, Labor Day weekend. Rachel

and I were at the Tipsy Turtle, a beachside spot in Montauk that lives up to its name, rows and rows of sloppy twentysomethings grinding against and falling all over each other, the midday sun illuminating their summer skin and goofy grins. Until a few months ago, we were still best friends, me and Rachel. Despite four years at different universities, we remained inseparable. She could be polarizing, sparking jealousy in some people and obsession in others. But for me, she was protection. I knew better than to cross her, to dare her to leave my side. When Rachel was on your team, you felt untouchable. And she leaned on me for stability, a steady hand in a life full of absence: parents, siblings, structure or concern or love. We were codependent, relying on one another to cloud our insecurities, fill the hollowed parts of each other.

I slid my body sideways to squeeze in next to her at the bar. It wasn't that long ago, but somehow it feels like a lifetime has passed since. We were staying at Rachel's mom's beach house. Fresh out of our undergrad programs, she still hadn't landed a job, but I had just started a psych program at a university in the city. The bar was packed with preppies from both our alma maters: friends, friends of friends, kids who graduated a few years before us.

"Two, please." Rachel flagged the bartender, pointing to a bottle of Jose Cuervo. It was only three in the afternoon. "To warm us up." She winked.

"So did you hear Ashley is interning at *Vogue*? I mean, her mom's connections totally got her the job, but still," Rachel said. I hadn't really stayed in close touch with the high school crew, minus Rachel. "Apparently her mom's company, you know, that diamond one, is spending, like, a million dollars advertising with them."

"Ashley Peters? Hmm," I said, squinting as sunlight pierced the bar. "That's unsurprising, though. She's had, like, her whole life handed to her." We both laughed, happy to make fun of someone else's silver spoon if it let us ignore our own.

The bartender passed us two shot glasses, a shaker, and a plate of limes. Rachel grabbed her glass first, then I followed.

"At least she's still nice," she said. "Maybe she'll be able to get us free shit. I bet that closet is loaded." I sprinkled Rachel's hand with salt, then mine.

"Maybe," I said, the shot crisp in my hand. I hadn't talked to Ashley in months, and most of my memories of her involved name-dropping the celebs she had met and the labels she wore. Rachel never begrudged Ashley's vapidity, almost like calling it out would spotlight her own.

"Oh, oh my god, and Drew Campbell," Rachel said, her proclivity for gossip never satisfied. "He's getting his MBA at Stanford. I know he went to Georgetown and all, but I honestly thought he was an idiot."

"Seriously? How is that even possible? Don't you need, like, real work experience?" I asked, the shot glass sweating.

Rachel shook her head. "He invented some insane app in college that, like, did something genius with the cloud and so he's in. Everyone's calling him New York's Zuck." I laughed, the idea of Drew, the kid who frosted the tips of his hair until 2007, representing the future of tech a touch too hyperbolic.

"Well, I guess, here's to being the losers of our class," I said, licking the salt off my hand. Just before we clinked, raised the glasses, and tossed our heads back in unison, Rachel's face went slack for a second, my joke, I realized, hitting too close. I swallowed the tequila, the sting softened by a quick bite of lime.

"You ladies celebrating something?" a guy in a sleeveless tank interrupted. His neon-green sunglasses hung around his neck by foam, eighties-style Croakies.

"Our future," Rachel said, placing her arm across my lap as she leaned toward him. "She just started grad school." She nodded toward me. "And freedom, for me. Because I never have to go to school again." She flashed him a smile, her lips shiny with gloss, her comfort zone returned.

"Ah, I remember those days." He moved closer. He smelled like beer and tired deodorant, with a hint of sunscreen. "You should really toast to the end of freedom. Real life sucks." He smiled as he spoke, a cocky look that was both charming and alarming. He adjusted his flat-rim hat, turning it backward, and leaned back into the bar. Rachel whispered something to me, but I couldn't hear with the blaring music and bodies on top of bodies all talking too loud. I could tell it was full of excitement, though. She grabbed my arm and gave me a look. "Hey, man," this new friend of ours said to the bartender, a surfer-looking fortysome-thing with leathery skin. "Can I get two Bud Lights? And two vodka sodas for the ladies?"

"How'd you know?" Rachel batted her lashes. Of course he knew. Even I knew our vodka-soda order was predictable and completely cliché. The dimples in his cheeks deepened with self-satisfaction.

"I'm Reggie," he said, his hand outstretched.

"Amanda," I said, grasping his smooth palm.

"And I'm Rachel." Her lean got more dramatic as she took his hand.

"Yo," Reggie said, elbowing the guy behind him, his eyes still on Rachel. "Yo, Jack. Meet Rachel and—" He turned to me. "Sorry, I'm bad with names. What was yours again?"

"Amanda," I said, unsurprised. Guys gravitated to Rachel. I swore something about her hit them on a pheromonal level. She knew it, too. She had game without even trying. Whenever we were together, they rarely noticed me. Usually, I didn't mind.

"Amanda," Reggie's friend said, now turned and facing us, his fingers wrapped around his fresh bottle of beer. "I'm Jackson. Jackson Huxley." He looked at me, not at Rachel, his stare direct and uncomfortable. It rattled me, his intensity like injecting sex into my veins. We didn't realize it at the time, but the jolt, the immediate need we both felt, was darkness seeing darkness, both of us filled with secrets.

"Amanda Brooks," I said, repeating my name. He wasn't conventionally attractive, like Reggie, who screamed Abercrombie-esque lax bro with chiseled biceps and golden hair shaved in the right spots and tanned skin from always being outdoors. No, Jackson was sinewy with sharp features, his hair dark and messy, his skin too pale for this place, his shoulders broad but bony. His eyes were electric amber, his cheeks wearing a hint of sunburn. Something inside me fluttered. He looked smart, but in a hot way. Our eyes locked and I confused lust and love.

"Amanda Brooks," he said, walking around Reggie and over to me. Rachel pushed past my other side, sidling up to Reggie. "What are we drinking to today?" He placed a hand lightly on the center of my back. He was smooth, that's for sure. I blushed.

"To new beginnings," I said, raising my glass. "And to toasting too many things in the span of five minutes." The room felt like it was spinning, or maybe Jackson's presence was draining all my perspective. We each took a sip. He told me he was working at an ad agency, one of the big ones, but was thinking about going to school to do entertainment law. "Truth is I'm shit at copywriting," he said. "Good at arguing, though." He smiled. I melted. He'd graduated a year earlier and was studying for his LSAT, with plans to take it the next fall, wanting to take a break before returning to nonstop lectures and cramming sessions and tests. I told him I was in grad school in the city with a focus on exploring cognitive psychology and how experiences shape our version of reality. I had never talked about what really happened at Catalpa. Not to my parents, or Rachel, or therapists. I had packed it away, folded neatly in a locked trunk in the back of my mind. That's common for kids who experience some sort of trauma,

I'd learned; they compartmentalize, blocking out the bad to live some semblance of a normal life. With time, that method works. At least it did for me. My career choice was the only nod to my past, but no one knew that since they didn't really know what had happened. No one questioned it.

"So, you're like a psychic," Jackson said.

I scrunched my nose, confused. "No." I laughed. "I said psychology." The music was loud, Rihanna belting about love in hopeless places pouring from the speakers.

"Yeah, yeah. But you're, like, studying how our brains work, no? You're literally reading minds." We were back by the bar, another round ordered.

"I guess, in a way."

"You wanna know what's on my mind right now?"

I nodded slow, biting my lip. He leaned closer, his lips hot against my ear.

"You." The world stopped, our closeness all I felt for an instant. I jumped when a cold glass hit my upper arm, the bartender pushing our latest round toward us. Jackson led me to an empty corner of the bar away from the dance party undulating in the center of the space. Reggie and Rachel were already making out, their hands touring each other's bodies as they danced. Jackson found an open high-top and we each perched on a bar stool, moving them close enough so our knees brushed. The more Jackson talked, the more enamored I became. He grew up in Georgia, in a small town outside of Atlanta. His dad was a Yankee; he'd been transplanted below the Mason-Dixon line for college and never left. His mom was born and raised in West Virginia, meeting his dad when she worked as an assistant at a bank in Charlotte. They settled in Georgia shortly after Jackson was born, when his dad landed an investing gig that he called "once in a lifetime." Jackson met Reggie as a freshman in college—I was right; Reggie played lacrosse there—and, though he wasn't an athlete, he became a fixture in the crew. He interned at companies like HBO and NBC thanks to his dad's golf connections. (When we met, Jackson wore a shirt with a small yellow logo in the corner. Augusta, I later learned.) He grew disillusioned, annoyed by the bullshit work he had to do. He didn't want to be a passenger on the sinking media ship. "I want to make the rules, not follow them," he said, chasing the statement with a swig of beer. He was a fixer, he explained. I wondered if he could fix me. Besides one almost-serious boyfriend, my relationships in college were all casual, all skin-deep, all more like Reggie. Athletic, lovers of the status quo, generic. Guys who never probed too much or asked too many questions, whose egos and mediocre minds kept them in their lane. Jackson wasn't like them. He wanted a big, important life. To change the things he thought were wrong in the world, to mold them to fit his worldview. I stared at him as he talked, fixated.

"It feels like you're looking into my soul," he joked.

I shrugged. "Maybe I am," I said, a devious smile crawling across my face. He was into me; I felt it. I wasn't sure about him yet. He was smooth, goal oriented, interested. But something made me hesitate. He was too—I couldn't put my finger on it. Not perfect. Too passionate, maybe? Even then, it was a little suffocating, his ability to harness all the energy in the room and repurpose it to further whatever it was he was talking about. I had never once cared about the media industry and their horrible business models, but the more he talked, the more I agreed, his charisma and confidence my drug.

As the sun started to set, Rachel and Reggie stumbled toward us, a mixed group of their respective friends behind. "My place, now!" Rachel slurred, waving her phone. Reggie dropped his arm around her shoulders and she leaned into him. I looked to Jackson, hopeful he'd want to come.

"Sounds good to me," he said, looking at me. Not at Rachel.

We piled into a taxi, one of the Hamptons' famously overpriced, slightly run-down vans, a lot like those we used to ride in at camp. The seats had too much bounce, our heads moving up and down in unison as we drove. There were screams from the back for the driver to turn up the radio—the *jams*—and loud sing-alongs during the fifteen-minute ride to Rachel's house. Jackson sat next to me, both our hands on our respective laps. Shoulder to shoulder with him, I felt the heat from his body, my every nerve humming.

When we got to her house, Rachel mixed a few pitchers of margaritas, her hand heavy with the tequila. Without the sun, the beach air had a bite; I changed out of my cover-up and into mini jean shorts and an oversized sweater, my body pulsing with excitement and alcohol.

I walked out to the pool, an aquamarine pit in a cove of trees. Everyone was already there, some doing gainers into the pool and others crowding the reclining chairs. Jackson sat on the edge of one, his back to me. I slipped next to him, stretching out so we were perpendicular. He turned his head and his eyes soaked in my smooth legs—thank god I had shaved extra carefully that morning. Sip by sip, I relaxed, drunk on salty air and Lisa Frank sunsets and this new guy.

The hills were alive with wildflowers and I was as wild, even wilder than they. That song. It made me cringe, memories of Sarah jumping on her trunk, hairbrush in hand, singing at the top of her lungs. Me on my trunk, silk pajamas and freshly show-ered hair, twirling and singing as loud. Sarah always insisted on Dolly Parton when we'd do a bunk dance party.

Rachel was already draining her third margarita and she stood up and started dancing, yanking Reggie's hand. Jackson and I watched, the huge backyard suddenly feeling intimately small, Jackson leaning closer toward me as the chorus neared.

"I hate this song," I muttered, tipping my head back and cloak-ing my tongue with the sweet tequila mix.

"Aw, come on now, little lady. No need to hate on Ms. Dolly simply because her roots run deep in the South. Do I hafta teach you a thing or two about good music?" Clueless, cute, distracting. I looked at him and tilted my head. His nose hooked a little to the left, an imperfection I wanted to explore. "Lesson begins," he said as he stood up and tilted a fake hat at me, "now!" He put out a hand, an invitation to dance. A smile broke out on my face.

Before I could put my hand in his, Reggie released Rachel with a spin and bulldozed into Jackson, who back-flopped into the pool, the bulk of the spray hitting Rachel. Too drunk to care, she peeled her sweater off. "*I grew up fast and wild and I never felt right in a garden so different from me,*" she mouthed, swinging it over her head and throwing it at me. She knew all the words, too; I'd mentioned it was a song we listened to at camp, one of the few things I shared with Rachel about that summer, so she'd gotten the CD and listened to it on repeat. She always learned what I liked and adopted it as her own. "*I just never belonged, I just longed to be gone, so the garden one day set me free,*" she shouted before cannonballing into the water. Reggie went next, the two quickly climbing all over each other.

"Amanda Brooks, your turn!" Jackson said, treading by the edge near my chair. I still hated swimming. I shook my head, tucking my legs under my sweater and hugging them into my chest. "You leave me no choice, m'lady!" He pushed himself out of the pool, scooped me into his arms, sweater and all, and jumped right back in. He didn't ask permission; he took me in his arms, like I was already his. The water was cold, stunning my lungs and rushing up my nose. The sweater weighed me down, sparking that too-familiar panic. I flailed, still in Jackson's arms. When we surfaced, he was laughing and I was near tears, coughing up water like a toddler in a swim lesson. I clung to him, my feet barely able to touch the floor. "Get me out," I said between coughs. "Please."

There was enough action around us that no one seemed to notice my freak-out, except Rachel. She swam over, placing her hand behind my head as I lay in Jackson's arms. "She's a horrible swimmer, asshat," she said, nearly yanking me from Jackson.

"Rach, stop," I said, suddenly embarrassed by my babyish re-action. "I'm fine. Seriously." I gently pushed her hand away and stood on my tiptoes in the deep water.

"Do you want to get out?" Her eyes were bloodshot from the chlorine and drink. "We can just chill on my parents' bed or something."

"No, no." I shook my head. "I'm fine, Rach." I raised my eye-brows, slightly nodding my head toward Jackson, who stood behind me, not speaking. I knew Rachel understood, yet she hes-itated. "I'm fine," I said again, this time with my teeth gritted, ignoring her concern, her helping hand. "I'm fine," I said for the umpteenth time as I turned to Jackson, who wrapped his arm around my waist and pushed me onto his back as he swam us to the shallow end. He grabbed my hand and pulled me out of the water, leaving Rachel in our wake.

"I can grab a towel. They're inside, right? If you sit, I can get you one?" He was flustered, unsure what had just happened. I bit my lip, the rush of foolish embarrassment hitting me as my adrenaline waned. I needed to change the subject, to not have this be a big deal. His most obvious flaw, how he always took things a step too far, was softened by my buzz and focus on winning him over, on making sure he felt forgiven, a habit I unconsciously perfected in the following months.

"Um, I could use a shot more," I joked. Though I wasn't really joking. Between the song and the water, that summer at camp was on my mind. Getting drunk and forgetting seemed like a good idea.

"Yeah!" he said, his tone more upbeat. Hopeful. His body re-laxed when he realized he had been forgiven, his own anger with

himself visibly relieved. "A shot. Yes!" I followed him inside, our
dripping bodies leaving a trail of water on the expensive hard-
wood floor. I grabbed two towels from a linen closet and threw
one at him, wrapping the other around my shoulders, my soaked
sweater leaden against my skin. The tequila was on the kitchen
island, cap off, an open invitation for us to drink. Jackson grabbed
two water glasses, filling each with a touch too much alcohol. Still
wrapped in the towel, I propped myself on a bar stool. I wiped
the undersides of my eyes with the corner of the towel, suddenly
aware my mascara had probably raccooned itself. Jackson handed
me a glass. "Bottoms up," he said, clinking his to mine before
we both opened our mouths and let the liquor slide down our
throats. This time, the shot hurt as it went down, my throat already burnt by the chlorine. I flinched at the pain. When I opened
my eyes, Jackson stared at me, worried.

"I'm sorry," he said. "I didn't—I wasn't trying to—" he stammered. His chest was splotchy; he was worked up.

"I'm not a great swimmer," I said matter-of-factly. I didn't
want it to become a thing. To be pitied—or questioned. "One
more?" I pushed my glass across the island toward him.

"Shit," he said, running his hand through his hair. He grabbed
the bottle, pouring a bit more into both our glasses. He walked
around the island and sat next to me, his suit soaking the stool's
cushion. "I'm glad I didn't accidentally drown you." He smirked
a little, putting the glass in front of me. "To cheating death."

He has no idea, I thought before taking the shot. I shivered as
alcohol trailed toward my stomach, the house's air-conditioning
raising my skin. "I think I've done, like, twenty toasts today." I
laughed, trying to break the tension. "I can't tell if there are endless things to celebrate, or if someone is trying to take advantage
of me." I looked right at him, a dare.

Instead of laughing, or kissing me like I had hoped, he put a
hand on my back. The motion was gentle, caring. "All right, that's

fair." He grabbed our glasses and dropped them in the sink. "How about a movie? Your pick since I'm the asshole who almost ruined your night." My stomach flipped. Watching a movie was code for so many things. Or he could mean he just wanted to watch a movie.

We went upstairs and I grabbed him some dry clothes from Rachel's brother's room. He was way older than us and ran a restaurant in Chicago; he rarely visited. He wouldn't miss them. Drunk and giddy, I slipped out of my wet clothes and lay on my bedroom floor in my swimsuit, watching the ceiling fan spin with excitement. The warm feeling I had all over—it was a new high. It felt invigorating, exciting, a foreplay of sorts. I grabbed my towel and opened the bathroom door. Jackson was in there, still dripping from his swimsuit, turning the shower knob.

"Oh—oh god," I stammered. "Sorry." I turned quickly, shuffling back to my room. I stood in there alone for a few seconds, catching my breath. But the alcohol, it made me brave enough to do things I wouldn't otherwise, to go for what I wanted with the same fervor I had before that summer. It made me hungry. I turned on my heel and walked back to the bathroom. Still unlocked, the door opened with a push. Jackson hadn't gotten in yet, his back to the doorway, both hands on his head. I walked up behind him, tugging at his waistband. He turned slowly, his hands suddenly on my face. "Amanda," he said so quietly, I almost couldn't hear. I stood on my tiptoes and kissed him, his lips warm against mine, his tongue gently slipping between. He moved a hand down my back, pressing the edge of my swimsuit bottom to pull me closer. I had been with other guys, crossed all the bases simply for the story, to prove I could keep up with Rachel, to do what I thought I was supposed to in a relationship. I had even had a few drunken one-night stands, the rushed, sloppy ones full of urgency and fleeting passion. This, it was different. My insides danced, every cell running on overdrive.

I pulled away, looking up at his face. So eager, so hopeful, so earnest. Turning, I shut and locked the door, never once letting go of his hand. The shower still running, he followed me inside, still in our bathing suits. He grabbed shampoo from the shelf, squeezing it into his palm, then rubbing it into my hair, massaging my scalp, bubbly lavender filling the room. I did the same to him, blowing the leftover foam at his face as he stuck his head under the faucet and the soap dripped down his body. We didn't talk, just laughed, our lips brushing skin, hands unsure what to do next. I grabbed the body wash, looking up at him, hoping we were on the same page. He stared back, unflinching, this complete stranger who felt so familiar. Who felt safe. I puddled a dollop in my hands, rubbing them together then on his chest. He stood like a starfish, arms out, following my lead. I lathered his arms, then his chest again, swerving my hands toward his waistline. I put a hand on each side of his trunks, shimmying them down his body, still looking at his face, only his face, while my hands wandered to do what I thought they were supposed to do, what I thought guys wanted. He closed his eyes, his expression one that seemed only meant for me. He grabbed my hands, pulling them back up and around his neck, kissing me as the warm water sprayed around us. Anticipation pulsed all over. Jackson pulled at the strings of my bikini top, then bottom. He kissed my sternum, my stomach, placing a hand on each hip as he moved toward his knees. For a split second, I felt self-conscious, until he hit the right spot and I thought I might pass out. I stumbled toward the shower wall, leaning in ecstasy. His fingers seemed to be everywhere, dancing as he stood up and watched my face for cues, the climax. I gasped when it came, the ease of it a total surprise. I later learned he loved to watch me come, to see how his touch could conjure a joy that colored my face. The way he made me tremble was almost as addictive as the sex itself. "I feel like a god," he told me. I opened my eyes, turning off the water and grabbing our towels from the ground. We were both quiet, smiling at each other. My heart was pounding, my cheeks and collarbone flushed, my lips buzzing. I stuck my head out of the bathroom door, then pulled his hand toward my room across the hall. We shut the door, locked it, and, again, he waited for my cue. I dropped my towel, walking toward the bed and looking over my shoulder. He stood, his towel still wrapped around his waist.

"Are you sure?" he asked, sounding surprised, excited, a beg for me to say yes. I remember thinking he seemed like one of the good guys, so worried about my wants. I nodded, sitting on the bed and watching him.

Something about Jackson Huxley felt trustworthy. That, combined with the tequila, made this moment revelatory. His affection flooded the cracks in my self-built wall, the ones I'd never let anyone get close enough to see or touch. Jackson's warm body enveloped me, covering my neck in soft kisses, each push a hammer, hacking and hacking at my wall until I felt it start to crumble, a rush of pleasure that made me dizzy. He collapsed on top of me, our skin sticking together with sweat. I wrapped my legs around his back, pressing them tight into his sides. I remember thinking I could have lain like that, my body entwined with Jackson's, for eternity.

When he finally climbed off me, pulling me toward him to spoon, he whispered, "Fuck, you're perfect," stumbling to find his next words. I laughed, unsure how to respond. My heart pounded as I turned away, hiding my expression. Elation. Excitement. "I want to do this every day." He traced a finger down my stomach, past my belly button, and rested his hand on the inside of my upper thigh, his head crashed into my shoulder. Fear. I felt utter and total fear. But for once, it was the good kind.

The memory of our first night together makes my head ache even more. How he called me the next day—not texted, called—with an invitation for dinner. A surprise to Rachel, her bar so low after years of playing various roles in cat-and-mouse dating games. The intensity of his attention, the immediacy of his adoration, the way he looked at me, like I could do no wrong. I rub my temples again, the circular motion an attempt to suppress all thoughts of Jackson. Isn't the best cure for a hangover a little hair of the dog? I crack open one of the canned Diet Cokes in my bag and pour half into a red Solo cup, then add vodka until I hit the brim.

"That seems like an appropriate beverage to drink while remembering a man whose life was ruined by alcoholism."

Catherine. She looks the same, though her cheeks are no longer chubby and the only trace of her braces is a thin metal retainer I glimpse behind her bottom teeth. She's wearing a plain crewneck shirt and jean shorts a touch too long to be stylish. Catherine's smile is tight, controlled. It says, *I don't want to be here.* I flit away my annoyance, the old feelings of insecurity ignited for a moment. I need her, I remind myself. I smile bigger, ignoring my headache, my phone, my resentment toward Catherine, and our entire crooked history.

I stand up, my arms open. As she gets closer, I smell cedar on her skin. It's a mature smell, so different from the fruity kid stuff we drenched ourselves in when we were at camp. Her frame feels solid, tight muscles hugging her lanky bones. Maybe she's still into hiking and scavenging and the other outdoorsy things she used to go on and on about. She does have that signature Silicon Valley prepper vibe.

"It's been so long!" I say as I pull away, my enthusiasm a touch too much.

"Not that long," she says. Her comment hangs in the heavy air, taunting me with its innocuousness. Is she upset? Angry? Catherine has always been a tough read. I respond with a half-hearted laugh, ignoring her comment. There's no need to dissect the past. Today is about the future. Mine—and hers. I need her, yes, but she needs me, too. She is right, though. It hasn't been that long.

We ran into each other on a random Saturday morning in New York in December at an unmemorable Starbucks somewhere near Washington Square Park. The air was starting to freeze, deep winter lurking in the droplets of each cloudy breath. I was waiting for my order when a familiar voice asked, "Amanda Brooks?" Immediately, I was taken back to that summer, Catherine's signature baritone unchanged by hormones and age.

"Wow," I said, my surroundings suddenly fading. "Catherine Wagner. Wow. It's been—well, forever." I awkwardly wrapped my arms around her gangly body. I remember she was wearing a T-shirt, some nonsense no-vowel company name splattered across its center, and a backpack, looking like she belonged in San Francisco rather than New York. "What are you doing here?" I said, pulling back. New York was *my* city and her presence felt like an intrusion.

"I interned this past summer at Google," she said, adding, "in San Francisco." Of course. "But we have post-program informational interviews during winter break this week, so they sent a few of us to New York. I'm focused on computer science, getting my master's in Boston. I just started." She still talked with a youthful excitement, like everything in her life was infinitely interesting and worth sharing. "I live in Boston," she said again, like she could read my mind. "I'm only here for a few days."

A man behind her cleared his throat, cutting between us to grab his coffee. He gave Catherine side-eye, likely annoyed by her chirping earnestness. My chest twisted in defense, and I glared right back at him. The sensation was primal. It was okay for me to make fun of, to judge, Catherine, but not him.

I turned back to her. "Right, wow," I said. Again. The only word I seemed capable of mustering. Here was this key piece of my past, this person I was bound to on a deep, frightening level, and we were making small talk. There were things I wanted to ask her, like if she also still had nightmares. Or if she had talked to Meg at all. Or if she'd shared our secret with anyone—maybe Barrett, or her dad. Yet I held back. Mainly because it seemed inappropriate to dive into these sorts of things in an overcrowded Starbucks in the middle of Manhattan. But also because Pandora's box isn't meant to be opened. I didn't need its havoc upending the life I had put together in my attempts to move forward and never look back.

"Amanda—skinny iced caramel macchiato," the barista shouted. I grabbed my order, hand already wet from the condensation. When I turned back toward Catherine, I realized she was holding a black coffee, iced. No visible milk, likely no sugar, all business and caffeine. My order suddenly felt frivolous. I held it by my side, fingers clawed around the cap.

"We should catch up," she said, moving a step closer. "Like, really catch up, you know?" She spoke the second sentence softer, the conspiratorial tones unmissable.

My heartbeat picked up, the thought of a one-on-one with Catherine too much to handle. At that point, life with Jackson was good. My professional future looked bright. I had no interest in revisiting the past. Still, I heard myself say *sure*. "What's your number?" I asked, pulling out my phone with my free hand. "I'll text you and we can get drinks or something this week before you leave."

She smiled and eagerly shared each digit. "That would be great. After you never answered our emails, I figured we'd never talk again," she said when I finished typing. "This meeting feels fortuitous. There are things you should know."

I didn't acknowledge her comment about the emails. I knew the ones she was talking about but pretended otherwise. And what did I need to know? She wasn't a part of my life anymore. Didn't she realize that? I was done with the past but also hated confrontation. So, yet again, I smiled. "Yeah, seriously. For sure," I said absently. "I have to go . . ." I motioned toward the door.

"Meeting someone for a project," I lied. "I'm in grad school, too." Catherine looked excited by this, her mouth open and ready to say something else. "I'll text you!" I said quickly, giving her a quick hug and moving toward the door. The last thing I saw was Catherine's confused face. Didn't she remember I couldn't be trusted? That she couldn't mean anything to me if I wanted any sort of normal life? I didn't care about being rude or hurting her in the moment, thinking I would never see her again. I didn't even save her number in my phone. She friended me on Facebook a month later. Why was she always doing that, extending an olive branch? I left the request in limbo, until I clumsily hit accept while going through my friend request list on my phone in February. When everything changed, I found myself wishing I had her number, not wanting to share too much on Facebook, sorting through old AOL emails and finally finding the ones she and Meg sent in the year after we left camp. The ones I read but left unanswered, until a few weeks ago, when I typed my first response in almost a decade, hitting send and praying they still occasionally checked their accounts.

"Want one? There's plenty to go around," I ask Catherine in the woods, the memory of our impromptu meeting fading as I nod toward the Tito's bottle lying on the blanket. Standing now, I see how pathetic the setup looks. Me, alone, red Solo cup in hand, drinking away my sorrows. It's a cliché, but fuck if I know how to better handle the shitshow my life has become, the uncertainty of my future despite a decade of carefully laying stepping-stones that seemed to distance me from my past. Planning was pointless, I realize. Jackson reminded me I was bound to that summer, no matter how much I tried to escape. So, for now, a drink seems like the easiest reprieve.

Catherine cocks her head to the side, debating the pros and cons of having a warm cocktail in the middle of the woods with me.

"Um, I'm good. I have to drive back to Boston tonight, so . . ."

I'm supposed to drive, too, back to New York that evening. Oh well. I have time to sober up before the trip home, I convince myself, taking a sip. We sit in awkward silence for a minute. I take another sip from my Solo cup, giving Catherine a closed-mouth smile. "It's weird to be back here," I say, the drink already putting me more at ease. So is her presence. She showed up. Just that feels like half the battle. She's a bit fidgety, uncomfortable in these woods, her hand gripped around her phone like it's a lifeline. I wish she would have a drink with me.

"Yes, it certainly is. It's triggering quite a few memories." She looks around, the same way I did when I first got here. "It feels a bit eerie, candidly."

She's right. It does, like Meg's dad's spirit is lurking, dodging behind trees as he watches us. As he tries to catch us. "Yeah, I know meeting here was Meg's idea and all, but I wish we could have met at the casino or something." I take another gulp from my red Solo cup, my phone vibrating once again. I pick it up, the notifications piling, then flip it facedown. "It's creepy here."

"We couldn't have met there. Too many cameras." She's paranoid, her pupils big as they jet around the woods, watching. Her eyes land on my phone, its vibrations impossible to ignore. "Who's that?" she asks, her face suddenly flushed.

"Him," I say, then pause. "You know, Jackson. My boyfriend." The real reason we're here, I want to add. I know she knows that, though.

She nods again and silence lingers between us. Catherine breaks eye contact, her sight line darting from my phone to the trees to her lap. She looks nervous. I get it; there's so much to say, to ask—from both sides—but it feels like sacrilege to start without Meg. "You know what?" Catherine says, the awkwardness easing in her voice. "I'll have some." She tilts her head toward my bag, the bottle of Tito's poking its head through the unzipped top. "But just a little. Only one drink."

I smile, a sly crack across my face. Like I said, we are twenty-three. No one ever drinks alone when they're twenty-three.

I wasn't always a big drinker. The consistent bingeing crept up on me, worsening the longer I've been with Jackson. He loves a stiff cocktail, a heavy pour. I usually don't, save the occasional big night out. Or didn't, downing enough cocktails to feel a solid buzz but never so many I lost control. That's what happens when life becomes too comfortable, though; you get sloppy.

For the past decade, normalcy is all I've craved. I had shut down when I got home from Catalpa: curling up in my bed, shades drawn for hours every day; answering questions monosyllabically, if at all; cutting meat out of my diet, the sight of cooked hunks of flesh enough to make me hurl. No one except my parents knew I was home since I wasn't supposed to be back in New York until the end of the summer, so there was little motivating me to leave the apartment. Worried, my parents suggested therapy. After all, I'd seen a man die, they reminded me, like I had somehow forgotten. I wasn't ready, I told them. They turned to sports, signing me up for daily tennis lessons. The structure was like an electric shock, reviving me and steering me onto a new path, one with schedules and weekly goals and purpose. I started playing more than ever, the aggressive pursuit of thwacking the ball over the net with graceful precision keeping me calm, eating up frantic energy. When I wasn't on the courts, I ran, punishing my body, pushing out the bad, the excess, the fat, like shedding it would shed my lack of control, my distaste for discipline, my rage. It felt good, having something to focus on beyond the image of blood seeping into the brown carpet of the RV on a loop. When school started again, I applied the same fervor to my studies, becoming a straight-A student, never too close to danger. Everything I thought I knew—being bold, daring, manipulative, mean—seemed too dicey. Restraint became my best friend, the thing that kept me feeling safe and in control. Oddly, it also made me cool, a nonthreat to Rachel's reign since I was openly indifferent to taking the top spot; a walking thinspiration board for the girls in our class fighting newly acquired muffin tops and the first signs of cellulite; a mystery to the guys, a challenge that drove them mad. I had finally earned a permanent seat at Rachel's table. I liked our friendship; it meant I was never really alone with my thoughts and I was never the focus, the one drawing attention. She was more than I realized, too: a force if crossed, but also fiercely loyal with a complicated home life, a girl who found a semblance of family in me. And maybe because I wasn't a threat to her, with no plans of my own to usurp her throne, we became closer than ever. With my setup—tennis, good grades, cool friends—I blended in. In college, I was a floater, never fully landing in a specific group. There was always a boy in my bed, but I never let it get serious enough to bring them home to my parents. I ran when things started to get deep, when they began revealing their hopes and dreams in the early-morning hours or suggested meeting their families, and hopped into the next relationship, the cycle enough to keep me from seeming too odd or unpopular. The closest I ever got to a serious relationship was Adam Rhodes, a premed student a year ahead of me with kind eyes and a dad bod. When he was accepted into med school in New York, I thought maybe, just maybe, I would keep him in my life. But I felt claustrophobic in the weeks leading up to his graduation, his parents'-weekend plans a laundry list of activities I began to dread. We broke up a day before senior week. I was everywhere and nowhere, just another girl too focused on school to ever really be tied down. It was enough to stave off my parents' abundance of careful how-are-you-doings and impromptu cell phone check-ins.

I didn't think I deserved to feel special—until Jackson.

He told me he loved me a month after we met, over al fresco rosé at a café in the West Village. It was magic hour, the city soaked in a golden glow. He had come straight from work, the top two buttons of his oxford undone and his hair a mess from hours of running his hand through it. Rachel and Reggie were there, too, their relationship, I proudly noted to myself, hardly as serious as mine with Jackson. We'd spent almost every waking moment together since meeting in the Hamptons. A lot of the relationship was sex, limbs twisted and arms around each other for hours and hours. It was also this deep reliance on one another, an obsession neither of us could have predicted. Physical, emotional, unexplainable. It felt like science at work. Jackson was quiet as I talked, not adding much. I had never experienced his kind of intensity, a never-wavering focus. He listened, absorbed, a student in the school of Amanda. After years of feeling invisible, mostly on purpose, I was suddenly seen. Some might have categorized his constant contact, his immediate need, as smothering, but I found myself wooed, the pace so speedy I had no time to question it. Instead, I found it addictive.

"So, like, did you already apply?" Rachel asked, referring to a summer internship I had my eyes on; I was in the thick of midterm prep and I had spent the day poring over textbooks and my notes in the library. I had so many big goals. One included scoring an internship at my university that summer that would put me on the path to join an esteemed research group in the psychology department the following year.

I shook my head, about to answer, when our waitress, a twenty-something with arms covered in a trail of trendy minimalist ink, interrupted. "So, what can I get you guys? More wine?" Two bottles of rosé at the center of our table, each nestled in a sweating metal bucket of ice, were nearly empty.

"Yeah, hit us with another round," Jackson said, his eyes on the menu. Our waitress looked at him, no notepad in sight. Her face was neutral, unreadable, like she was indifferent to our very existence. *I'm from here; I have as much street cred in this city as you,* I wanted to shout at her, my need to be liked by everyone I deemed cool still quietly persistent. But I said nothing. "And I'll have the veal orecchiette," Jackson continued, still not looking at our waitress, his finger trailing from the pasta section to seafood, where it stopped. "She'll have the halibut."

"What, you can't order for yourself?" Rachel joked, draining the last splash of wine in her glass.

"Amanda likes halibut," Jackson said, a defensiveness in his tone. "Right, babe?"

"Since when?" Rachel asked, her head cocked to the side, her smirk smug.

She had known me forever, and therefore knew I wasn't much of a fish person. Jackson prided himself on his foodie palate, though, so I never stopped him from picking out my meals when we ate out. As I searched for an answer, Jackson talked first, completely missing the tension between Rachel and me. "What about you, Reg?"

"Nah, man, I gotta run," Reggie said, looking at his phone, then at the waitress. "We're good. Just food for those two." She nodded, turning for the kitchen.

"But I thought you were free all night." Rachel's cheeks darkened a shade, a few anxiety splotches appearing on her collarbones as she suddenly forgot about the great halibut inquisition and channeled her focus from me to Reggie. "Where are you going?"

"I have shit to do." He shrugged. "Jack, Venmo me. Cool?" He pushed back his chair, Rachel's face stunned. "I'll text you later," he said to her, half-heartedly kissing the back of her head before walking down the street.

"What the fuck?" she said once he turned the corner. "Um, does he think I'm a fucking joke or something? Jackson, who is he going to see? I know you know," she pushed.

Jackson shrugged, his lips tight. "I think a work thing."

An awkward silence stewed between the three of us, Jackson

obviously wanting to avoid the topic, Rachel fuming that her best friend's boyfriend wasn't working harder to win her over, and me not sure what to contribute. Rachel pushed back her chair. "Well, guess I'm out, too. I'll Venmo you, A."

I gave a weak nod and said goodbye. She stormed down the sidewalk, her strut the tiniest bit loopy from the wine. "That was sudden," I said once she was out of sight. "What's Reggie's deal?"

"I dunno," Jackson said. "I think he's sort of realizing Rachel is, well, a lot. And you can't really blame him."

"I mean, she can be sometimes," I said, trying to diffuse his words with a small laugh. "But, like, she's a really good person. Deep down, you know?" He said nothing, taking another sip of wine. "Maybe it was all my talk about academia?" I wanted it to be true that I had taken up too much space with my words, that my ambition was overwhelming to Reggie, that it wasn't my best friend's flaws that scared him away. I was afraid Rachel couldn't handle another rejection, another setback on the perfectly drawn path she'd mapped for herself. I knew Jackson had never questioned my love of goals. It was part of his appeal; my life without them was messy, complicated. Dangerous. Goals, especially professional ones, kept me focused on my future, not my past. All the past had for me was trouble. Jackson found my ambition endearing. "I know internship talk can be boring." I looked down, my fingers dancing in infinity signs on the table's crisp linen.

"No," he said softly. He reached across the table, his hand resting on my free one. "No. Not at all. It's cute when you get all excited about work." His hushed tone made me anxious; I'd never heard him use it before. He looked off to the side, then back at me. "Don't do that. Don't minimize yourself to lift up Rachel. You don't need to do that. You're perfect, really," he said, his lips crooked. I let out a girlish giggle. I couldn't tell if it was performative or real, but it seemed to please him. "I love you. You know that, right?" He squeezed my hand a little tighter, rubbing his thumb along my palm. I felt my eyes welling, these three words more than I ever expected, as he blubbered on, saying how much he enjoyed every minute with me. How, in less than a month, I had changed his entire view on relationships, on being with one person forever. How he wanted to make sure I knew how much he appreciated me. And didn't I realize how much he loved me? The swirl in my chest intensified the more he talked. I didn't deserve his love, his trust. I was a bad person, one with a dark past he knew nothing about. A past I didn't so much regret as want to hide, worried that someone might pick at the glue damming it from gushing into the present, upending the normal life I'd built for myself. I knew I should end it with him, right then and there. This had gotten too far, our hookup. I felt myself slipping, losing the control I had spent years perfecting and slowly revealing the deeper parts of myself I usually kept hidden, my desires and aspirations and feelings. Hearing those words, though—they erased my apprehension. The rush they gave me was intense and all-consuming, my chest tied in a series of sheepish, frenetic knots. Why couldn't I be impulsive and follow my gut? Sure, last time I had done that it had ended with a man dead. But this was different. Jackson was safe, reliable, unconditionally there for me. That's what love meant, no?

"I love you, too," I said, sandwiching his hands with mine, Rachel and Reggie now completely out of mind. He scooted his chair around the table and kissed my cheek, my forehead, then my lips so tenderly I felt like I might die. I didn't want to, though. For the first time since that summer at camp, I had something— someone—to live for.

We met each other's families after Thanksgiving. Jackson's parents preferred dinner at a steakhouse in midtown, the booths spacious and tables covered in crisp white linens. Downtown was too far from their hotel, and they didn't like cramped spaces

with overpriced portions meant for mice, he explained after I
suggested a few New York staples. They were in the city ahead
of the winter holiday, his mom a fan of New York only when it
was bedazzled and intoxicated with Christmas spirit. "Manhattan
is usually a touch too brusque for my taste," she confided after
three glasses of Pinot Grigio at dinner, her slight twang suddenly
sharp. His dad ran the family office of a storied Georgia family
called the Warners, their massive wealth ballooning all the more
with each new investment he made. Jackson didn't agree with his
dad's politics—the family Mr. Huxley worked for was known to
support candidates with silver hair and a passion for overturning
Roe v. Wade—but they got along well enough, usually opting to
talk about sports over current events. Jackson's mom had been a
kindergarten teacher until he was born, her miracle child who
arrived after six years of trying. They seemed like lovely people,
polite and polished, Jackson's dad's Northeastern roots buried by
two decades in the South. Mr. Huxley mainly talked about their
country club, name-dropped his friends' kids who he was almost
positive went to my alma mater—"Class of 2005, I think," he
said, his thick hair gelled into a crisp wave against his scalp, "or
maybe it was 2007"—and Bill Belichick, who, both Mr. Huxley
and Jackson agreed, despite their loyalty to the Falcons, was the
best coach in the league. Mrs. Huxley complimented my Chanel
purse, borrowed from my mom's closet, and asked me about my
studies. The conversation never got too personal, froth scraped
but not blown away. Overall, it went well. Jackson promised they
liked me—loved me, even, though it was hard to imagine either of
them using those actual words. Fawning emotions didn't seem to
be their strong suit. We had dinner with my parents the following
week. I still lived at home, saving money while I worked toward
my master's. My parents gave me plenty of space, but ever since
my summer at Catalpa, they wanted me to assure them that everything was fine and I was stable—even if deep down we all knew

that wasn't true. The appearance of Jackson in my life seemed to be the first time they were truly convinced I was not only stable but happy. My mom mouthed "He's cute" as she gave him a welcome hug. My dad winked at me from the living room while he talked to Jackson, my mom and I at the kitchen island doing the dishes. It felt cleansing, like Jackson gave me a new start.

To celebrate successfully meeting the parents, we cracked open a bottle of champagne at his apartment that weekend. I spent most days and nights at his place, two drawers in his dresser and one in his bathroom reserved for my things. The first bottle quickly turned into a second, this time red. We were pure effervescence, consumed by the love we felt for each other and the love we felt from our families. Jackson turned on a portable speaker and started playing Ed Sheeran.

I shook my head. "No," I said. "This is too cheesy."

He ignored my resistance, putting out his hand. "Amanda Brooks, may I have this dance?"

I laughed, the room around me starting to blur from the alcohol. My hand placed in his, he pulled me off the couch and we started swaying, the intimacy of the moment drawing us closer and closer. He tilted my chin up, giving me a soft kiss. I closed my eyes, savoring the moment. I knew I had to tell him about that summer at camp. It was only fair—and, after all, he loved me. Love forgave all, right?

"Jackson," I whispered, my eyes still closed. "I have to tell you something."

"Shh," he said into my ear. "Just shh."

He clumsily spun me around, both of us laughing at our ridiculous moves. Then he swept me into his arms, one around my back and one under my knees. He carried me to his bed, laying me on top of the comforter so he towered over me like a cloak of protection. That's how I felt in that moment: protected, understood, vulnerable. Totally and completely his.

"Oh, wait!" he suddenly said. "Can't forget the most important part." He ran to the coffee table and grabbed our wineglasses, both half empty with what was left in the second bottle. My phone, plugged into its charger on my nightstand, buzzed. I glanced at it quickly, a text from Rachel.

How'd the big meet the parents night go?

"Who's that?" Jackson asked, craning his neck to get a glimpse of my screen as he placed the bottle on his nightstand and crawled onto our bed.

"Oh, no one. Just Rach," I said, flipping the phone upside down and ignoring her message. I'd get to it tomorrow.

"When is she not texting you?" Jackson laughed, passing me a glass. I didn't need any more, I knew, but we toasted and smooshed our purple-stained lips together, falling on top of each other in bed and tangling ourselves in the sheets.

"Um, we hit that out of the park," I slurred. "I can't believe it. I don't deserve this. Deserve you." I poked Jackson's stomach, his skinny abs tensing with laughter. He rolled his eyes, draping an arm over me. We were lushes sinking in a sea of down feathers.

"I'm not a good person," I murmured, shaking my head. "Not good like you."

"I don't know why you say shit like that," he whispered. I'd done it a few times before, always after too many drinks, the guilt of my secret clawing its way up from the depths. "There is nothing you could do that would make me fall out of love with you," he said, his voice sincere. "You're stuck with me, babe." Jackson pulled me close against his chest. "You're stuck with me," he repeated. "I was about to say that I think you should move in."

"What?" I asked, unsure whether I'd heard him right. I sat up, my head cocked to the side.

"You. Move in. With. Me," he said more slowly, his dimples deepening as he spoke.

"Seriously? You don't think it's too soon?" I asked, the room suddenly spinning.

"You're always here anyway. Why not?" He walked toward me, grinning. "I mean, no shit I want you to be mine twenty-four seven." I wanted to be his. I *was* his. And moving in together would solidify that. Nothing had to change. Nothing would change. In fact, it would only get better. I needed this world of coupley milestones and declarations of love; they affirmed I wasn't damaged goods, that I could be like my picture-perfect parents. Jackson gave me entrance to a club I didn't think would want me because of my past. But it did. I basked in the acceptance, my insides fluttering with excitement. This was it—my fresh start.

"Yes, of course! Let's do it," I said, jumping to my knees and throwing my arms around him. "I'm all yours."

I saw Catherine at Starbucks days later. At the time, it seemed pointless reigniting a relationship with her. Now I'm kicking myself. We're taking sips of our drinks, struggling to find anything to talk about. She doesn't seem to want to talk about Jackson, at least not yet. I have no desire to do so until Meg's here. Catherine's vibe is different than it was months ago. It's not as curious or excited. Which makes sense, considering the context of today's reunion. Still, there's an uneasiness to her, an underlying instability that reminds me of my own. Maybe I missed it when I saw her last winter. Yes, that's it, I tell myself, hoping I'm right.

"So," I say, drumming the now-empty red Solo cup in between my hands. Catherine pulls a portable radio out of her bag, turning it on so grainy music plays through its speakers. "Have you seen Meg since that summer at camp?"

I don't think she has. I spent a night stalking Catherine's

Facebook profile after I accepted her friend request, and again before I reached out to her and Meg two weeks ago. It said she had studied computer science as an undergrad at Penn State, her profile full of pictures of hackathons and *Star Wars* memes. She wrote status updates asking for recommendations of good neighborhoods in Boston or if anyone had a friend looking for a roommate. Her dad was still alive, more gray and tired than I remembered. She had a group of seemingly nerdy friends, girls who graduated from Aéropostale graphic tees and shapeless denim in high school to Gap basics and skintight colored jeggings postcollege, their virgin hair woven into braids or messy buns, frizzies framing their faces. There was no sign of Meg or of some troubled past. She seemed happy.

She shakes her head as she takes another sip. "Not in person, no."

I look down at my lap, my dress resting smoothly against my flat stomach. Jackson likes that I count calories, balancing my intake with exercise, never letting things spiral too much. Rachel used to call me a drunkorexic, teasingly. Sort of. She had gotten a slight belly in college, her boobs two engorged balls of beer, so I didn't really care what she said. Jackson tells me it's sexy I'm in control of my body, that I make it do what I want. I can't shake the feeling of pride in making him proud, even now. I blink extra hard, forcing myself back into this conversation. The heat and hangover and alcohol are making my head spin.

"What's she like, Meg?" I ask, genuinely curious. When the three of us talked by phone, she had been a bit quiet, letting Catherine do most of the talking, a reversal of sorts.

Catherine looks uncomfortable again, shifting her weight from one butt cheek to the other. "She's, well," Catherine starts, "she's the same, in a way. Her personality remains jagged, but I've found her to be quite frail as you get to know her. She's never really had anyone look out for her."

"What about Laura? Isn't she still in the picture?" I ask, their faces the night everything happened vivid in my mind. I want to know what I missed all this time, what to expect. Out of curiosity—but also to comfort my own middle-of-the-night anxieties. Are they angry? Vengeful? Have they moved on?

Catherine nods, her fingers pressed against the blanket and scratching at the fleece. "My understanding is that Laura was a guardian, little more. Between unexpectedly becoming a parent and losing a good chunk of her income with the camp closing, she was pretty focused on working to support Meg. So Meg was left alone a lot. Physically, but also with her thoughts, reliving that night more often than either of us, I'm sure."

"Hmm," I said, nodding as if I could ever understand what she had gone through these past few years. "Why do you think Meg agreed to meet with us?"

"It's in her best interest. It's in all our best interest," Catherine says, picking harder at the fleece.

"Did she say that to you?" I have no idea what they've discussed, realizing for the first time that they likely talked— planned, even—before answering my initial email.

She looks up, her locked gaze so sudden it almost makes me jump. "Do you talk to Sarah still? I wonder about her from time to time," Catherine says, changing the subject. I haven't heard that name in years. Sarah, in a way the catalyst of it all. We're friends on Facebook, stalking one another from afar. That's it, though. She means nothing to me otherwise.

I shake my head. "The past." I lift my Solo cup in the air. It's light, a single sip left. "Fuck it, right?"

She raises her red cup to mine and mutters, "If only," toasting as her eye contact falters once again.

I laugh, tilting my head back with the last sip. "You know it's bad luck to do a toast without locking eyes, right?"

She looks at me, and for a second I could swear I catch

something shameful across her face. I only notice it because of its familiarity, a mirror reflecting my own flickers of buried emotion. It's gone in an instant and now I'm second-guessing what I saw. I realize I'm drunk. Not tipsy, but full-blown drunk. I should have eaten breakfast.

My phone buzzes again. I flip it over, Jackson's name bold and loud across the top as he calls for the twelfth time. I cringe, holding the side button on my phone until it goes completely black.

"Is that Jackson Huxley again?" she asks, nodding toward my phone. Her drink is about halfway done.

I nod back. It's sort of weird she knows his full name; I think I only ever referred to him as Jackson. Whatever. I push away the thought, focusing instead on topping off my cup with another round of vodka and Diet Coke.

The music playing from Catherine's radio is old, the kind of music our parents like. It's relaxing, though, Paul Simon's voice bumping along to an easy melody that embodies summertime. I look up and close my eyes. There's something magical about being day drunk, the tingling sensation that you're in this world but also slightly in another. The sun spilling through the leaves seems a bit too bright. A light trying to help me out of the darkness. I hold back a giggle, the alcohol making me optimistic about whatever will come next.

"Hail to Camp Catalpa," I start singing, a laugh escaping my lips at the same time. "Hail to her colors true." Catherine cocks her head as I sing. I keep going and she finally joins in, our voices in shaky harmony. We sing Catalpa's song, the one we practiced and practiced that summer until every single word was seared in our memory. When we finish, we hear a slow clap.

"Ladies, that was quite the performance," a voice says. We both look over. Moving against the trees, a girl in an earth-colored tank top and an off-white, billowy skirt seems to float, her orange hair swirling as she nears. It's Meg.

— 4 —

THEN

. . .

A rock, a steel flint, some tinder, and the forest floor. That's all you need to start a fire. Well, supposedly that's all you need, according to Chrissy, the campcraft counselor. I doubted that was the case, considering I'd been ferociously spinning a sturdy wood stick between my hands for eons, its bottom pressed firmly against the flat "beginners" rock Chrissy gave me, a wisp of hairlike cedar bark circling it. The fire eluded me; I couldn't summon so much as a spark.

"This is pointless," Sarah said, throwing her stick down in anger. Our cabin sat in a circle, each girl crouched above her caveman-esque setup. My hands were raw, the skin fragile and about to blister.

"I'm with you," I said, putting my stick down by my side. I transitioned from squat to cross-legged, my shoulders slumped in defeat. Larry kept spinning, unwilling to relent, never one to give up on the tiniest shred of potential even if the project was an obvious lost cause. Sydney had tried to start a fire maybe twice before giving up and carving doodles into the muddy ground with her stick. Amy's fire would never start, her tears soaking the flint. She hadn't stopped crying since our first night at camp, when she wailed for hours about missing her parents, her face speckled with red. Her sniffles were at first irritating and now a regular part of our daily routine. Everyone ignored them. We treated homesickness like a disease, the tiniest reminder of your parents or siblings or school friends enough to unleash a torrent of tears and ruin a perfectly good day. A few feet from the rest of us, Catherine and Barrett conspired like two witches concocting a spell. They worked in tandem, twirling their sticks with harmonious grace.

"Any luck?" Barrett asked Catherine.

"No! I'm baffled," she replied. I watched, peering their way, hoping their movements held the answers to this frustrating test. "I assure you I have tried every motion possible, but I have not had my eureka moment." We were in the small cove outside the campcraft hut, surrounded by tall pine and box elder and white ash trees. There was something otherworldly about the intimacy of the space, the screams and laughter from the field muffled by the thick brush circling us. But the campers who were drawn to the space ruined its magic. Campcraft was for losers. The fire-making part was the singular fun thing we had done there all week; our earlier lessons focused on memorization and identification, like school in the middle of summer. Plus, I didn't see why I needed to know why moss grew on the north side of trees or the difference between wild cherries and American bittersweet berries. We were at a camp with running water and two cooks. We were hardly roughing it.

"Look!" Barrett shouted, pointing to her setup. A spark of orange grew into a true flame, devouring the tinder. Catherine sprang up, grabbing kindling to add to the pile. She gently massaged the fire, strategically positioning twigs so enough oxygen flowed, until it caught and swelled into a roar, red hair swaying in the stagnant summer air.

"Incredible," Catherine said, her eyes fixed on the bundle of flames. "Truly incredible."

We all started moving toward the mini-campfire. Even Amy stopped sniffling, her mind distracted by this small natural miracle. Chrissy's hand darted toward her back pocket, only to re-emerge empty.

"Crap," she said under her breath. "Okay, you guys hold it right there. I'm going to the hut to grab your cards so I can mark off Barrett's fire skill. Do not move! Or breathe on the fire." She sprinted away, leaving the seven of us alone. The fire was gentle, crackling and quietly eating the wood and forest rot it was fed, its power small but growing. Next to me, Sarah looked bored, her tools askew by her side. She pushed up the cap on her water bottle and tossed her head back, a waterfall of clear liquid pooling in her mouth. The excess dripped down her chin, which she wiped with a smirk. The rest of the group was transfixed by the fire, their eyes locked on the morphing creature. Instead I watched Sarah's face, illuminated with mischief. "Oops," she said, pretending to fumble her water bottle in her wet palms, grabbing it after a few volleys from hand to hand. She caught it and squeezed. Hard. Water streamed out from the cap's opening, aimed square at Barrett's fire. There was a scream, from Barrett maybe. I didn't see who because my eyes locked with Sarah's, her smile inviting me to join the joke. My face froze in shock. Even to me, by that point a regular perpetrator of casual cruelty, this was *mean*. I only had experience with Rachel's queen bee–isms, and they were subtly exclusionary and passive-aggressive, never explicitly malicious. "Oh my god, I am *so* clumsy," Sarah said as Chrissy ran back out, cards in one hand and pencils in the other. "Sorry, Barrett. I'm sure you'll be able to do it again."

Barrett's face glowed with rage and indignation. "Shove it, Sarah. You're full of shit."

"Whoa, whoa." Chrissy stood between the girls, putting a

hand on Barrett's head. "We don't speak to each other that way, okay?" Babysitting, parenting, whatever you wanted to call it, the counselors were constantly dancing on the line between keeping us from getting into trouble and keeping us from ripping one another apart.

"It really was an accident," Sarah said, this time to Chrissy. And even after having seen what she'd done, I almost believed her. She seemed so wholesome. It wasn't until I got older that I began to understand this privilege, the power and influence girls who look like Sarah have over the world. They were given the benefit of the doubt, even when their actions clearly were wrong. After all, I'm one of them.

The gong rang, its chime telling us to move on. We all stood silently, waiting for Chrissy's direction. She shrugged. "You'll get it again next class, Barrett. I'll mark you as passed, regardless."

"You have got to be kidding!" Barrett exploded, unsatisfied until Sarah was apprehended. She followed Chrissy into the campcraft hut, yelling about Sarah's plans of sabotage. The incident had already flittered from Sarah's mind, her attention on Larry and Sydney, who were yodeling at the top of their lungs as they walked away from the campsite, each note an octave higher than the last and rippling off their tongues, an inside joke from last summer I still didn't really get. Sarah joined in, screeching louder than the other two.

"Amanda," she said, "I bet you can't go higher than this." Her vocal cords vibrated at their highest range, cracking the slightest bit as her note reached its peak. Camp was full of bets, of who could be better or best. I started yodeling, too, our group a goofy cloud of noise, minus Amy, who shuffled quietly next to us. Over my shoulder, Catherine was still sitting by the extinguished fire, her expression one of disbelief—and, I thought, maybe one of anger.

Packed shoulder to shoulder along benches facing the open center of the Great Hall, campers in all blue on one side and all green on the other shouted competing chants at the top of their lungs. A little over a week into camp meant it was time for team selection night, a Catalpa tradition that lit each girl's veins with excitement, their loyalties to their teams finally unleashed for the summer, anticipation about inducting new campers at an all-time high. There were lots of first-time juniors, and we were ushered to the front, both sides rowdily cheering as we walked down the center of the hall to take our seats. The lights were dimmed, the darkness pushed out by fat candles melting atop tall brass candelabras. Laura jumped up onstage, a flashlight up-lighting her face as a quiet hush came over the room.

"Good evening, Catalpa girls!" Laura yelled. "Welcome to the 2003 team selection ceremony." She was wearing her counselor uniform of all white and carried a wood walking stick, carvings chipped into its body from the ground up, and a glowing candlestick. Legend had it that the stick was a Native American tribe leader's and had been gifted to the camp by the town's mayor after fifty successful years in business. It was total marketing bullshit, but campers ate it up. Sometimes Laura let them hold it, the carvings signifying stories about friendship, family, and community. There were two chairs on either side of her, their wood frames cradling worn canvas. A large stuffed animal sat on each: Greensy was an ancient-looking turtle whose head, legs, and tail flopped around his overstuffed center. Bluesy was a teddy bear, also looking like he had seen better decades, his short hair a collection of matted tufts. Both were covered in fabric patches, each hiding the incisions previous captains had made to sew their final letters to the team inside the animals' stuffing for eternity. Notes from the previous summer's captains were the only ones not sewn inside; instead, they were stored in the little heart-shaped pocket on each animal, letters written in bubbly cursive and slanted print oozing with declarations of passion and friendship and forevers. "I'm very excited to introduce you to your new captains: Alison Bonn and Emma Zolner!" The hall shook as Laura hugged each girl and they took their respective seats in the captain chairs. Like Sarah and Larry predicted, Ali was the Blue Team captain and Emma, the Green Team.

Ali stood up first and the whole camp grew quiet. She walked to the front of the stage, a paper in one hand and an unlit candle in the other, next to Laura. Her face was solemn, a deep serious-ness assigned to the task at hand. "This summer we make an oath to lead, to love, to learn. Wind, water, and earth will help us on, asking nothing in return." She really was stunning, Ali. Her eyes sparkled aquamarine even in the dark. I got Sarah's obsession. I started to feel it, too. *Pick me,* I thought. *Please pick me.* She turned to Emma, who joined her at the front of the stage, Em-ma's curly hair tucked neatly into two braids that hung past her compactly square shoulders, ones that had helped her become a camp legend the previous year when she led the Green Team to victory during the final canoe sprint in the War Crew competi-tion. "We ask Mother Nature to bless us with strength, her power unparalleled. May we channel her vigor, beauty, and might, her integrity upheld." Together, they spoke in unison. "Two sides, not unlike, we make each other strong. Pushing each other toward excellence, we fight until all is won." Laura turned to each, press-ing the flaming wick of her candle to theirs until those candles, too, produced a swaying flame. Silence filled the room, the only noise distant katydids rubbing their wings. Laura stepped for-ward, teetering on the edge of the stage. "Camp Catalpa salutes the Green and the Blue Team captains of 2003. Ali, Emma—congratulations." She turned to each girl with a nod. "Now, let the games begin!" The hall erupted in cheers again, veins popping from girls' necks as they chanted at the top of their lungs. *"We are the Blue Team girls, we wear our hair in curls, we wear our dungarees, a-way above our knees . . . ,"* one side yelled. *"Thunder—thunderation—we're the Green Team—delegation—when we fight with—determination—we create a—sensation—thunder . . . ,"* the other tossed back. Laura brought two glass fishbowls filled with scraps of paper: one for each captain, the teams already presorted. Still, the not knowing which team you were on, nor when your name would be announced, heightened the evening's drama. My name was swimming in one of those bowls, ready to hear its fate.

"Good luck," Catherine said, hyperly slapping my thigh as Laura stuck her hand into the bowl. "You seem like a Green Team girl. I hope I am, too." She smiled, not realizing the insult she'd dealt. What did she mean, I seemed like a Green Team girl? I bounced my leg, shaking her off.

"Thanks, but, um, no thanks," I said, my response drowned by the chanting.

Name after name was called, the Greens or Blues cheering as the girls joined them. I sat nervously, my ankles crossed and my fingers sweatily entwined on my lap. *Please let me be a Blue, please let me be a Blue,* I willed. Catherine and Amy had already been called—they were Greens, hilarious additions to the athletic-looking group, their unformed bodies awkwardly perched on the newbie bench. Each time Ali put her hand into her fishbowl, I felt my stomach flip. With hope, with anticipation, with this desperate need to fit where I wanted to fit. I felt an urgent need to be with Sarah and was terrified of being not only separated but her competitor. When Ali announced my name, a waterfall of relief cascaded over my body. The cheers, just for me. The hugs from Sarah and Sydney and the older campers I didn't know that well but already looked up to. The blind loyalty and pride I immediately felt toward the Blues. It took everything to not cry in happiness, the overwhelming feeling of camaraderie a whirlwind.

As I was hugging Sarah, my chin nestled into her shoulder,

I saw Meg in the doorway of the Great Hall's entrance, her legs crossed as she slouched into the frame. Her arms were also crossed and I recognized the expression on her face: longing, the feeling of being so close to the action yet not truly a part. We locked eyes for a split second, then I broke contact, hugging Sarah tighter as we all bounced, a collective organism of cheer.

That night, Sydney and Sarah threw blue shirts and shorts and accessories at me, twisted bandanas and stretchy armbands. Then Sarah dug through her trunk and tenderly pulled a glossy river of blue silk from its spool and cut, at the slightest angle, an eight-inch ribbon. I brushed my hair into a ponytail, and like I was a queen at coronation, Sarah delicately knotted the fabric into a bow around my hair tie.

"Did you see Laura's creepy niece, or whatever she is, like, watching all of us from the shadows?" she said as she tugged a bit tighter at the bow.

I was embarrassed Meg and I had had something of a moment. I was still trying to process what her presence, her constant lurking, meant. There was an allure to her, to wanting to know more. This was an opportunity, though. "Oh my god, yes," I said, my arms still tingling from all the Blue Team hugs. "Something is weird about her, don't you think?"

"I think she's pretty," Sydney said as she stepped into a pair of plaid boxers, always rolled a couple of times. "Like, in a Spinelli way."

"Oh my god, dweeb. From *Recess*?" I laughed, Sydney's brain always drifting to corners of pop culture none of us thought about regularly.

"Why are you so obsessed with her?" Larry asked, ignoring me and Sydney as she threw a balled-up sock at the back of Sarah's head. Only Larry could ask a question like that without pissing off Sarah.

"What?" Sarah's cheeks turned a shade darker. "I'm not. She's such, like—I mean she's creepy. You guys have to agree. Total loser. Like, what is her deal, you know?"

Sydney shrugged, moving by Sarah's side and petting my ponytail. "Like I said, I think she's pretty."

"Ew, no," Sarah said. "She is not pretty. She's a freak, a total stalker. I mean, did you not see her teeth? They're so crooked and gross."

Sydney shrugged again, still stroking my hair.

"Stop being a loser," Sarah said, but without her usual brashness, before she turned and crawled up to her bunk, not saying anything else.

Our first color war match was the next day. The sport was Newcomb, which is basically volleyball in slo-mo. Sarah leaned over the shared sink area between cabins 5 and 6, staring into the copper-studded mirror while applying blue war paint under her eyes. Two French braids trailing her back, Sarah stood next to Sydney, who was coating stripes of her hair with blue mascara. Both were shirtless, their chests covered by training bras, the ones we had all begged our moms to get us—stretchy white half tanks with lots of coverage and little support, easy to jokingly stuff with balloons or secretly fill with balls of toilet paper. Catherine was the only one who didn't own a bra. The first night we were at camp, undressing with our backs to one another, most of us modest and trying to stay covered, Catherine took her entire shirt off, her nipples raised by two tiny lumps of fat. I found myself staring; we all were. It was weird, her lack of awareness. Larry put one of her bras in Catherine's trunk the next day, something that I now realize must have caused Catherine deep embarrassment, but at the time we thought was a kindness, a gentle suggestion that she hide her swollen bee-sting chest.

"Excuse me." Larry bumped past the two. Her hands were

covered in green war paint and she stuck them under the faucet. She didn't make eye contact and focused on the running water, streaks of green bleeding toward the drain. The pre-competition air was tense.

"War paint!" I said, scooting past Larry and between Sarah and Sydney. The blue jar of goo was cold as I scooped a glob and spread it on my fingers, tracing them across each cheek to create four perfectly parallel lines angling upward. The blue paint intensified my eyes.

"That looks really good," Larry said, looking up from the sink, breaking her pregame routine.

"Good? Um, it looks amazing." Sarah grabbed the tin and held it toward me. "Do ours!" Sarah grabbed a paper towel, drenched it in water, and rubbed it across her cheeks, erasing the thick rectangles of paint under her eyes. Then, without warning, she turned to Larry and wiped the towel across her left cheek.

"Are you for real?" she said as Sarah turned into a mini-mom, scrubbing Larry's face like it was covered in food. There were few barriers between the two, friends for as long as they could remember. Going through childhood's biggest milestones and bumps together bonded them in a way I couldn't comprehend. Not then, at least. Larry, the ultimate good sport, understood why Sarah acted out. She didn't absolve the bullying or the obsession with popularity, but Larry got it, had witnessed enough of Sarah's home and school lives to see past the act and, perhaps naively, believe it was nothing more than a phase. Such an attachment is rooted in love and care and heavy nostalgia. I only know this because it's what I have—well, had—with Rachel.

"Shh," Sarah said, still scrubbing. "You'll thank me later, even if you'll be my sworn enemy once the game starts." Larry swatted at Sarah's arm, a pesky fly buzzing around her head.

"I got you, Larry," I said with a laugh, and threw her a soft towel, pulling Sarah away. Larry huffed, stomping back to her bunk. "Your turn, crazy lady. Prepare to look amazing."

"I want to look fierce. Like Braveheart, you know? Scare all my competitors." Sarah flexed her arms, a warrior ready for battle.

"Hold on, this requires more tools." I ran to my trunk, rummaging through its contents to pull out a small paintbrush. "I stole this from the art hut. Don't tell anyone!" I held my finger to my mouth as I spoke and looked right at Sarah. Sydney watched as I dipped the paintbrush's head into the blue mess, then traced Sarah's closed eyes with a mask of swirly blue strokes. An artist at work, I stood back and added a touch of color here and there. "You look *insane,*" I said, sending a chef's kiss into the air.

Sarah's eyes blinked open, taking in her reflection. She stared at herself, tilting her head to one side, then the other, me and Sydney watching. She turned to me. "You're a genius. I *love* it!" She grabbed my arm and made me do a quick spin, my wet paintbrush hitting Sydney's torso.

"Um, hello?" Sydney said, pointing to the blue streak. "I'll forgive you if you do mine, too." She went into the cabin, where the rest of the girls lounged lazily on their beds; sat on her closed trunk; and jutted her chin upward expectantly. I dipped the brush back into the tin, painting Sydney's face but making sure hers wasn't as good as Sarah's. I wanted Sarah to see she needed me to look the best. When I was done, we put on our shirts, tie-dyed socks, and bandana headbands, a blue army. Sarah grabbed my hand, then Sydney's, and pulled us toward the door.

"Bye, soon-to-be losers," she said to the rest of the cabinmates. Larry gave a half-hearted wave from her bed, where she sat cross-legged while stretching her arms. Catherine's and Barrett's noses were buried in books; they didn't look up. We ran to the boathouse, where the Blue Team met in the hour before games, giddy with excitement and still holding hands. We didn't need Larry; we could be the new trio.

Warm from the midday sun and lack of air-conditioning, the boathouse was filled with other juniors. Ali and the pep captain, a pert fireplug named Janice Craig, sat on a bench in the front. The rest of us gathered on the floor, awaiting instruction. Ali talked about teamwork, about not giving up. The things we needed to focus on—communication, reaction time, strength. And, of course, the main goal of the game, to have fun. She said this to a room full of burgeoning athletes, save a few campers whose parents had underestimated Catalpa's focus on sports. Winning was all any of us cared about. Across the campgrounds, on the dock in Senior Row, the Green Team was meeting for their own pump-up speech.

We marched to the volleyball court, Janice our leader. She wore a blue tank top and Soffe shorts, and her limbs were covered with blue words: *Blue Team Girl; Forever Blue; I* ❤ *Bluesy*. She led every single cheer and chant at the absolute top of her lungs yet somehow didn't lose her voice. It had taken me a week to learn the camp's fight song—and now I had a whole slew of cheers to learn. It didn't matter as much; there were plenty of returning Blue Teamers whose volume made up for my lack. Sarah and Sydney were transformed, bulls gearing up for a run, the color green their signal to charge. The Green Team was on the other side of the court, Larry towering over the other juniors. Catherine and Barrett looked bored, half-heartedly cheering with the rest of the team, and Amy—well, she added nothing. She ended up leaving camp early a few days later. No one missed her.

Newcomb is a game for sloths. The greatest challenges at that age were serving and throwing the ball over the net, which was a few feet taller than even Larry. It seemed to go on forever. We rotated in, served, caught a few balls, tossed and missed a few others, rotated out. It wasn't until Catherine started serving that we woke up. She tossed the ball in the air and hit it with her fore-arm. It arced toward Kimmy, a petite first-year junior, who put her hands in front of her face to avoid getting knocked out by the serve. The ball hit her palms and fell to the ground. Point for the Green Team. That small win transformed Catherine, a sudden determined focus washing over her face. It was surprising, the reality that even she was susceptible to that sort of power. She glowed as she targeted the weaklings, her strategy quiet but ef-fective, like taking them down provided her a fleeting moment of respite from her own miserable stint as the weak one. Serve after serve, enough points accumulated that we lost the game.

Back in the boathouse, our shoulders hanging in defeat, Ali con-gratulated us on an "amazing effort" and said we'd get the Green Team next time: "The next game—softball—is in a week!" she said, cheering. "And I have faith that you girls will bring it." Sar-ah's arms were crossed and her lips tight during the speech—and as she stormed back to our cabin ahead of Sydney and me. When we got there, we heard the door to the bathroom slam.

Larry walked in just after, laughing with her arm around Catherine, the hero of the day.

"Lar," Sydney said. "We have a Code Blue."

Larry's face dropped and she pulled her arm back to her side. "Ugh, of course we do."

"Has she done this before?" I asked. Sydney and Larry were already heading back to their beds, disinterested in the Sarah show.

"Duh," Barrett said. "This is Sarah's thing. Every time the Blue Team loses a game, she storms around camp, is a brat through the daily activities, sometimes locks herself in closets, bathrooms, the equipment hut, like the true deranged person she is." It usually only lasted a couple of minutes, sometimes an hour. She wanted attention, maybe, or was angry about not getting enough atten-tion. The counselors were clueless, rarely at the cabins during the day, instead running around camp pushing girls from activity to activity. "It's one of the million reasons why I can't stand her," Barrett said, loud enough that Sarah could likely hear her through the drafty wood wall separating the outhouse from our cabin.

"Should I apologize?" Catherine asked, back to her sheepish self.

"Don't think so highly of yourself," Sydney said, letting out a low humph. "It's not about you, trust me." And then in a softer voice, "Besides, all you did was play well."

"Yeah, she just needs time." Larry threw a towel toward Catherine, then grabbed her shower caddy. "Guys, lunch is in, like, five minutes. I'm starving. Shower time!" she sang, swinging her caddy over her head. The war paint on our bodies had melted, drips striping our faces and limbs, towels over shoulders and shampoo in hand. We all had the same one, shaped like a fish with fruity insides, except Barrett, who used a scentless concoction of oils and glycerin, and Catherine, who used Head & Shoulders, making her an easy target for jokes about phantom flakes on her shoulders. I followed but stopped when I passed the bathroom door, tapping lightly. Larry had been so dismissive, so sure that she had the answer to best help Sarah. I wanted to prove her wrong, to show her that I alone could fix Sarah, that I could offer her something Larry couldn't. What that something was, I had no idea.

"Hey, Sarah—you in there?" I knew she was, of course, but felt shy, dumb even, as I waited for an answer. There was nothing. I could smell the stale air through the cracks in the door. "It's sort of gross to lock yourself in there. You're probably giving yourself the plague or something," I joked. Anything to get her to respond. But still, nothing. "Sarah—it's almost lunchtime. Are you going to come out?"

"I'm not hungry." Progress. I was pleased, at least for a second. I wanted to help her, for her to lean on me and commiserate about our loss. To be her confidante, if that's what she wanted.

"But they're serving BLTs! You've been telling me about this meal since camp started. Maybe dessert will be peanut butter swirl ice cream."

"Go away. I don't want to talk." Again, silence.

My eyes started to burn, the rejection levering a swell of embarrassment. I ran across to the shower cabin and slipped into the last stall. Anger started to bubble in my belly, an irritation toward Sarah matched with a pull; I wanted to make her happy. Why wouldn't she just let me? I had this deranged idea, the result of tween insecurity and competitiveness, that the summer would be a total waste if I wasn't her best friend by the end.

Dressed in regular clothes, paint hiding in the crevices of our nails after scratching it off our bodies, we waited outside the food hall for lunch. My stomach growled. Dan the Handyman came out, his thrice-daily routine of blowing into a trumpet to herd us into the cafeteria in full force, a few notes always squeaking as he blew. We sat at preassigned tables, each with a counselor at the head and a mix of campers from all rows. Sarah usually sat at a table a few over from mine; sometimes we'd catch each other's eyes and make faces. Her chair was empty today. I globbed peanut butter onto bread, topping it with bacon. A BPB, I liked to call it. Bacon peanut butter goodness. It was dry in my mouth. That's when I saw Larry, with two sandwiches in her hand, talking to Laura by the doorway. I looked away as she walked outside, like I had stumbled on some secret rendezvous. I felt my face tingle with frustration, once again feeling like no more than an observer unable to break through and make Sarah realize she wanted to be *my* best friend, not Larry's. A thick lump formed in my throat, the telltale sign that tears might come next. Ashamed, I mumbled something to my table about feeling sick and grabbed my plate, then beelined for the kitchen. We weren't supposed to be in there unless we were on dish or scraper duty, but the Nancys, the two chefs who had been working at camp since my mom went there, both named Nancy, were juggling cartons of ice cream and chocolate syrup as they prepared dessert and were too busy to notice me. As I put my plate behind them, I saw Meg raiding the fridge. I paused, plate in hand, and stared at her as she grabbed a can of whipped cream and a jar of something. She looked about my age, maybe a little older; her boobs, way more pronounced than those of the girls in my cabin but not as big as those in Senior Row, gave her away. Her legs were dotted with scabs, scars from itchy mosquito bites. Her oversized T-shirt and Umbros weren't that different from the ones we all wore, though hers had a slight gray sheen, and her hair was a bright red mess of a bun on the top of her head. She had a few streaks of uneven sunburn hissing against the pale skin of her arms and legs. I had never been so close to her, the freckles splashed across the bridge of her nose visible. Maybe I was looking for an outlet, or my own way to get Sarah out of her self-imposed lockdown. I walked over.

"What are you doing?"

She jumped, the touch of my hand on her shoulder enough to give her a scare. "What the tit," she said. "Hello, do you not believe in some goddamn personal space?" She paused, sizing me up. "You're a junior, right? I saw you in today's game. Cool war paint," she said, her smile a truce.

"Thanks." I smiled back, suddenly shy. "What's that?" I pointed at the can in her hand, glossy red liquid sloshing.

"Maraschino cherries," she said, putting the whipped cream down and screwing off the top of the jar. "Want one?"

I put my hand up, motioning that I was good. Her who-gives-a-crap vibe reminded me of Grace. We both smiled again. "I'm Meg, by the way."

"Amanda." As I spoke, a man walked in through the kitchen's back door near the fridge. "Go," she said, panicked, hiding the jar behind her back. "Go!" she said again with more urgency. So I did as told and ran back toward the dining room, crashing into a counter in the kitchen as I watched over my shoulder.

"Meg," he spit, "what the hell are you doing?" He resembled a puffier version of his daughter but looked about twenty years older, with a scruffy beard and messy salted hair. His eyes were tired, sagged down by deep bags. He wasn't unattractive—but there was something that seemed a bit wild about him. Almost feral.

Meg spun her head toward him, hiding her spoils behind her back. "Nothing," she said, her tone flat.

"Put those back," he said, his tone calm but serious.

She shook her head and started to walk past him, hands still full.

"I said put those back." This time, his voice was loud. Not a yell, but a deep bellow. "You want your aunt Laura to think you're a thief, huh? You're already on thin fucking ice," he said as he grabbed her forearm, his fingers digging into the skin so hard her grip eased and the glass jar cracked against the tile floor, lumpy goo turning the tile grout red.

The Nancys finally looked up, spotting both me and the disturbance. "What are you doing in here, hon?" one asked me. Meg's dad was already dragging her out, not wanting to draw more attention, the mess still untouched on the floor. She looked over her shoulder, our eyes locking. The air suddenly felt chilled, like the Nancys left the freezer open after unloading all the ice cream.

I dropped my empty plate on the counter. "Sorry," I mumbled, and nearly ran out of the kitchen, a pit in my stomach about what I had witnessed between Meg and her dad. I had never seen a grown man treat a kid that way, the meaty smack of his hand as it grabbed her arm echoing in my ears. I could have used it as gossip to share with Sarah and the crew, yet it all felt off, wrong,

like I'd witnessed something I shouldn't have. I was quiet the rest
of lunch, picking at my ice cream, feeling weird but unsure what
to make of it all. By the time I finished, I shifted my thinking toward Sarah and Larry, that part of my brain like leaving algebra
for third-grade math. A problem that seemed solvable, or at the
very least familiar. Still, deep down, Meg's dad and his strong
grip loomed, a boogeyman right under our noses.

After lunch, during Rest Hour, Sarah was back in her bunk,
quiet and furiously writing a letter. Likely one full of grievances,
addressed to her mom, carefully folded and licked and sealed
with a kiss (we all SWAK'ed our envelopes home; any excuse to
smear glittering color on our lips). Larry was back, too, eating
her sandwich in bed. Of course Larry had been able to coax Sarah
out of the bathroom, despite being on the team that had sparked
Sarah's fury in the first place. They had known each other so
long, their personalities familiar and predictable to one another,
their closeness impenetrable, like sisters'. I felt irritated, forgetting about seeing Meg less than an hour earlier, and stormed out
to the Roost looking for a distraction. Sydney, ever unfazed by
Sarah and Larry's bond, asked me to wait up. She was looking
for a letter from Greg, her boyfriend. They hardly talked in real
life, as most relationships at age twelve go, but wrote each other
lengthy letters on lined notebook paper, the margins of Sydney's
covered in metallic gel-pen doodles. She wore a bracelet he had
given her right before she left for camp, a puka-shell thing that
looked clunky on her skinny arms. She told me all this as we
walked to the Roost, her bubbly and me stewing. When we got
there, there was a box with my name on it, Rachel's in the top
left corner with her return address. Something about getting a
package at camp felt so pure and joyful, like Christmas morning.
It was already open—the counselors opened all packages before
they gave them to us, making sure contraband like Skittles and
jars of Nutella didn't make its way into our cabins—and the toy

animal inside, a fluffy bear, was cut open, stuffing spilling out from the incision.

"What the—" I started to say, picking up the bear with two hands. It was an overly gruesome cut, the bear forever maimed.

"Oh no! You got raided," Sydney said. It had happened to her before. Parents or friends would try to sneak us candy. You had to be strategic, filling boxes of beads with noisy candy like M&M's or stuffed animals with soft ones like Fruit by the Foot. The counselors were pros at sniffing out candy; after all, most had been campers once, too. And they had found all the candy Rachel had sent me that day. I left the Roost defeated and hot, the ripped-apart bear hanging from my fingers. Sydney called after me, an unopened letter from Greg held delicately between two fingers. I couldn't be near her joy. We'd been at camp for almost two weeks and what did I have to show for it? A gutted stuffed animal and an angry friend. The bear seemed like a harbinger of more bad news, an omen that meant my summer was doomed. I didn't know where to place my anger; I tried to send it to Rachel, for shipping me the package in the first place. Why hadn't she been more careful when hiding the candy?

I clenched my fists, my fingers fiery with frustration, and stormed down the dirt path back toward Junior Row, veering off a dozen yards before the first cabin. I let out a small, angry grunt, throwing the bear into the dirt and stomping on him, the ball of my foot twisting and turning as I pummeled him into the ground. Frustration coursed through me. It was the kind that would make me cry as a kid, the livid helplessness that comes when things never seem to go your way. I wanted to scream, to shout at the top of my lungs and release the greedy demon that seemed to keep me from being content. Why couldn't I be like Sydney, skipping around and daydreaming about fairies? Or Larry, big and solid and reliable? I didn't want to be Sarah. I knew her flaws, how polarizing her personality could be. But I needed her to like me. It was an addiction, one I hated in myself. I grunted louder as I dug my foot deeper into the ground.

"Um, what are you doing?" I heard over my shoulder. I froze, not wanting to see who had caught me. How would I explain what I was doing? It was childish. I knew that even then. I loosened my fists and slowly turned. Meg's face was scrunched, forehead twisted. "Did that bear go all Chucky on your ass or something?" She tossed a Skittle in her mouth, the bright blue package crinkled in her hand, and she tried not to laugh. Her bemusement infuriated me more.

I stormed past her, leaving the bear in a pile of dirt. As I took a few steps, my composure returned and I felt inertia pull me back toward Meg. Who did she think she was, making me feel like the stupid one? I stared at her for a second, soaking her in. Sydney was right. She was pretty, in a disheveled Pippi Longstocking sort of way, flaming strands of hair falling out of her ponytail, freckles smattered across her sharp cheekbones. Her eyes were dark, though, colored by a coldness I felt as I stared right into them. They made me feel uneasy. She stared right back, though, not wavering. I sensed we were equally interested in one another, intrigued yet distrusting. To me, she was a possible pawn in my game with Sarah, but more so a mystery, a young girl with an old soul, the type of wisdom only gained from living beyond your years. I wanted to know more, to rip her story open. For Sarah, and for myself. To her, I was a way in, the only girl at camp so far whom she'd really talked to, young enough that she wasn't intimidated but not so young a friendship would be weird.

"How do you even have those?" I asked, pointing at her Skittles. "Do you get special treatment because of Laura or something?"

"Ha," she said, raising the pack to me. "Yeah right. Want some? The tropical ones aren't even that good."

I put a hand on my hip, looking for a fight. "Are you okay, by the way?" I asked as casually as I could. Part of me truly wanted to know, and part of me wanted to put her in her place.

Meg cocked her head to the side, confused. "What are you talking about?"

"Earlier, I mean. I saw your dad—it was your dad, right?—grab you in the kitchen." She knew what I was talking about. My delivery was arrogant, like I had something on her way worse than burying a teddy bear. I don't know why I asked in that tone, the connection I felt seconds before shattered. Her eyes turned icy.

"Why—" she started, then stopped. "You don't know shit." Her voice was quiet, less confident than it had been seconds before. She picked up the bear and gave it to me. "Your secret's safe with me, psycho," she said, nodding toward the imprint in the dirt the stuffed toy had made and giving me a wink. It was cocky and condescending, a reminder that I was the stupid one. Not her. She had the power. Not me. It was such a small thing, her seeing me having a tantrum over the bear, but it felt bigger and embarrassing. I didn't want anyone to know, especially not Sarah. It was like Meg somehow sensed my insecurity, my obsessive need to fit in—yet she saw something more in me. An anger. And it seemed like she liked it. At least enough to keep it between us. Meg turned and walked through the bushes, heading toward the woods in the distance. The entire interaction left me disoriented, off-kilter. Confused about what I had seen in the kitchen, what Meg's quiet words meant. I spun around, the dirty bear in my hand, and started running back toward Junior Row. There was an underlying sense of unease, the kind that takes over when you're about to go to bed and have an irrational, unexplainable fear that something will crawl out from the darkness between your mattress and the floor and grab your ankles. I tried to shake it off with each bound. As I turned the corner, I physically ran into Sydney.

"Oh my god," she said, her hand placed at the center of her chest. "You gave me a heart attack. Oh my god." She took a breath, then giggled wildly—and before I could even speak, she started telling me about Greg's letter. He had broken up with her, told her long distance was too hard. And like that, I was pulled back into the world of small dramas. It felt comforting and predictable, a place I understood. Preferred, like my twelve-year-old brain couldn't handle more than what Sydney was sharing, the scope of Meg's world incomprehensible, like a PG-13 horror movie I watched with hands over eyes so I wouldn't have nightmares. I smiled as she told me that Greg was a bad kisser anyway, using too much tongue and slobbering all over her chin.

"Gross," I said, my mind drifting to my, not Meg's, reality, like how to get Sarah's attention back. How to make her like me the way she liked Larry.

"So what's up with Larry and Sarah?" I asked, trying to sound casual.

"What do you mean?" Sydney twirled, facing me as she walked backward.

"Well, like, they're best friends, right? But so different. Like, I don't get it."

Sydney paused her strut for a second, fingers to chin. "Hmm," she said. "I see what you're saying, but Sarah also is way meaner this year than she was last summer. Lar told me I have to excuse it because her parents are, like, in a bad place or whatever. My friend Monica DeAngelo's parents divorced last year and it was so bad. Like, all the parents were talking about it and people at school talked and stuff. So I sort of feel bad for Sarah." I nodded, not feeling sorry for her so much as bad for myself. How could I ever compete with Larry? There was too much history, a tangled mess Larry helped Sarah deal with outside the confines of Catalpa; I needed something big, something to really woo Sarah.

"Let's sing." Sydney veered the conversation back to the goofy, her specialty, weaving her arm through mine and starting to skip. How easy she made it look, pushing a grievance out of her head to make room for positivity. I wanted to be like Sydney, to have her be enough to satiate my insecurity. My obsession was too far gone, though; I convinced myself the only friendship that would be enough was Sarah's. *"The rain in Spain stays mainly on the plain,"* she began. I joined, both of us skipping and belting the lyrics in our best cockney accents. We burst through our cabin door, Sydney drunk on giddiness and me hoping our loud revelry would make Sarah jealous.

"Girls, it's Rest Hour. Respect the silence!" Betsy said, looking up from the notebook on her lap. She glared at both of us for an extra beat, a mall cop on the prowl. I had already forgotten about Meg, my obsession with Sarah so strong it tunneled my vision. I grabbed a notepad and pen before crawling onto my bottom bunk. Sarah was above me, still writing. My notepad was purple, a border of daisies framing its lined center. I tore off the bottom half of a sheet and scribbled a few quick words. As I wrote, my moment with Meg vanished from memory. It seemed ancient, as if it had happened years ago. I filed it away, storing it as a card to show to Sarah if I ever needed an extra edge, ignoring the tug that it was actually so much more than that.

The message I wrote for Sarah was simple:

Plan: Ruin Catherine's Life
Meet me after Rest Hour to learn more

I slid the note under the top bunk's guardrail, right onto Sarah's mattress. My heart clamored against my chest, beating faster and faster as I waited for her response. I had a general idea of what the plan entailed, a vague and shameful outline that involved a few harmless, I told myself, pranks. Would they be enough? After what felt like ages, she poked her head over the edge and threw the paper, crumpled in a ball, back at me to get my attention. I looked up.

"Hell yes," she mouthed, using her fingers to make a slicing motion across her neck.

Girls learn at a young age the easiest way to make a new friend is to find a common enemy, a girl to gang up on. Catherine was about to change my relationship with Sarah and, though I didn't know it at the time, my entire life.

April 23, 2014

[Blocked Number]

Hi, Jackson. Did you find what you
were looking for?

seriously, who is this?

if this is reggie im gunna wreck you

cut it out

I don't know who Reggie is. You
don't need to know me. But I know
Amanda.

pls just leave us alone

this is gettin creepy

Hint, hint: Check her old FB
photos. You'll find him there.

who

hello?

April 29, 2014

Hi, Jackson. Feeling sad from all
those lonely nights?

> wtf who is this???

> have u been watching me

> seriously stop or im
> calling the police

But then what would you
 learn about your sweet Amanda?

It seems she's been quite occupied
by her studies, don't you think?

> shes a good student so what

> what do you want

This is about what you should
want. Did you not find anything
on her Facebook?

Such a pity. I thought you'd be a
better detective.

> i looked, ok?

> i don't even know what im
> looking for

Try her album Spring Break 2012.
He's in there. Nothing like revisiting
the past, don't you think?

who is

??????

5

NOW

• • •

Everything about Meg is bigger, more pronounced, than I remember. Her hair flows past her shoulders in two loose pigtails. Rings clutter her fingers, all silver and mood stones. And her skin is almost translucent, save the freckles sprinkling her arms and chest and cheeks, the same ones I remember from that summer. "So, who's ready to squash the motherfucker trying to ruin our lives?"

"Jesus Christ, Meg. Shh." I look around, panicked, despite our obvious isolation in these woods. The only sign of the campground's previous life is a singular fifties-style trailer, all metal and rounded sides and rust. Everything else is mossy land and trees. Meg was always unfiltered, an in-your-face personality with splintered edges. Guess that hasn't changed. I hop up and give her a hug, our bodies so different than the last time we held one another. Catherine does, too, but they embrace a bit longer. Their touch is genuine, making me apprehensive as I see the strength of their bond. There's so much about both of them that I don't know. Maybe this reunion wasn't the right move. I twist my earring again. "Want some?" I nod to my Solo cup, then pause, realizing my mistake. Does she drink? Is she also an alcoholic?

"No, I'm good." She swats away the bottle and joins us cross-legged on the blanket. "But please carry on. God, Laura would lose her shit if she knew I was meeting with you two. She still loves rules. You can take the counselor out of camp . . ." Meg shrugs. Catherine and I exchange a look, knowing we—well, our parents—caused the demise of her aunt's pride and joy, Catalpa.

"Yeah, I figured," I say, "so thanks for still coming." I mean it. Catherine puts a hand on Meg's forearm as I speak.

"It's great to see you. A hundred emails and ten years later," she says, the sincerity in her voice irritating. It's obvious she favors Meg, that they have gotten closer since that summer. There were more emails beyond the initial ones I ignored, the ones they both sent after my and Catherine's parents told us to never talk to Meg again. I followed their orders, not wanting to create a deeper friendship with either of them, even though I now wonder if it may have helped me understand how things had gotten so fucked up that summer. It turns out Catherine didn't. I am surprised. She always seemed like more of a rule follower.

I'm jealous. It pricks at my skin like an annoying mosquito, biting and leaving me itchy and uncomfortable. They have had each other all these years, while I isolated myself and let our past simmer, its scent eventually so strong it became unbearable and I had to share our secret. With Jackson, whom I loved, trusted. Maybe if I had just answered their emails, this all could have been avoided. But I can't dwell on what I could have done. That's not what today's about, I remind myself. It's about what I can do now. What I need to do, which I haven't really mapped out beyond guaranteeing their silence.

I don't have Jackson. I don't have any real friends, not even Rachel. And I don't want to drag my parents into this, potentially implicating them (as accessories after the fact and all that). I'm alone, I realize. Catherine and Meg are my only options.

Rachel was never a fan of Jackson, her distaste for him growing as we went out with Jackson and Reggie and their friends more and more. When Jackson and I were together, everything around us seemed to fade. We were addicts, clinging to each other with an intense need. She told me to be careful, to not lose myself in some guy I hardly knew.

We made our relationship Facebook official by October, and a few weeks later Rachel first tried to warn me. A girl he went to college with, a regular at the open bars and apartment parties we went to with their posse, befriended Rachel while in line to use the bathroom at a cruddy spot in the Lower East Side. The uncoupled girls always found each other, sharing bronzer and heart-to-hearts. When this girl realized Rachel was my friend, Rachel told me her eyes grew wide.

"Tell her to watch the fuck out," she had said. "Jackson is not a stable person."

Rachel pushed, wanting to know more, the alcohol turning this girl's tongue slippery with gossip. "He made a girl transfer when we were sophomores. Kelsey Margraff. I didn't really know her, she was just a frosh, but I saw them together a bunch. Jackson and Kelsey had this, like, on-and-off thing and I do know he was super obsessed with her. They were always together, making out everywhere or, like, screaming at each other. Never an in-between. And at some point, I guess she ended it and apparently he, like, pushed her down a flight of stairs in one of the soph dorm buildings. She took the next semester off and last I heard she was at a college in her home state."

I knew about Kelsey. Jackson had already told me, had ad-mitted in the past that he was drawn to crazy girls. They had a tumultuous relationship, one full of ups and downs and accusations of cheating, Kelsey telling everyone she could that Jackson was a pig, a psycho, abusive. He said she once chucked a beer bottle at his head; another time she showed up, unannounced, to his family's summer home at Kiawah for a full week. He said she was a pathological liar, absolutely batshit crazy. There was another girl before Kelsey, one from high school. Alexis Fulton. They got super drunk at a party in the woods the summer before they left for college and were fighting because Alexis had been putting quarters on the top of the wheel of his car at night to see if he drove anywhere. If he cheated. That night in the woods, Jackson pulled her aside, a few steps outside of the glow of the bonfire, and broke up with her; when he turned to go back to the party, she ran after him and tripped over a thick tree root, breaking her ankle. She told everyone he had pushed her. When he told me all this, his tears were real, the scars his exes had left so obvious. Jackson told me he liked that I was so sane, so real, so different from the crazy bitches he met at school or in New York. I liked the pedestal he put me on, the way he overlooked my flaws. With Jackson, I wasn't the broken one, the unstable girl to be avoided. He'd been with those kinds of girls and he told me I was better than them, exceptional. The supremacy of that feeling was dazzling, an elixir that robbed me of perspective. His pattern of pitting me against other women, of encouraging me to only see their most monstrous defects versus my most faultless features, was so flattering it kept me from realizing what was even happening.

"Jackson told me about Kelsey," I said to Rachel, a bite in my tone. "I know all about her, and trust me, that is not the story. She was nuts. Like, certifiable." I didn't mention Alexis.

Rachel nodded slowly. "I just want you to be careful, okay?"

"Why are you doing this? What is your problem with Jackson?" I felt anger rising, a defensive tide ready to typhoon.

"Nothing," she said, hands raised. "No issue. I just thought you should know what I heard."

We didn't talk about it again, but in the following months I felt her watching, her eyes following Jackson in and out of rooms, warning him to be careful. It had been eating away at me, pissing me off. We danced around the topic, like if we both ignored it the tension would somehow resolve itself. Things came to a head in February, when Jackson and I moved into our new apartment. I had been living with him in his studio since early January, most of my things still at my parents' place in midtown. We immediately started apartment hunting, landing on a shoebox in a Tribeca high-rise, doorman and elevator included, steps from some of the city's buzziest restaurants. Our place was on the fourteenth floor and Rachel helped me lug my things from my parents' place uptown. Her complaints about sore arms piled up by the time we reached the apartment door. Jackson was at work, unable to muster a day off, so Rachel volunteered to help. I reminded her she could leave anytime. She was my best friend, though, and a nervous one at that. I guess she wanted to stay close, to make sure the darkness she was positive Jackson hid never revealed itself.

"Ugh, Amanda, what did you pack?" Rachel asked as she rolled a huge black duffel filled with my shoes down the long hallway.

"We're almost there," I said, my hands shaking from the rush. This was our third trip, my bags lumped outside the door of the new apartment. My apartment with Jackson. Our apartment, one we chose together, another step in our relationship. My insides fluttered as I pulled out the key the broker had given me earlier that day, its polished silver like a camera flash capturing my excitement. When I turned it in the lock, it was like I turned on something bigger, propelling me into a fresh phase of life, one of new memories and firsts and positive, thrilling things.

"Oh my god," I said to myself, but loud enough that Rachel could hear. "I can't believe this is really happening."

"Yeah, yeah," she said from behind. "Keep moving. You can gush about Jackson later. I need to sit down, pronto."

We dragged my bags in. I hadn't brought everything I owned, just the basics. After all, we were in Manhattan. Space was limited.

"Okay, as much as I want to unpack every last one of your precious Chloé flats," Rachel said, pulling the final bag and kicking it to the side of the entrance, "I would so rather get celebratory drinks."

Jackson would be home from work in hours. Our furniture was getting delivered a few days later, but we'd promised one another we'd have a romantic night popping champagne and sleeping on an air mattress in the center of the empty space. I hesitated.

"Girl, no," Rachel said, wiping her hairline and wagging a finger in disapproval. "I did not drag fifty zillion of your bags out of the goodness of my heart. We're getting drinks—and you're paying."

We ran across the street to a small wine bar, the late winter air biting the excitement out of my cheeks. Like most spots downtown, it was overcrowded but charming, full of gorgeous people who smelled faintly of cigarettes and expensive lotion. Rachel ordered a bottle of Pinot Noir, a compromise between my love of whites and her preference for heavy reds. When the bottle arrived and our drinks were poured, we knocked our glasses together.

"I wish Jackson was here," I said absently as we put our drinks back on the table. After work, he had an important client dinner, hence the delayed celebration that night. Almost a year out of school, Rachel was still job hunting and hadn't had much luck. The process had nibbled at her confidence, the various styles the companies said no—"Call us when you have more experience" or "Have you looked at our intern program?"—chipping at the way she'd long viewed herself. Rachel now had a slightly desperate undertone, a five o'clock shadow she couldn't shake no matter how often she tried; she wanted me to validate her, to remind her that she was still someone important, someone with sway. Instead, I gave all my attention, my worship, to Jackson. I felt Rachel give me an annoyed look when I mentioned him, one with traces of upset. "Too, I mean," I added. "This is really fun." She took another sip of her drink.

We finished the first bottle way too fast. We thought we drank because we were young with an excuse to celebrate, not thinking about limitations or hangovers, but really it was avoidance, the wine a way to make things light and easy. Rachel ordered another as I checked my phone. I started to protest—Jackson had just texted that he was on his way home—but she put up a hand and shook her head. "No," she said, wagging a finger in my face. "Don't be lame, Amanda. Seriously." She rolled her eyes, her ability to make me feel uncool still strong enough to get me to stay. When the bottle arrived, we clinked glasses again. The small tea candle at the center of our table waved from the heated air pouring out of the bar's ancient vents. I stared at it, hypnotized by its sway.

"So, I have to ask—and I know you will never tell me, but I have to ask," Rachel said, her words slightly slurred. We hadn't been drunk and alone in months, I realized. She was always a third wheel to me and Jackson. "Does Jackson have, like, a huge dick or something?"

"Huh?" I looked up, confused, and laughed awkwardly. "Do you want to have a threesome, you perv?"

"Ew, no," she said, making a face. "No offense. It's not that he's not hot. But he also, like, isn't? And you are so into him. Like so, so into him. And honestly, he's sort of an ass. So I'm trying to figure this"—she made circle motions in the air—"out."

"Um," I was unsure what to say. "How is he an ass?"

"Where do I start?" Rachel's eyelids were heavy, the wine lubricating her thoughts. "He always comments about what you're eating and tsks when you have anything with bread. Like, when's the last time you had a pizza?"

"I don't even like pizza," I said, my eyes narrowed.

"Not true, but whatever. I have more," she said. "He never hangs out with our friends. Ever. It's always parties at his friends' apartments, nights out at the bars they're at—"

"Okay, you're just pissed because of Reggie." I held up a hand, wanting her to stop.

"No, that's not it. And you know it. I know you know it. He seemed too good to be true early on, and he totally is." She took another sip from her glass. "Oh, another thing. He's a complete mansplainer. I swear to god he'd tell me I put in my own fucking tampon wrong if he had the chance. And when anyone pushes back, he acts like we're being hysterical. It's so fucking weird."

He had done the things Rachel detailed, but not in the way she was remembering. She had misunderstood. I stared at her, not wanting to respond. Why was she doing this, trying to take away my happiness?

"And remember his ex I told you about? I actually met her, randomly at a bar last month. She was visiting April Foley, you know that small girl Reggie and Jackson went to college with, who's always sort of around, the one who looks like Jennifer Aniston a little? Anyway, April is still friends with Kelsey, Jackson's ex or whatever you could even call her, and she's a nice person, you can tell. Not crazy at all. I told her my best friend was with Jackson and about that girl who warned me to warn you and she told me the whole thing. They got in a stupid drunken fight and he got pissed and shoved her down a flight of stairs. A fucking flight. She said he's completely nuts and he, like, flipped a switch when he got fucked up and turned all Hulk. The next day, he told everyone she made it up because she was mad he broke up with her. And now she has some deal with his family so she can't press charges. He's not a good guy, Amanda. He's a total and complete liar. Reggie even told me that Jackson's 'weird' with girls. That was his exact word," she said. "'Weird.'" Both her elbows were perched on the table, her wineglass nestled between her two palms and held right below her lips. She looked satisfied, happy with her performance. It made me all the more irritated.

"What does that even mean?" I asked, the comment so obtuse I couldn't make sense of it. "And, like, who cares what Reggie told you. He's the one who's full of shit, hooking up with other girls behind your back." She was quiet for a moment, her finger ringing the tip of her wineglass, a nerve hit. I took a deep breath. "If you were that bothered about all this, why are you bringing it up now? I mean, I just moved in with Jackson. What are you expecting me to do? Get all my shit and move back out?"

"I don't know," she said, her voice serious. "I—I wanted to make sure you knew. That you've thought this through."

She was wrong. Selfish. Envious. It was as simple as that. "You know what—what is your problem?" I asked, my voice high-pitched with anger. "Just because Reggie doesn't give a shit about you doesn't mean you need to try to ruin my relationship." Their hookup had lasted for months and had recently fizzled officially; I knew it was a sensitive subject. I took another sip of my wine, hoping my glare would pierce through Rachel and get her to shut up.

"Please," she spit back, her look of concern replaced with one of anger. "This is not about Reggie. This is about Jackson, Amanda. I know you're smarter than this. I know you see it. You two spend, like, *all* your time together. It's not normal. Like, do you not think that he's sort of controlling?"

"No," I said, "but I do think you're really fucking jealous." She was silent for a moment, her resignation evident. But I wasn't done. "You're a loser, Rach. A big fucking loser who can't get a boyfriend or a job. No one wants you. Don't try to ruin my life because yours sucks. It's pathetic."

Rachel's face fell and a small tear creeped over her lower line of lashes. She wiped it away, looked up at me for a millisecond, and pulled her purse, which was hanging over the shoulder of her chair, toward her. She started riffling through it, grabbed her wallet, and threw some cash on the table. "You can Venmo me," she said, standing up. She didn't make eye contact. "I'm tired, I'm going home."

"What?" I asked, following her out the door. "What the hell just happened?" I said, louder. We were on the sidewalk outside the bar, the frigid city air electrocuting my skin after a few hours in an overcrowded wine bar. The taxis and cars streaked by next to us, their lights like shooting stars noisily painting the background. I grabbed Rachel's arm, trying to catch her attention.

Rachel pivoted toward me. "Are you insane? What happened?" She was shrieking. "You just berated me. Oh my god, you're just like him. Don't you even try to fucking gaslight me. I'm going home, Amanda. I'm over this," she said, pointing at herself, then me. Rachel stepped closer, her nose inches from mine. "I'm over your narcissism. Your delusional idea of your life. Your obvious self-loathing. I'm over it. If you want to ruin your fucking life by ditching everyone for a total sociopath, fine. I'm done helping you."

I stood still, stunned by her outburst. She hailed a cab and hopped in before I could even respond. My face felt hot, the confusion welling tears I'd never expected. This was supposed to be a happy day, one full of celebrating this glorious new chapter in my life. A future with someone I loved. Rachel was my best friend; she was supposed to be excited for me.

I ran across the street, my face wet. In the elevator ride to our floor, I stared at my reflection in the mirror, eyes puffy and rogue streaks of eyeliner dripping from the edges. I took a few calming breaths, wiping my messy face until it looked somewhat normal. When I walked into our apartment, Jackson was inside, sitting cross-legged on the floor with an open bottle of champagne by his side. He was typing on his computer, which was perched on his lap. He looked up, his expression one of annoyance. "Where have you been? Next time you're gonna blow me off, you could at least text," he said. "I started without you." He took a swig straight from the bottle.

It was too much, his disappointment. I started to cry again.

"Babe," he said, putting the bottle down and hopping up. "What's going on? I was gonna say welcome home, but come here." He walked over to me, wrapping his arms around my shoulders, pulling me into his chest. I started shaking, sputtering "Rachel" and "wine bar" and "jealous."

"What a cunt," he said, shaking his head. I paused for a second, the word so strong it unearthed a stinging, repressed memory. He guided me toward the crook of his shoulder, and I forgot about it immediately. I looked up at him, blurry through my tears. She didn't get this powerful connection Jackson and I had. *Fuck her,* I thought. "She's always been jealous of you."

"You think?" I asked, closing my eyes and leaning my head on his shoulder.

"Yeah, it's so obvious. I mean, look at her life. It's a disaster."

He was right. How had I not seen it before, how she'd morphed into a desperate parasite? She needed me, but I didn't need her.

"I love you," he said, stroking my head. "And all my friends love you. You'll bounce back from this. What do you even need her for?" He rested his head on top of mine, pulling me even closer and saying, "For me, this is enough. You're all I need."

I dug my head deeper into his neck, a puppy showing unconditional love to its owner. He was right. He was all I needed.

Rachel texted me the next morning.

> hey girl
>
> sorry about last night
>
> i was a jerk, going through a lot with the job hunt and reggie and stuff . . . mani/pedi later today?

We had gotten in drunken fights before and this was usually how they were resolved. But being with Jackson made me feel a new kind of untouchable. It was obvious she would never understand that. I refused to have her negativity ruin the one good thing in my life.

I didn't answer. Not that text, or the twenty-plus she sent in the weeks after. I should have, though. Because Rachel had been right.

I have always been a sidekick, drawn to people with big personalities who make my decisions for me. Grace, Rachel, Sarah. Jackson. With Meg and Catherine, it's different. They aren't those types. They're observers. They see things others don't, quietly listening, processing, calculating. At camp, Meg made it seem like I had chosen her, that I'd volunteered to help her. But I know that's not true. She had to have sensed my anger, my quiet discontent. My petulant rage. Catherine? She has ice in her veins, a coolness in the most stressful of situations. They aren't going to tell me what to do, I know, but they're my complements. Together, we'll figure something out.

We're in a circle, all three sitting on my blanket. I wish someone would speak and tell me what to do. Instead, they're looking at me expectantly. "So what are we doing here, Amanda?"
Catherine asks the obvious question, the one I'm not sure how to
answer. I thought seeing Meg and Catherine would make some
massive, once-hidden plan unveil itself. I open my mouth as if I'm
about to talk, then take a sip of my drink. I don't know what to
say. It wasn't my idea to meet in Pennsylvania, to suffocate from
the weight of this heat and our past. The location was Meg's idea,
so why isn't Catherine directing her question at her? I convince
myself that's what her question means, though I know it's not.
What can I say, though? They're here, right in front of me: my
supposed answers to everything. As I look at them both, I see no
solution, no easy way forward, of everything clicking into a plan.
It's like we're kids again, the woods looming around us, making
us feel small and in over our heads.

Catherine rolls her eyes at Meg, an I-told-you-so move. She
starts to get up, brushing small grains of dirt from her skirt. "I
can't believe I drove all this way," she mumbles.

"Wait!" I say, jumping up to my feet. I wobble, my feet slippery against the soles of my sandals. I'm sweating: from the heat,
from nerves, from my hangover-turned-day-drunk. "You can't
drive," I say, pointing to the Solo cup in her hand. She looks at
me as she tips it over, pouring a near-full amount of liquid out.
The ground drinks the puddle, a small refuge from the dry heat
spell making us all crazy. She starts to turn but Meg, still sitting,
grabs her hand.

"I just got here, Cat," she says. "Don't be a shithead and bail.
You can't." She's speaking in code, hinting at something beyond
my situation. I shift my weight, the edges of the trees around us
softening. I pour my drink out, too, staring at Catherine. Her lips
purse, tight and annoyed. But she sits, so I do, too.

"Jackson wouldn't just take me down," I say, looking at each of them. "It would be all of us. He knows about you guys. If I don't do what he says, he will ruin me at whatever cost."

"Which is what?" Meg asks, her arms crossed. The question doesn't feel pushy; it's more a nudge, a detective angling me toward the right answer. I bite my lip, not sure what she wants me to say. The answer, I know, is to stay with him, to pretend none of this ever happened, beg them to keep it all buried in the past. I can't say it out loud, though, unsure how Meg will handle such an answer. She's stronger than me, always has been.

"Are you sure you're not being dramatic?" Catherine's voice is small as she asks the question, like she's afraid to offend not only me but also Meg.

We both ignore her. Meg places a hand on mine. The touch makes me jump, sobering me the slightest bit. They're here, I remind myself. They want to help. If not me, then themselves. I have no choice but to trust them. "What did he do to you? He didn't—"

I shake my head, predicting what she's asking. "No, he hasn't hit me. I don't think he would. It's more emotional, you know? Like gaslighting or whatever people are always talking about. That's what my friend Rachel called it. He makes me feel like all our issues are totally in my head," I say, a tear welling in my right eye. "Like, it's so messed up. He was my person—and now he's, like, this monster or something." I wipe the tear and there's a trail of wet in its wake.

"This is not your fault, Amanda." Meg's hand is still on mine. Catherine looks at it, then at me.

"One might contradict that statement and say quite the opposite." Her arms are crossed.

"Cat, come on." Meg takes her hand off mine, rubbing her forehead.

"Should we be worried?" Catherine asks, pulling at the skin on her elbow. The motion's mechanical, like that patch of her arm lacks feeling. I gulp the lump in my throat. It hurts going down. I don't know the answer, so I don't say anything. Catherine gives Meg an intense look, an encrypted message I can't decipher. I worry she'll leave again, so I push my phone at her.

"Look," I say, holding it out like a weapon. "Look at these. He's insane." I toss the phone across the blanket, between Meg and Catherine. Meg picks it up and starts scrolling as Catherine inches closer, looking over her shoulder. They're reading my text history with Jackson, our entire life together in bubbles of light gray and blue. Meg slides her finger, reviewing the outline of the rise and fall of my relationship with Jackson—the flirty texts sent when we were getting to know each other, the I-love-yous and sentimental words of encouragement shared on bad days, the trickle of accusatory texts, then the deluge. My phone log currently has twelve missed calls from Jackson. He had promised me a break this weekend, some time to think; he is always reasonable when sober, always willing to meet me where I need. But everything is worse when he's drunk.

"Jesus," Meg says. "What the hell did you see in this guy?" I pull my knees into my chest, hugging them and burying my chin in their crook. Catherine has my phone now, her finger flicking the screen up, up, up as she obsessively scrolls.

"So what's your plan?" Catherine says, her grip still around my phone in her lap.

"What do you mean what's my plan?" I ask. "I already told you. I don't have one."

"I'm calling bullshit," Meg interrupts, popping her head up as she holds her palm flat in the air. "You asked for this reunion. Which, to be fair, I'm not that upset about. I've wondered about you all since that summer. It's sort of a relief to hear not everything is perfect for you while I'm stuck working as a waitress at a shithole casino swarming with dudes like my dad."

"Well that's a sort of fucked-up thing to say." I grimace, wondering if Meg's on my side or here for the satisfaction of seeing me suffer. Catherine's trying not to laugh. I squint at her in a glare.

"Whatever." Meg waves it away, her rings sparkling in the sun. "You know what I mean." There's an ethereal quality to her, like the cool girl in high school who knew everyone's star sign before it was so mainstream.

"Really, Amanda." Catherine looks at me, her eyes dark. "Why are we here? What did you say to him?"

I feel tired and dizzy, my buzz a touch too much for the seriousness of the conversation. "I—I guess . . . ," I stammer, now realizing the truth is lame and anticlimactic. "I mean, I guess I wanted your promise that you would stay silent."

This time Meg lets out a small laugh. "No shit," she says. "No fucking shit. Of course we'll stay silent."

"Yes," Catherine says, once again looking at me with a tad too much intensity. "We never told anyone. And we'll never tell. Ever." Her tone is accusatory. But she doesn't get it. I didn't tell just anyone. I told Jackson. I could trust him. He had promised.

My secret started to unravel with a knock on my bedroom door the summer after I graduated high school, when my mom wanted to talk. It was weeks before I headed to college, three hours north in Connecticut. I was so ready to leave, to not have my parents watching my every move. Ever since they had found a handle of vodka in my closet several months earlier, hidden behind lines of stiff leather boots and crisp white sneakers, I had felt their eyes continuously lingering. We'd had a talk when they found it, about how I was too young, alcohol was dangerous, how I could ruin my future if I got caught up with stuff like that. I nodded the whole time, apologizing and saying it wouldn't happen again. They pulled me into the kitchen and I watched them pour the handle in the sink, gulping as it emptied. They got stricter about my curfew and I stopped keeping alcohol in the house. It wasn't like I was a heavy drinker; I just needed enough to relax, but I hated the feeling of being out of control or drawing attention to myself as the drunkest girl at the party. I had more sleepovers, usually at Rachel's dad's; he was rarely around. I pushed the limits on the rules, knowing my parents didn't want to seem too overbearing or uncool; they had been teenagers once, too, they told me that night I first got in trouble. I couldn't stop going out, chasing the rush of a party, how a loud room full of careless people could always make me forget myself. No matter how much I wanted to please them, it wasn't enough to make me want to stop. Until they cornered me that day in mid-July. My mom was the ringleader, I could tell, sitting me down on the couch and sucker-punching me with her concern.

"We've noticed you rely on alcohol in social settings quite heavily," she started. My dad sat quietly next to her.

"Um," I answered, unsure where this was going.

"We're—well, we're worried about you, Mandy bear," my dad said, his hand reaching out and layering mine.

I hated the nickname. I was too old for it by then. I pulled back, tucking my body into a crack in the couch. If only I could completely disappear in there. "I don't know what you're talking about," I said. And I didn't. I wasn't doing anything abnormal. Every other eighteen-year-old I knew partied. That was normal. *I* was normal. I had worked hard to be normal, to not stick out or attract suspicion. People don't ask questions when you fit in.

"Well, I was cleaning up your room the other day and your computer turned on," my mom said. "I saw the pictures Ashley Brown posted from the party you were all at. It looked—it looked a bit wild, honey." I knew the pictures she was talking about, Ashley Peters sprawled across me on a couch, my tongue pointy and sticking out, Ashley Brown on the other side, giving me bunny ears, Rachel in the background with one hand holding a red Solo cup and the other giving the camera the middle finger. I hadn't even been drunk, or at least not nearly as bombed as everyone else.

"You went through my Facebook? What are you, some sort of Big Brother stalker?" I felt the rage I usually kept so bottled up getting hotter.

"It just happened, Amanda," my dad interrupted.

"You don't really think I am stupid enough to believe that, do you?" Lately, I had felt my tone toward my parents creeping closer to hostile. I loved them, really, but I hated the lack of freedom their existence meant, the questions and worrying they showered me with. "I wasn't even drinking at that party. You guys are being insane."

"We want to make sure everything's okay with you, Amanda," my mom said, her face serious. "We know you struggle with big changes. Ever since . . ." Her voice trailed off. We rarely talked about that summer and what I had seen, and on the scarce occasion it did come up, they referred to it as "the Incident."

"Your father and I, well, we think you should defer college for a year," my mom said. "Maybe travel, take a step away from New York and the craziness and the parties. I'm not sure you're ready for college."

"Are you fucking kidding me?" I asked, incredulous. They had to be kidding. My whole high school experience, grades had been their priority. Good grades meant a good future. It had been their focus and I excelled. I had done what they wanted, hadn't I? Hours studying and straight As to show for it. Why was it such a big deal if I had a healthy social life? "I'm going to college in September. I'm not giving up everything I've worked for because you're worried about me."

My dad stayed quiet. I knew he agreed with me; he wasn't one to push for lovey-dovey solutions. He was the one my GPA mattered to the most, the one who cried—actually cried—when I got into an Ivy. "Amanda, there's a troubled side to you that seems to want to come out when you're surrounded by people with the wrong priorities," my mom continued. I felt dizzy, my peripheral vision zooming more into focus. "It's not good to keep that bottled up, sweetie. You've still never really talked about your feelings after seeing that man die at summer camp—"

The mention of camp was too much. There was a reason we didn't normally discuss it. It made me shut down, turn inside myself so tight that no one else could get in. I uncurled my legs and ran to my room, wanting the conversation to end. Did they want to upset me? To bring me pain? I slammed and locked the door, crawling into bed. The memories began to unblur, the ones I'd been able to push out of my day-to-day. A beer can cold and crisp against my palm. The fear surging through—no, shaking—my limbs. The blood, darker than I expected. My eyes stung, hot and wet and overwhelmed. I knew I couldn't stay in bed all day, even though I wanted to. And I knew my parents weren't being unreasonable. I just didn't like what they were offering. The whole finding-yourself thing that came with a gap year required too much vulnerability and self-exploration, two traits I very much avoided. I pushed myself out of bed and shuffled to the door when I heard a knock. It was my mom; I unlocked, a sign of defeat. She followed me as I turned around and crawled back into bed. She sat on the edge, rubbing my back as she talked me through her reasoning.

"Honey, I couldn't forgive myself if I didn't point out that you're in extreme mode. You're wild and happy with your friends but sullen and moody with us. I bet you know you're not making great choices." She paused. I didn't. I was blending in, being a normal teenager. Why didn't she see that? My argument was pointless, though; I knew it would lead to a circular conversation, one I would never win so long as I was still a teen with no real income or independence. "It's not healthy to keep so much bottled up, Amanda. I worry about you in college with all those unexplored emotions."

I rolled onto my other side to face my mom and curled my body against her back, resting my head on her lap. "I want to start school with everyone else. I don't want to stick out as a loser." She petted my hair, gently stroking the side of my face like I was a kid again, one with endless possibility ahead.

"Okay." She paused her motion, then turned to face me. "If we're going to do this, and your father and I are going to pay for your college, there will be rules." I pushed myself up, listening. "I want you to see someone."

"See someone?" I asked, confused by what she meant.

"Yes, a therapist. Once a month. To talk. To open up about what's eating away at you. What's going on"—she tapped my head—"in here."

I nodded, not saying anything, the tears rolling down my face once again. My mom hadn't given up on me; I didn't want to give up on me, either. That's how I ended up sitting across from Dawn Kestler during my freshman year of college.

My parents found her through a friend of a friend whose daughter became anorexic when she was a freshman at the same university. Dr. Kestler specialized in teen and young adult addiction. (My parents decided my problem was alcoholism. It's always easier to go after the lowest-hanging fruit, not the mess of trauma that's snowballed after years of never being addressed.) Dawn was pretty: thirtysomething, tall and slim, always wearing a perfectly pressed silk button-down and stone slacks. I imagined she lived in a shingled Cape Cod with hydrangeas out front, a sure sign of success in Connecticut. When we met, I noticed the serene color of everything in her office: grays and light greens and ocean blues. *This is a safe space,* her décor tried to say. I knew better but still liked the calm I felt every time I plopped onto the slate couch across from her.

"Amanda," she said at the start of our first session. "As you know, your parents called me to set this all up." *Great,* I thought. Even in this supposed safe space, my parents were still here. "They've shared their concerns, which I appreciate. But these sessions are about you. So let's start clean. Tell me, why do you think you're here?"

I looked down at my fingers knotted on my lap. She was good. Attentive. Not trying to push her or anyone else's opinion on me. I shrugged. "My parents, really."

"Okay," she said. "And why your parents? What is it they want from you?"

"Perfection." I laughed. "They want me to be like them. Super perfect." Dr. Kestler looked at me, waiting for more. Silence is funny that way. It's uncomfortable; you can't help but want to fill it. "It's not possible. I'm not cut out for that sort of perfection."

"And why is that?" she asked.

I paused, the trap she was setting apparent. I steered the conversation away from my parents. "Well, I mean, is anyone my age cut out for that? Like my roommate. She's a mess," I said. "She drinks. A lot. Honestly, everyone in my class seems to."

"You're all young and on your own for the first time. Exploration is natural. How do you feel about it, though?"

I shrugged again. "They all joke that bad decisions 'don't count if you don't remember them.' Do you think that's true?"

Dr. Kestler tossed my question back. "Do you think it's true?"

That mentality was such an easy way to breeze through shame. My roommate Elsie always said that bumper sticker of a phrase; it bounced off her tongue with such ease, like it was obviously true. And wasn't it? Didn't she always brush off the bad behavior that came with alcohol, her antics nothing more than silly mistakes? The liberation that attitude allowed. The I-don't-give-a-fuck-ness of it all. An okay to growl, to fight, to love, to hate, to screw around—and, in the morning, to slough it off, a snake shedding itchy skin its body tired of. That didn't seem like such a bad thing. Why did they all get to forget and I didn't? "Like, logically, no. But in practice, it seems like that's how everyone feels. And who am I to argue? I mean this girl on my floor, Margeaux—she puked all over the bathroom a few nights ago . . ." I started to tell her about different people I had met since starting college, mainly discussing those who seemed more screwed up than me. That was how most of our sessions went, me talking about other people, her trying to parse why my thoughts about them were relevant, me never really diving too deep. It was nice, our monthly sessions. They weren't revolutionary, but talking to someone removed from my past, trained not to judge, calmed my underlying anxiety. Plus, I was making my parents happy. It felt like I was checking all the boxes, following my parents' rules without upending life too much. Since I was over eighteen, they couldn't receive updates or be in touch with the doctor themselves unless I gave permission, which I didn't. Doctor-patient confidentiality and all that. Still, each month for four years, they wired $250 into my bank account and asked me for updates when we'd talk on the phone, and each month I strolled into Dr. Kestler's office and talked about anyone but myself.

When I graduated from college and moved back to the city, Dr. Kestler recommended Deborah Neuhaus. Dr. Neuhaus was older than Dr. Kestler, with cardigans and clip-on earrings and over-curled hair chopped above her ears. Her office was old, too, lined with wood veneer and windows covered in yellowing privacy shields, the air always a few degrees too warm. After my first visit, I learned to wear layers. I liked her, though. She felt comfortable, cozy. I started seeing her before I met Jackson. Something about her soothing voice and unassuming temperament was like a grandmother coaxing me with treats, getting me to abide by her guidelines without realizing it—and she won my trust. I wanted to impress her with how good my life was, only sharing the positive stories about Jackson, never mentioning the parties or his blacking out. I didn't even tell her about my fight with Rachel, not wanting her to think poorly of me or to know too much. She was like a beloved principal. Prim and proper but kind, someone you wanted to impress. So instead I mainly talked about the things I was learning at school.

"Have you heard of jury nullification?" I asked her during one of our later sessions. It was March, around the time of midterms, and I was tired, off my game. At that point, I had started seeing her consistently every month, my parents thrilled by my enthusiasm toward therapy (and the fact that their insurance, which I was still on, helped cover the cost). We had discussed jury nullification in my moral psychology class that morning, using the examples of mercy killer Jack Kevorkian's acquittal and that of a parent who accidentally left their baby in the back seat of the car on a hot July day. Wasn't living with a lifetime of guilt enough? Not all who were guilty had harsh intentions. That's what I told myself, at least.

"I have. What about it?" Dr. Neuhaus asked. Her lips were pursed and her head tilted. I think she liked talking to me as much as I liked talking to her.

"Well, it's the idea that a defendant committed a crime—and self-defense isn't a strong enough argument legally, but it's all they have. Like, they may have hurt, or even killed, someone—but they were in the right ethically because that person was hurting them or others. So even though they broke the law, the jury can agree to declare them not guilty." I spoke a little too fast, the words tumbling over my tongue.

"Interesting. Why is this concept so important to you?" The room felt still. I pulled at the collar of my shirt, the overly warm temperature making me uncomfortable.

"Um, it's just interesting, I guess," I said, trying to maintain eye contact but struggling. "It rarely happens, you know. Jury nullification. Which is unfortunate, especially for women."

Dr. Neuhaus leaned forward, her arms propped against her knees. "Yes, it seems that would be unfortunate. Did you learn these statistics in school?"

"No," I said, waving away the notion. "Well, the jury nullification part, yes. But the self-defense cases against women. I've been following those since I was a kid. It doesn't seem to work out that often for them."

"What was it about self-defense cases that intrigued you when you were a kid? Does this have anything to do with your summer at camp?" Her question didn't seem to presuppose guilt, but my mind immediately fell into a conspiracy theory spiral, its columns of rationality near gone by that point. I had never mentioned camp. Had Dr. Kestler told her about it? Maybe I could threaten to sue, a betrayal of doctor-patient confidentiality. Then I remembered the tablet Dr. Kestler had handed to me at the end of our last session. I had been in such a rush to get outside, distracted by finals brain and the last days of college, sloppily signing the form, which must have passed on my full file to Dr. Neuhaus. I cursed myself for inadvertently planting seeds for a conversation with Dr. Neuhaus I didn't want to have. I gulped, realizing I had said too much. Would my words trigger a deeper look at my life, at my private internet searches, the ones I did late at night and always cleared my browser after; my obsession with the *Post*'s crime stories; my fascination with *Forensic Files* and *Law & Order* and *The Killing*?

"I'm sort of tired today," I lied, my paranoia growing by the second. "I have a headache, actually." I started to gather my things, scrambling to get away from Dr. Neuhaus. Her presence felt dangerous, a truth serum I needed to avoid. "I'll see you next month, okay?" I smiled, giving her a little wave as I ran out the door. Her face was stunned but not surprised; there was a hint of regret, the knowledge that she, too, had crossed a line.

"Bye, Amanda," she said, her expression back to stoic professional. "See you next month." She didn't push me to stay and keep talking. But she would be ready to pounce during our next session instead. I felt it.

I paced around Central Park the rest of the day. The place was serene, perfect blankets of snow from the previous day's storm draped across the fields, the people little black dots floating across the white backdrop. I walked until my nose was numb, the cold air an escape from the anxiety brewing inside. When I got home shortly before sunset, Jackson was sprawled across the couch, feet up, work clothes half undone. We had only been living together for a few weeks, but already our apartment felt lived in.

"Hey, babe," he said, putting the TV on mute. "Where you been?"

"Wandering," I said, my voice giving away that my head was somewhere else.

He turned around, watching me as I threw my bag on our kitchen table. "You okay?" The room felt too small, my secret and its weight causing the walls to cave. I wanted to scream no, to tell him every single detail about that summer and what happened to me, Catherine, and Meg. And Meg's dad. Jackson loved me, I knew. That had to mean I could—should—tell him, that he would still want to be with me despite what I'd done. Instead, I said, "Do you want to get drunk? I want to get totally shit-faced tonight. Do we have wine?" My words were speedy as I opened the fridge.

"You know I'm always down," he said, getting up from the couch and snaking his arms around my waist, holding me from behind. I smiled, nuzzling my cheek against his, his embrace like a magic trick. His arms strong around me dulled my anxieties, my tendency to live in the past. It brought me into the moment, reminding me of the good in my life, that everything would be okay so long as I never left him.

Two bottles of wine later, we sat on opposite sides of the couch facing each other, my legs on top of his. Mouths stained like vampires after a feast, we slurred and grinned and unwound, our guards relaxing. "I'm glad we're drunk," Jackson said, his hands wrapped around my feet, his thumbs gently circling against my arches. "I like watching you loosen up. You don't do this normally."

I stuck my tongue out at him, the tip a dark maroon. "A little slurring never hurt nobody."

He smiled, his head tilting the tiniest bit. His thumbs were still circling, hypnosis on my feet. "Midterms go okay?"

I tossed my head back, laughing at the suggestion. I had aced them, I was sure. Schoolwork was the one thing I could control. I never let it slip. "God, no, it's not about that." I was smiling in a deranged way, too much to drink mixed with anger at my secret. I could feel it pushing to get out, my resistance waning. "I was at my therapist," I started.

His thumbs stopped, pressing harder into my feet. "Therapist? Since when do you go to a therapist?"

"Oh," I said, waving my wineglass carelessly. "Yeah, I go to a therapist. Once a month, for, like, a few years now. It's not a big deal, or wasn't. She pissed me off today." The room started to spin a bit.

"Why didn't you tell me?" Jackson looked angry, his eyes dark. "We don't keep secrets from each other." He pushed his thumbs harder, like he didn't notice he was still gripping my feet, his touch a heavy bite. "Do you have other secrets I should know about?"

"Ouch," I said, shaking my foot away. "You never realize how strong you are when you're drunk." I pretzeled my legs, rubbing the sole of my right foot. "Sorry." I shrugged. "I didn't think it was a big deal." That was a lie, but what else was I supposed to say?

"Of course it's a big deal." Jackson's family believed in pills—

especially small white ones with Vs and Zs and Xs—but not therapy. It was too soft, too emotion-driven, too exposing for their
way of handling things. "Why are you in therapy?"

I was quiet now, afraid of what I would say next.

"Amanda." Jackson crawled toward me on the sofa, dropping
his head in my lap and looking up. "You can tell me anything.
You're supposed to tell me anything."

I stared down, his eyes as big and open as he was claiming his
heart was. "I know, I want to, but—"

He said my name again, placing his hand under my thigh.
"Why don't you trust me?"

"I didn't say that," I started.

"So tell me. I promise this will be our little secret." He smiled,
completely unaware of what I was about to share. Maybe it was
the wine, or the naïveté that comes with falling in love for the first
time, but I did. I told him everything.

When I finished, he was sitting up, his face serious like his
drunk was wearing off. "Who else have you told about that
summer?"

"No one," I said, shaking my head. My eyes were watery. Not
from recollecting and sharing what had happened, but from the
relief that came with sharing, finally, this secret that had weighed
on my conscience for years. How scared I felt, but mainly light.
I knew Jackson was on my side. Sharing my darkness wouldn't
backfire; we understood and supported each other. He promised.
"Well Catherine and Meg know, obviously. But they'd never say
anything. They're sort of guilty, too."

"Mm-hmm," he said, unconvinced. "Have you talked to either of them since—" He paused, maybe not wanting to say "you
killed Meg's dad" out loud. "Since that summer," he finished.

"Not really, no." I didn't tell him about running into Catherine.
Not because I wanted to hide anything. Honestly, it just didn't
register as significant. I never thought I would see her again.

"Okay." He paused, his eyes angling upward and right as he thought. I waited, ready and eager for his guidance. "You won't go back to Dr. Neuhaus."

"But she's been great—" I began. It had felt so good to tell Jackson, the block of guilt crushing my life noticeably lighter; how would it feel to tell even more people? Dr. Neuhaus would understand. I was sure of it. "If I did tell her, I think she might help me. Not saying I will tell her. But if I did."

"Amanda." He grabbed my shoulders and shook me, a wake-up call. I was sure he meant to be playful, but it was all a touch too hard. "Do you want to end up in jail?"

That had always been an underlying fear—someone revisiting the case, connecting dots, claiming it wasn't self-defense, that it was premeditated from the moment I read Meg's journal, dragging me back to Pennsylvania. The more distance I put between myself and that day, the less likely it seemed. Still, it ate away at the deepest parts of my stomach; the acid of the secret slowly burned a hole inside of me. I shook my head.

"You will stop seeing her." His voice was stern, protective. "I'm part of this secret now, too. I'll make sure no one else ever finds out."

He was acting so paternal, a pack leader aggressively protecting the runt of the group. I laughed, the whole situation's weight still not apparent to my swirling mind. "Duh, like, at this point they would only find out if you told them."

"This isn't funny," he said, his voice low. "You killed someone, Amanda. I know you, I know you're a good person. But you think a jury will care about that? They'd love to lock up a girl like you. A bunch of redneck hicks with fucking chips on their shoulders." He was still in his work clothes, the top three buttons of his light blue shirt undone, the grip of the wax he spread through his hair every morning softening. His eyes were wide as he talked, the concern so obvious. But I wanted him to be wrong. I had been so young, so scared. I had spent years mapping through all the excuses I could share with the police, if they ever did come knocking. Jackson was right, though. I was a murderer, destined to rot in the tortuous limbo of carrying my secret. I was bad, so unworthy of his love and lucky he had shared it with me. Now he also carried my secret, helping me manage the weight. He would keep me safe. "It's our secret now. If I need to get my dad and Mr. Warner involved, I will." I cringed, not wanting to know what other secrets his dad and his dad's boss had buried. He reached for my hand, wrapping his fingers around my palm. "I will protect you, okay?" he said as he burrowed his lips into my neck, his hair tickling the bottom of my ear. "Forever," he whispered.

Forever, I thought. *Forever.*

The next day, Jackson didn't ask to talk about what I had done. But when we looked at each other, I knew things were different. Deeper. I smiled at him, grateful for his trust. For his protection.

Dr. Neuhaus emailed me after I missed our next session. I told her I had decided to go a different route, that I was trying a new therapist. Her response, as expected, was kind. "Should you ever change your mind, you're always welcome here, Amanda." I teared up a little reading it but shook off the emotion. Therapy meant remembering the past, analyzing all those built-up feelings and that tucked-away trauma with a microscope, slicing each memory until my body bled itself clean of secrets. Of guilt.

Not going meant forgetting, keeping the past where it belonged.

I was wrong to trust him. It's always a gamble, trust. Bet it all, and with the tiniest slip, you lose everything. I stare at Meg and Catherine, my eyes still misty from talking about Jackson. A hint of a headache pokes through my buzz, that horrible combination of the night before, heat, and exhaustion. I gnaw on the edge of my cup, now empty, and my fingers tighten, the flimsy red plastic seeming like my only retreat from this hellscape of a scenario. I'm still not sure I can trust Meg and Catherine; their promises of staying quiet are just that, promises. But what other choice do I have?

They didn't push me to share more details about Jackson. Not surprising. Any girl who's been alive for longer than a few seconds knows that some men hate to lose control, and the insane lengths they'll go to to make sure they don't. "Well," I say, genuinely unsure where we go from here. "That's what I came for, I guess. Your word."

The concern dances along Catherine's face, microscopic beads of sweat glittering in the sun. Meg starts to shake her head. "No," she says. "That's not it, Amanda. You have to leave him. You know that, right?" I do and I don't. I haven't figured out what comes after this meeting, what I do once I'm back in New York. Jackson is out east with Reggie this weekend. I told him I'd be gone, too—that I was going offline and needed a weekend to think. We hadn't gotten in an official fight, but it only took a few hours until Jackson's chain of stalkerlike texts and calls began. It's obvious he's day-drinking, each beer adding an extra dose of vitriol to his messages. I know I can't go back to that. I am too scared to. I am also too scared not to. I simply shrug at Meg's question, noncommittal and a bit defiant. "Didn't you have something you wanted us to do?" I ask, changing the subject as I suddenly remember our back-and-forth about meeting here. Meg needing to be close to work, pushing us to meet in the woods, back where it all began. *Let's throw my dad a proper funeral.* Her email was so odd, cryptic in its own way. When Catherine quickly responded that she'd be there, I didn't think I had much leverage to change the location, to push again to meet in New York, or at least anywhere besides the dark Pennsylvania woods. "Do you guys have some bigger plan you're not telling me about?" I look at Catherine for confirmation. She's quiet. So quiet, minus the occasional zinger. I want her silence, but this kind of quiet makes me uneasy.

"Have you ever had your aura read?" Meg asks, avoiding my question. Catherine rolls her eyes, like she's heard this spiel before. I shake my head, unsure where this is going. "I did two years ago, at this weird tech confab the casino hosted. And the woman said mine was black. And you know black is basically the evil aura. Like, what a fucking nightmare to be told your aura is black when you've been through all the shit I've been through. How am I supposed to react to that, you know?"

"Okay," I say slowly. "So what does that have to do with us meeting here?" I look at Catherine, hoping she might help with the answers. She's quiet still, instead looking at Meg. Regret is tickling my mind, threatening to consume it. Have I made a very stupid choice trusting these two with my life?

"When you reached out, I realized this is my chance to purge. To cleanse myself of my shitty, rotten, dark-as-fuck past. You, too. And you, Cat. We all can." Catherine is nodding, still quiet and letting Meg do most of the talking.

I bite the edge of my cup harder, the plastic crinkling against my teeth. "So what are you trying to say?" I ask.

"Ladies," Meg says, her grin growing, like it's admiring her own brilliance, "we're going back to Catalpa."

6

THEN

. . .

"What do you think about this?" A can of shaving cream, its bubbly pink top popped off, was in Sarah's hand.

"It's perfect." I held Catherine's hairbrush above the sink as Sarah pressed down on the top of the Skintimate can, foamy gel snaking through the brush's teeth and piling into a raspberry-smelling dollop. We smirked, our conspiratorial high giving us excited chills as we placed the sticky mess inside Catherine's cubby, nestling the can next to her brush, covering our tracks, creating plausible deniability. It was just before dinner, our cabin empty, the other girls and Betsy already showered and waiting for Dan's trumpet outside of the dining hall.

A few days earlier, I had stolen a cup from the kitchen. Sarah and I filled it with daddy longlegs, propping a book on top to block all the oxygen from entering. Daddy longlegs were always crawling in the corners of our cabin, their frail legs scaling our bunks. I wasn't scared of them; girls at camp said their venom was toxic, but they were too small to bite humans. It was easy to underestimate them, to think they weren't worth fearing. Even then I knew that creatures like that could still create harm if used in the right way. We picked each spider up with tenderness, knowing they were destined for something greater, dropping them into the glass until they were piled to the brim, twitching and writhing. I woke up early, before our cabin was coated in yolky sun, and I gave Sarah, snoozing above me, a shove. She rubbed the sleep from her eyes, propping her head on the safety rail of her top bunk. "Do it," she mouthed. I tiptoed toward Catherine's bunk, cup in hand, and turned it upside down, the dead spiders scattering across her face, resting on her hair. An hour later, reveille played on speakers across camp, each of us slowly rolling out of bed.

"Oh my god, Catherine!" I shouted, everyone else except Sarah still in a half dream.

"What—" Catherine started to say, lying on her back, but stopped. One of the spiders fell into her mouth when she opened it. She sat up, spitting it across her bed.

"Ew!" Sarah screamed. "You're covered in spiders!"

The whole cabin filled with excitement. Even Betsy jumped out of her bed. Disgusted screams bounced from bunk to bunk, Sydney curling up in a ball in hers, Larry grabbing her pillow and leaning over her top bunk to whack Catherine's face, Betsy trying to calm everyone, Barrett yelling that they were harmless, to be careful, to not kill them. She didn't realize they were already dead. "Get them off!" everyone, all at once, seemed to shout. Sarah and I couldn't stop laughing, the whole scene too much.

"Maybe if you showered more, Wagner, you wouldn't be such a spider magnet," Sarah said, Catherine pulling the last spider from her hair, her expression blank as she dropped it on the ground and crushed it with her socked foot.

"That's enough, Sarah," Betsy said, the only counselor who saw through Sarah's performances.

I didn't feel bad pouring dead spiders on Catherine or filling her brush with shaving cream. I felt energized, excited to share the moment with Sarah. She was a walking adrenaline rush, every decision I made with her leading to a temporary thrill, then another, then another, each growing stronger as our behavior became worse. Without Sarah, Catalpa would have been fun in the simple, pure way all camps are. With her, Catalpa became an emotional amusement park, every situation a roller coaster, the track constantly built seconds before the car sped forward. It was addictive, this game we played.

"You know," Sarah said, tapping the last bit of goop onto the top of the brush, an inedible sundae, "I'm sort of bored with this stuff." I didn't know what she meant. I stared back, waiting for her cue. "It's amateur." Her boredom terrified me; I felt her slipping, moving away from me, back to Larry. That's how things worked at that age. You had your temporary besties, all shiny and fun until they weren't. But I wouldn't let her discard me.

I walked over to Catherine's trunk and unbuckled the latch. Her underwear was sitting on top, perfectly rolled into tight cylinders all lined in a row. I grabbed a handful and threw them at Sarah. She looked taken aback, curious. "That," I said, pointing to the shelf behind her. "Hand me that paint. The red."

She paused for a moment, then understood. "You are so bad. Oh my god, I love you." Our war paint kit came with all the colors, including a watery maroon. We rubbed Catherine's underwear in it, smearing the soiled bottoms with the clean ones, making sure every single one was streaked. The warning gong for dinner started to ring. We sped up, sloppily putting the cap on the paint and pushing the little tin to the back of the shelf, hidden. My hands were covered in red, a telltale sign I was guilty. Sarah waited for my direction, the first and last time she ever did. "Go throw them, dummy. Fast!" I ran toward the sink as she ran outside and pelted Catherine's stained underwear at the roof of our cabin. I heard soft thuds as I watched the red swirl toward the drain, leaving a subtle trail of destruction in its wake. That nagging feeling, the one deep in my stomach, hit for a second. But then Sarah came in, breathless and grinning.

"That was awesome. You are awesome," she said as she sloppily rubbed her hands under the faucet, too. She then put her arm around me, dragging me from the sink, ignoring the hint of paint still lining her cuticles. She never assumed she would be caught, that she could be caught. Plus, she had to clear her table's dishes tonight, dunking the glasses in a vat of soapy water; the red would be gone before anyone noticed. We raced to the dining hall, making it just in time for the first trumpet note, our cheeks flushed, hearts pounding, appetites thick and hungry for more. We made eye contact throughout dinner; as Sarah shuffled to and from the kitchen to clear dishes, my skin prickled from the high.

The counselors never came back to our cabin after dinner, always off setting up for Milk Line, which happened at dusk on the Owl's Perch, where we met with showered hair and oversized sweatshirts and silk jammie shorts for graham crackers and cold glasses of milk. So when we got back to the cabin after dinner, it was just us, a bunch of twelve-year-olds all scared and fascinated and embarrassed by womanly things like periods. Catherine's underwear, bloodied and staring us all in the face, made everyone laugh. First nervously, then loud when the group realized they weren't alone. The *Ew, gross*es and crimson wave jokes came next. And the ID—well, that was Sarah. "Sick. Catherine—are those yours?" She pointed to one pair that hadn't made it to the roof. It dangled from a bush in between the two cabins, Catherine's name written in permanent marker on the waistband. "Try to keep your lady juices to yourself, puh-lease." She wove her arm through mine, pulling me with her as we walked inside the cabin. Larry's mouth was open, slack with shock. Sydney rolled her eyes and started climbing up toward the roof. I didn't see

Catherine's face. Maybe I intentionally avoided looking at her; it would confirm my underlying suspicion that I was the villain in this situation.

Barrett stormed in, Catherine slowly following behind her, head down. "What is your problem?" She ran behind Sarah and shoved her, Sarah's shoulder bulldozing into my back as she fell to the ground. I whipped around, eyes small and lasered on Barrett. "What is wrong with you two? You are disgusting, terrible human beings," Barrett said. "Rot on the bottoms of tree logs."

I felt the hot rage creeping in. I wanted to hit her straight across the face. Somewhere deep down, I knew she was right and I was wrong. But she didn't get to be the one to tell me that. She didn't understand why I needed to do this, how Catherine was the lowest-hanging fruit. "What are you talking about, Barrett?" I asked, my voice acidic. "We didn't do anything." I raised my hands, clean of paint. "Stop trying to pin everything on us. It's annoying."

Sarah nodded, picking herself up off the floor. "Yeah, and maybe lay off the steroids." She didn't flinch. Actually, Sarah seemed to beam, as if causing Catherine pain provided her a respite, however temporary, from her own. Catherine stayed quiet; she didn't even cry. It was unbelievable, like the crueler we were to her, the less she cared. It had to have been a defense mechanism, her way of compartmentalizing and shutting down so she could shake it off. At the time, it was infuriating. It meant our game could never end; Sarah wouldn't be satisfied until there were tears.

A few days later, Catherine was smiling again. She came back to the cabin with a shiny sphere in her hand, which caught the light every time she moved. Barrett was close behind, beaming. That's the thing with camp; you could hate your cabinmates one day and seek their adoration the next. We were like a band of cousins, stuck together and forced to forgive one another's flaws due to inescapable proximity and fear of our counselors' wrath. We didn't have the opportunity to *not* speak to one another. "Guys," Barrett said, making the whole cabin—Betsy included—huddle around Catherine. "She made this herself. Alone! With her bare hands." Barrett put her arm over Catherine's shoulder, flexing her other arm. "My hero."

It was a compass. Tiny, compact, its needle moving with the magnetism of the poles. I was impressed. Really. I hardly knew how to read a compass, let alone make one. "Wow," I let slip out. Sarah stepped on my toe.

"To be clear, I didn't make the container. They already had these in the campcraft hut," Catherine said. "But I made the compass itself, which is really all that matters. We took a magnet, placing it in the center of the plastic gauges we marked up with all the right degrees, and put a sewing needle in the center." She pointed at the arrow under the lens, its head wobbling back and forth like an unsettled scale. "It was surprisingly easy, actually, but I can't wait to use it. I only walked a few feet with it near the campcraft hut."

"Man, this will come in handy tomorrow night!" Betsy said, stroking the glass top of the compass. "You girls do know what tomorrow night is, right?"

Survival Night. We'd all heard about it, but no one—not even the returning junior campers—had been before. You weren't allowed to go until you were in your last year of Junior Row, so we were all novices. The older girls told us it was *amazing, unreal, insane*. A night under the forest canopy, the sky's stars sparkling above, the lake a soothing soundtrack as you fell asleep in your tent. Dinner—usually burgers and hot dogs, followed by s'mores— was made over an open fire. Plus, the counselors let you stop at a gas station on the way there to stock up on five dollars' worth of candy. I dreaded it; again, I was not a woodsy kind of girl.

That night, I woke up to the sound of heaving in the bathroom. I tiptoed out of my bed toward the cracked light and saw Sarah bent over the toilet, Betsy rubbing her back. "You okay?" I asked, still slightly outside the door frame. I didn't want to get too close; I always felt queasy around sick people.

Sarah looked up, tears streaming from her eyes. "Obviously not." Her face was a shade of green, her eyes bloodshot.

"Honey, you should go—" Betsy started, and Sarah put up her hand and turned back to the toilet, spilling out her insides. Betsy waved me away and pushed the door shut. I heard her call the infirmary on her walkie-talkie. Illness was no joke at camp; if one person had a virus or bug, it could quickly spin out of control, so they often quarantined those who showed the slightest sign of sickness near immediately.

In the morning, Sarah wasn't in her bunk bed. I told Larry and Sydney what had happened, and the three of us walked to the infirmary together.

"I guess Sarah won't be coming to Survival Night," Larry said.

"I guess not." I paused for a moment. Without Sarah, what would we even talk about? It was freeing but mainly discomforting. Sydney I could deal with. Larry? She was harmless, but we had nothing in common. Nothing. And there was that part of me, small and twisted and ugly, that hated her simply for being Sarah's best friend. Her true best friend.

Sarah was in a bed in the infirmary, a cold washcloth on her forehead. She looked so small and helpless as she gave us a weak wave. Larry pulled up a chair on one side of the bed, and Sydney and I sat on the other.

"They're not letting me go tonight," Sarah said. "I actually don't feel that bad, but I have a fever." She touched the washcloth on her head, making the statement all the more dramatic. "Probably from the heat."

"Did you talk to your mom?" Larry said, patting her arm. Sydney and I were silent, unable to contribute.

Sarah nodded. "You know Barb," she said. "She was, like, about to drive up here to take me home."

Larry laughed, an all-knowing guffaw filled with years of memories and inside jokes about Sarah's mom. I looked down and picked a scab on my knee. I hated when they talked about home, their shorthand a glaring reminder of their bond and all the ways mine fell short.

"We'll miss you," Larry said. "It won't be the same, that's for sure."

"Bring you back a s'more?" Sydney asked, and Sarah's face turned a slight shade of green.

I looked up, back in the game. "Watch the mention of food, Syd," I said, nudging her. "We'll miss you, though, really." I gave Sarah my most genuine look, my eyes almost pleading for her to have a miracle recovery.

"Thanks for coming, you guys, but they'll get mad if you stay much longer. You know, worried I'll plague the whole camp or something." She laughed, but it was dainty and sickly.

We nodded, saying our goodbyes and walking toward the exit. "Wait, Amanda—one last thing." I walked back over to the bed while the other two waited by the door. "Get me Catherine's compass," she whispered. "That would totally make up for missing the entire night."

Maybe I was her puppet. Or her partner in crime. Either way, she made me feel chosen. So I said yes.

Survival Night began at the front of camp, all the girls from junior cabins 5 and 6 lined in a row, our knapsacks packed with a change of clothes, mess kits, flashlights, and whatever else we could fit snug to our backs. None of us knew what to expect. We were jittery with enthusiasm and knobby with nerves. It was late afternoon, the sun encouraging overhead. The sky was clear, the air still, the drought in full effect.

I climbed into one of the camp's forest-green vans, sliding to the back row and sinking into the worn cushion. Sydney and Larry followed, then the rest of the girls, some completely quiet, others chatty and giggly. Catherine was in the row in front of us. She turned to Barrett. "This is going to be spectacular. I have a list of plants and animals to identify, thanks to Chrissy's checklist." I craned my neck as she rustled through her bag. Her compass caught my eye, buried in a side pocket beneath her notebook. "Maybe I'll finally be able to start a fire without you."

"In your dreams," Barrett said. "Anyway, that's my super-power. Yours is navigation, remember?" She bopped Catherine on the forehead, the two giggling with delight.

Betsy got in the driver's seat, turning around and giving us all a huge smile. Chrissy, the campcraft counselor, who went on every overnight, sat in the passenger seat. I remember thinking how foolish they looked, two almost-adults getting childishly pumped up about a night in the woods with a bunch of kids.

"Wait!" someone shouted from the trail leading to the van. "Wait, I'm coming!" It was Meg, her ponytail bouncing as she sprinted to us.

"Megan Perkins!" Betsy said, rolling her window down. "You're lucky you made it or Laura might have killed you. Get in, get in, get in!"

Meg flung open the creaky old door and crawled along the open side of the van. There was an available seat in the last row, but no one squeezed to make room. She sat in the aisle, on the black carpeted bump above the back-right wheel. Meg was panting, her chest rising and falling like a spastic accordion. "Girls,

Meg's here in place of Sarah!" Betsy said, cheerful and vague. We all stared, waiting for an explanation, then turned our eyes to Meg. Suddenly aware we were watching her, Meg turned, making a face. "Take a fucking picture, why don't you?" she said with a defensive bite. She looked forward again, her eyes focused on the back of Chrissy's seat.

"Whoa, Meg!" Betsy said, turning in her seat. "Catalpa girls don't talk like that. Cool?" Meg nodded, her face red, and was silent once again. An object of intrigue for us all, this mysterious redheaded girl; we started to whisper.

"Okay, girls! First stop." Chrissy broke up the murmurs by pulling a bunch of five-dollar bills from a brown paper bag. "Flaherty's." We all knew about Flaherty's, the local gas station a mile or so from camp. Five dollars got you far there, and Survival Night was an opportunity to load up, to gorge. I bought Tootsie Rolls, Skittles, Cow Tales, and a Coca-Cola. Larry went all in on the chocolate, Hershey's and Asher's this and that spilling from her arms. Sydney got Jelly Bellies and cotton candy, the weird wispy kind that comes in metallic blue packaging, all sticky sweetness. Catherine and Barrett strategized about their purchases; I watched them snake the aisles, calculating what they could get with their combined ten dollars, what they would share, what they would eat individually. Meg tucked the five dollars into the side pocket of her bag. Everyone else left with small paper bags rustling with candy. I handed her a Tootsie Roll, giving her a small smile. She looked at it for a second, then at me.

"Huh, you're not so bad," she said, pulling off the wrapping and popping the candy in her mouth.

"Um, who said I was?" I asked. I knew she was right, that other Juniors around camp had talked about me, but it was always in relation to Sarah. And there was a power to being discussed, your existence interesting enough to be a topic of conversation. I didn't mind the gossip. Not then, at least.

Meg turned to me and grinned, the Tootsie Roll flattened against her top row of teeth. We both laughed, shy and unsure. Maybe she wasn't so bad, either. I chewed on the end of my Cow Tale. It felt like years since we'd had sweets; most of the bags were empty, scrunched wrappers littering the van floor, before we even arrived at the campsite.

Survival Night took place on a strip of woods, maybe a mile wide, between camp and the neighboring campground. The van cruised directly into the woods via a gravelly mud path, bumping along until it stopped in the middle of nowhere. We all hopped out, the trees towering around us, fat green leaves climbing up their trunks. My feet bounced against the forest floor, a layer of moss on top of decomposing leaves. The sound of lapping water grew louder as we moved deeper into the woods. We were quiet, the spirited chirping of the birds, purring of crickets, and power of the kingly spruces leaving us in awe. The pureness of it all felt overpowering; it was so much bigger than my silly plotting. I closed my eyes as I walked, letting the gentle rustle of the trees wash over my eardrums, calm my anxious need to make Sarah happy. I tripped on a knotty root, bumping into Barrett.

"Watch it," she said, her snarl containing enough hate to feel visceral. I stuck my tongue out at her.

"Do you think there are, like, spirits in these woods?" Sydney whispered. I hadn't thought about it, but once she said it, it felt true. That sense that something bigger was there.

"Save the ghost stories for the campfire," Larry said, putting her arms around both of us. "Thank god Sarah's not here to scare the crap out of us." She had gained a reputation for telling the best ghost stories, her depravity knowing no bounds.

"Oh god," Sydney said, her big brown eyes staring right at me. "Please, please, please don't. Not out here." When Sarah had made everyone in cabins 5 and 6 do the Bloody Mary test a few days earlier, the lights turned out and all of us crammed near the sink mirror, spinning and chanting and cradling our arms like we were holding a baby, a few girls screamed and Sydney cried. Sarah couldn't stop laughing.

"You gotta toughen up, lady!" I said, giving her a push. It was nice without Sarah. Not as strange as I expected. Like we didn't *really* need her. Meg floated a few feet behind me, not fitting in but also not sticking out. We were out of our normal environment, which put everyone on similar footing. Even this stranger none of us knew.

The campsite was a small clearing, with a circle of rocks at the center and cut-up trunks, all laid horizontally, radiating around. "Okay, girls," Betsy said, putting the huge cooler in her arms down. "We're here. Before we set up—and you each will be setting up your tents yourselves—" We groaned. The tents were ancient, stubborn, stiff, and nearly impossible to prop up. "Okay, okay," Betsy said, quieting us. "There are a few key rules to follow. We've gone over these before, but they are important, so let's do it again. Who knows what you should not have packed?"

Catherine raised her hand, always excited to be called on. "No perfumes or scented items of any kind!" She smiled, knowing she was right.

"Good job, Cat," Chrissy said. Those two had a bond, and Barrett, too. A bunch of future Eagle Scouts, if only the club allowed girls. "And what do we do with food?"

Barrett this time: "Everything—even our candy—goes in the bear bag. To keep the bears away!" She threw her arms up, running toward the cabin 6 girls while growling. My secondhand embarrassment bubbled while watching her.

"Yes, Barrett," Chrissy said, pulling the bear bags from the plastic crate at her feet and throwing them at Barrett.

"And, of course, the buddy system is extra important out here," Betsy said, her clipboard perched against her hip. "But this time, you don't get to pick." She exchanged a look with Chrissy, excitement with a dash of mischief. Sydney pinched my triceps; I snaked my arm through hers, signaling that I wanted her as my buddy, too. I didn't, though. I wanted Catherine as mine, to be close to her the entire overnight. Close enough I could get into her stuff, take her compass, and stash it away in my own backpack.

They announced the pairs, all duos no one wanted. Sydney with Barrett, Larry with Marissa Cabot, the weird girl from cabin 6 who didn't like anyone touching her things, ever. Except me. I got exactly what I wanted: I was with Catherine. I moaned when they announced the pair, grabbing Sydney's arm tighter and mouthing "Kill me," not wanting to be too obvious. But then Chrissy added a twist; they were short a tent, so there were two groups of three. Meg would also be sharing a tent with me and Catherine that night. Meg's presence added a layer of complexity to my plan. It didn't seem insurmountable, though. I could already imagine leaning over Catherine's light snores, unzipping her backpack, and slipping her compass into mine. Catherine looked at me with a forced half smile. "I guess we're tentmates."

"We are!" I said, my enthusiasm a bit overdone. "This will be fun, right?" I put my arm around her shoulder, like we all did with each other. Her body stiffened slightly. Meg was on the other side of the crowd. She gave us a thumbs-up, her lips tightly curling.

Catherine wriggled out from under my arm. I followed her to the pile of old tents Betsy and Chrissy had brought. Ours was a putrid green, not unlike the mattresses we slept on back in our cabins. They all used to be a rich forest color, but age had waned their brightness. Catherine got to work setting up our tent. I told her I would supervise, that she should holler if she needed assistance. Meg started helping Catherine, holding a pole while Catherine snaked it through the fabric. Betsy and Chrissy circled peripherally, making sure we were all progressing. I grabbed another pole when they walked by, pretending I was helping. Catherine didn't even notice my faking; she was focused, determined to finish the task at hand. Meg stared at me a second too long, her eyes near rolling. The tent smelled musty, like overheated plastic and earthy moss. The three of us climbed inside, snug in the small space. We unrolled our sleeping bags and nestled our backpacks in our respective corners. I watched as Catherine pulled out a notebook and her compass, its glistening luring me in.

"Why are you staring at me?" Her matter-of-factness caught me off guard. Red filled my cheeks, my plan already crumbling.

"Um, please. Why would I stare at you?" I played dumb, tried to make Catherine feel self-conscious. "You're not that interesting."

She shrugged, then climbed over my sleeping bag to get out of the tent, compass in hand.

"Why do you hate her so much?" Meg asked, her hand smoothing her sleeping bag.

"What? I don't—" I began to say. I didn't hate Catherine. Meg didn't get it. This wasn't about Catherine, who had been unfortunate enough to get in Sarah's path. Sarah was the goal. But I would never admit how important it was to me that I be Sarah's best friend.

Meg laughed, big and windy, in my face. "You do. But whatever," she said, crawling to the tent opening. "I just call 'em like I see 'em." Her shirt hung away from her stomach, revealing a sliver of skin. There was a light purple mark near her right hip bone. She saw me looking and quickly tucked in her shirt as she left the tent.

I followed, grabbing my mess kit. My teeth were coated in a film of sugar, all our stomachs still full of candy, but it was dinnertime. And at camp, you always followed the schedule.

Chrissy and Betsy had made a fire and put a small grill rack on top. Catherine and Barrett ignored us all, taking notes on the tree bark in the area, the varying leaf species, the animal tracks etched in the dried mud. The rest of us scavenged the woods for thin sticks we could spear through hot dogs and marshmallows. It was a trite competition—who could get the best roasting stick—but one that persisted and we all loved. Larry won, like always, her stick a skinny, near-straight piece of smooth birch. She offered it to another camper, one with a near-broken spine, Larry's saintliness never taking a day off. It irked me, how good she was. The sun was starting to set, a shock of electric pink floating above, broken up by the occasional wisp of cloud. An orange glow washed over the whole scene, and I almost let myself relax into the friendly warmth of it all. Almost.

"*Pals, dear old pals,*" Sydney started singing. It was one of the songs from our green Camp Catalpa books, a song about the lasting impact of friendship.

"*We'll always beeeeee!*" I joined in, crooning the final word.

"*Sharing together, friendships that never ever ever sever. Faithful and true, we'll be to you. Forever more we'll be just pals, dear old pals!*" By the end of the song, everyone was singing in unison. The last part of the song—that final *pals, dear old pals*—was the best. We sang it as high as our tiny vocal cords could go, tossing our chins to the sky and belting the words.

"Guys, that was beautiful!" Larry made a fake face of adoration. The counselors brought out the food. Armed with our roasting sticks, we plunged our hands into the packed cooler, bees swarming their hive. Chrissy and Betsy shouted *slow down*s and *watch it*s as we elbowed one another to get the goods.

I speared my roasting stick through a fleshy hot dog and stood next to Catherine, who was carefully, cautiously rolling her hot dog above the flame. "Hey, roomie," I said, smiling at her. She smiled back but kept her eyes on the dog. We roasted together in silence, the other girls' chatter keeping things from feeling awkward. Catherine's eyes were glued to the fire.

"What's that?" I asked, her back pocket stuffed with pieces of moss and bark.

"Nothing particularly noteworthy," she said, suddenly engaged. "But, in a way, isn't it all noteworthy? Earth, nature—it's all remarkable."

"Yeah, I guess so." Catherine was perhaps the most profound twelve-year-old I had ever met, certainly more profound than any of my friends. There's another life in which we became friends and her thoughtfulness grounded me. A life where I was more concerned with substance than popularity. But, too bad for our intertwined future, that life wasn't this one. "It's kind of gross, too." I pointed my foot toward a slug oozing across a nearby rock.

"True. Though the beautiful can't exist without the gross. It's like a massive Rube Goldberg machine, each plant or animal or microorganism a crucial building block for the next." She looked up at the trees, dreamy. I followed her gaze; a cardinal bounced from one tree to another.

"Whoa," I whispered.

"You know, you don't have to be nice to me just because Sarah's not here." She was looking at me now.

"I—I'm not," I stammered. "I mean, I'm not mean to you normally?"

"We both know that's not true," she said, rolling her hot dog one more time. "But at least my dinner tonight isn't going to be ash."

"Wha—" I started to say as she hit my roasting stick with hers. I looked down; my dog was on fire. I spastically pulled it toward my lips and blew. I locked eyes with Catherine, looking at her, really looking at her, for the first time since our first day at camp. Her eyes' curiosity was piercing, like they would always, always be looking for answers. She giggled, then I did, too, louder and louder, smoke wafting between our faces. The pit in my stomach flipped; she didn't deserve my bullying, she was simply a smarty-pants who loved a mental challenge. I had heard, through camp gossip, that Catherine didn't have a mom. No one knew if she had died or if Catherine's parents were divorced; we just knew it was her and her dad, and they lived on a farm near Penn State, and she was here on one of the coveted camp scholarships. Sydney had a big, picture-perfect family in the Lehigh Valley. Larry's parents were together but slept in separate rooms, and Sarah's were divorced. (Sydney said they split up while she was at Catalpa last summer, so she left for camp with one home and returned to two.) Everyone here had a story, a background, a reason for who they were. Parents were often the start, and then friends, and teachers, and circumstances. We were only twelve but already complex. The adults didn't always see that, but we felt it. We knew we were more than kids.

The rest of the group had plopped on the logs around the fire. Sydney and Larry motioned for me to join them, pointing to an empty spot between them. I nodded at Catherine, who went toward Barrett.

"So are you guys finally friends?" Larry asked, ketchup smeared on the sides of her mouth.

"Who, Catherine?" I asked, placing my shriveled dog in a bun. "Don't be ridiculous." I didn't want Larry to report that kind of nonsense back to Sarah, trying to angle her way back to the best friend spot.

"Your hot dog looks gross," Sydney said, her nose scrunched. "A little burnt weenie." We all started laughing, toppling into one another as we chewed.

"Stop, I'm going to choke!" Larry said, a line of mustard now on top of the ketchup on her face.

Across from us, Meg sat on the same log as Catherine and Barrett, an awkward amount of space between them. We all ate with glee, the freedom of the night mixed with the sugar from earlier making us woozy. Even Meg looked at ease. The sun almost set, an eerie, magical blanket of purple swept over the campsite. Chrissy stood up, dusting the crumbs from her hot dog off her legs.

"Okay, girls, who's ready for s'mores?" Every single camper shot her hand up, me included. We circled around the fire, the post-dusk haze coating the forest. A few stars shimmered in the sky. The fire lit all the girls' faces, shadows dancing across their noses and chins as the flames shook. It was the perfect setting for a little horror.

"What about a ghost story?" Meg shouted, the girls' chatter quieting. We were taken aback, her presence still new, her brazenness boosting the mood like a sugar rush. There were a few groans, mainly from the cabin 6 girls, who were all wimps. Mostly there were big, anticipatory eyes. Call us masochists, but most of us loved to freak ourselves out. Something about the lack of parents, the billowing trees, the mysteriousness of the forest, camp lore—together, it felt like sacrilege to *not* tell ghost stories. And without Sarah, we needed a storyteller.

"Go ahead," Chrissy said, waving Meg on.

She started. "Many, many years ago, at a camp just like Catalpa, there was a terrible counselor. Her face was covered in warts, and her hair was missing patches. She had a hunchback and hobbled around camp, and she hated kids."

"Wait," Catherine interrupted. "Why would she be a counselor if she hates kids?" For once, I didn't feel annoyed. I was never the one to raise my hand and ask questions, but I wondered the same thing.

"Good question." Meg stood up and started to circle the fire for dramatic effect. "Magda—that was her name, Magda—was the ugly sister to the camp's owner, Maggie. Everyone loved Maggie; she was kind and generous and super beautiful. Their whole lives, Maggie had been kind to Magda, even though Magda was a miserable troll to everyone she met. When they got older and

Magda couldn't find a job, Maggie said she could work at the camp. The thing that Maggie didn't know was that Magda was a cannibal." A few let out quiet gasps. "That's why her teeth were so sharp," she said, using her fingers to make fangs, "and her hair was falling out—because you can't eat your own species without it impacting your looks." She paused, letting us all take in the image.

"You can always tell when people are cannibals because they look half human, with bloodshot eyes and bumpy skin and vampire teeth and thin, scraggly hair," she added matter-of-factly. Back then, we really did believe that bad behavior, crimes, would beam through your skin like spoiled eggs—smelly and flawed and slightly rotten. We saw it in the books we read and the cartoons we watched. I now know that's not true, that some of the worst people usually dazzle brighter than saints.

"But Magda didn't care about her looks. She was addicted to eating children. Like, she had to have them. So that summer, she kept to herself for the first half of camp. She watched the little girls devour cornflake chicken and pizza, sloppy joes and chicken nuggets galore." Everyone's eyes got wider. Those were all our favorite meals.

"She watched as they got fatter and fatter. Then, one night, she took her cabin—all seven girls—for their camp's version of Survival Night. They were miles and miles away from camp, away from the safety of having Maggie around."

I took a bite of my s'more, its sticky contents dripping down my face. Even Chrissy and Betsy were staring now, transfixed. She was good. "The next morning, Magda returned to camp. She cried to Maggie, telling her the girls were attacked by grizzly bears and she had tried her best, but none of them survived," she said.

Catherine raised her hand. Meg pointed at her, and the rest of the girls gave her a look. "Where did this take place?"

"Not that far from here," she said.

"But there aren't grizzly bears on the East Coast!" Catherine was adamant, wanting to solve this crime before I could solve it for her.

"Yeah," Barrett echoed. "There are only black bears!"

"Um, okay, detectives," she said, giving them a devilish smile. "Because Maggie also knew that area and those woods like the back of her hand. Like you, she knew there weren't grizzly bears. But she trusted her sister—that was always Maggie's flaw, she trusted too much." She looked at Catherine again. "And she asked if they could go to the site together to gather the girls' belongings. They drove in silence. Well, kind of in silence. Magda breathed heavily like a bulldog, full from her meal the night before." She panted a bit, slow and measured and creepy.

"When they got to the campground, Maggie saw the remnants of a fire. There were bones, bones that looked like they belonged to twelve-year-old girls. 'Magda,' she said, turning to her sister. Magda's eyes lit up and she showed both rows of teeth to her sister, grinning as she hissed, 'Thanks for a great summer, sis.' Then she ran off into the woods!"

"Eww, I don't like this," Sydney said, shaking all over like it would somehow make the story stop.

"Well then you won't like what I'm about to tell you. The camp shut down, obviously, and Maggie was so racked with guilt that she eventually went crazy and had to live in an institution. For years and years, Magda was never seen again. But a few years ago, some campers in upstate New York say they saw a hunched woman with wolflike teeth and tattered clothes wandering around the woods by their camp. It was Magda, looking for her next meal."

"Meg!" Larry shouted. "That cannot be true." It felt like she was saying it more for herself than anyone else.

"It is." She nodded, strolling back to her place between Sydney and Larry. "I did the camp tour with Laura. You know, when we go around to different school fairs and try and recruit new campers? So I met people who saw her. They're campers at Camp Silver Lake in New York and they saw her there. I swear on my goddamn life." She put her hand on her heart. "She might be in these woods right now."

"Hogwash!" Catherine shouted across the bonfire. Her face was lit with excitement, unable to hide how good it felt to play detective. All the campers started shouting, wanting to know more details. A chill breathed on the back of my neck, something feeling off in the forest.

"Okay, okay!" Betsy interrupted. "Magda is not in these woods. You all are safe, don't worry. There is nothing in these woods that will hurt you." She gave Meg a *Be quiet please* look. "Except bears, which is why we need to clean up! And then it's bedtime, girls." We all groaned but followed the order, getting up from our seats and looking for trash. "Meg, a word?" Betsy said quietly, pulling Meg aside, probably yelling at her for getting the group riled up or cursing again. I watched Meg nod as I used a stick to pick up lingering wrappers.

"I'm sort of jealous she's in your tent," Sydney said as she bent over to pick up what was left of a crinkled chocolate bar. We were all shuffling around, throwing the uneaten bits of our hot dogs in the dying fire and collecting whatever wrappers we could find. Meg seemed to be apologizing, saying "I'm sorry" over and over until Betsy seemed happy. When Betsy turned, Meg stuck her tongue out at her back. I looked down, pretending I hadn't seen. "She's kind of cool and funny. Like, I don't care what Sarah says. I'd be friends with her."

I nodded. "Yeah, maybe I'll learn more about her. Who knows," I said. "Sarah would probably say she's gonna steal my stuff or something."

Sydney paused, a half-eaten s'more in her hand. "Sarah can

sort of be a bitch, especially lately." I didn't say anything for a
beat, and Sydney turned pink. "Oh my god, do *not* tell her I said
that." We both smiled, an unspoken agreement, the need to tiptoe
alleviated without her here, everything suddenly lighter.

All trash went back in the cooler, which Chrissy zipped in a
cloth sleeve that attached to a rope. Several dozen feet away, she
threw the rope, which had a carabiner at its end, over a high tree
branch and hoisted the cooler in the air, the white blob swaying
in the darkness like a ghoul.

Back in our tent, I shimmied my body into my sleeping bag. Despite the day's heat, the mountain air always cooled our nights,
and that day's breeze really picked up after sunset. Catherine sat
cross-legged on her sleeping bag, a flashlight in one hand as she
scribbled furiously in a notebook with the other, crossing it out
and starting anew on a blank page. Meg was already snug in her
sleeping bag and used her hand to prop up her head.

"What are you doing?" she asked. I was a little curious, but
mainly exhausted, and wanted Catherine to turn off the light.

"I have been taking notes about the plants and last summer's
leftover cicada exoskeletons on the forest floor, plus noting the
direction the moss is growing on the trees," she said, pointing to
the ripped-out notebook pages by her side. They had scribbles all
over. "I built this compass the other day"—she held it out for Meg
to see—"and used it to figure out how many degrees away from
north we are, then compared it to the degrees away from north
when we're at camp. With all this information, I think I can figure out how far away we are from camp." Catherine was very
serious as she explained her process. "I have a rough ballpark, but
I'm basically there." She was so obviously thrilled with her work.

"Damn," Meg said. "So you're the really smart one?" I was
facing away, my head a few inches out of my sleeping bag, but

I could feel Catherine's pride, the shine that came from being seen.

I didn't care how far away we were from camp. We were probably a little more than walking distance—and if you followed the river, you would always get back. Anyway, we had a van. And counselors. And so many other reasons why this math problem was pointless and the umpteenth example of Catherine's being a brainy show-off.

I turned to my other side, my head sinking into my pillow. "Guys, can you please turn off the light? I want to go to sleep." I was cranky but mostly determined. The sooner we went to sleep, the sooner I could steal Catherine's compass.

Our little moment by the campfire wasn't enough to change my mission. Sarah's friendship was too important to me. Obsession pulls you into its eye, the windy chaos it's causing just beyond those borders apparent to everyone but you. My quest to become Sarah's friend may have started simply, but it was now fueled by momentum, a snowball. I needed to please her, to gain her total acceptance—and I promised myself that once I did, I would be done with the pranks. I would be better. I turned away from them again, yanking my blanket above my head. I heard Catherine scribble a bit more, the pencil chafing the paper. And then, the click of her flashlight.

In the darkness, Meg's voice sounded small. "What's it like?"

Catherine and I were both silent, not sure if she was talking to us or in her sleep.

"Camp," she added, her whisper gentle as a child's. "What's it like to be a real camper?"

"But you're a camper," I whispered back.

"Not really. Not like you guys. I'm like a tourist here." I didn't understand. Laura, the owner of the entire camp, was her family. Didn't she feel at home at Catalpa? Didn't she have total freedom there, roaming the paths however she wanted? I now understand her desperation as she grasped for something stable, comfy, her own, mainly because I found myself searching for the same things after that summer, my own sense of stability suddenly untethered.

"I like it," Catherine said, interrupting the quiet air with her squeaky voice. She was a horrible whisperer. "I don't have any siblings and now it feels like I have dozens. Some are great, some are pleasant, and others, well . . ." She trailed off for a moment. "Overall, I would give Catalpa a seven. Maybe an eight if I figure out how to start my own fire before summer's over."

"A big family of sisters," Meg whispered back. "That sounds really nice." Her voice was dreamy, the activity of the day finally catching up.

"I do, too," I heard myself say, agreeing with Catherine. "I like it, too, I mean. Like, there's a ton of lame stuff like the morning assembly and swimming and the food is kind of horrible—"

"Whoa," Catherine interrupted. "Do not dis cornflake chicken." We all started to laugh, her passion taking us by surprise. For a second, all I heard was the laughter, the clicking bugs, and the rustling of restless branches. It felt like magic, a bond forming I never would have expected.

"Girls!" Betsy's voice snapped me back to reality. "It's bedtime! No staying up all night gossiping!" She shined her flashlight at our tent, the inside suddenly a sickly green. I saw Meg for a flash, her body curled inside her sleeping bag. She looked so young, unguarded, and vulnerable.

We all buried our heads into our pillows, not wanting to get in real trouble. My mind reeled in the dark quiet, a jumble of thoughts: wondering when I should make my move; if I should take Catherine's compass tonight or tomorrow morning; how I could lie if I got caught, saying something like how I saw Catherine drop it in the woods earlier that day. But also wondering about Meg, worrying about her, the nagging sense that something was off, and thinking maybe I wouldn't take Catherine's compass, that I'd put an end to it all right here, right now. There was a rhythm to each string of thoughts, and they slowly, surely, lulled me to sleep.

A few hours later, I woke in a panic, with the disorienting sense of not knowing where you are. When I heard Catherine lightly snoring, her soft breaths filling our tent with hot air, I remembered. In my haze, I went on autopilot, my mission my sole focus. I quietly pushed myself up, rubbing the sleep crud from the corners of my eyes. It was pitch-black in our tent, which was so small I didn't have to crawl around to find what I needed. I reached over Catherine, feeling the air until my right hand hit a backpack. It was heavier than expected as I slowly lifted it over her sleeping body. With my left hand, I unzipped the tent. The air was cool outside, a breeze starting to pick up. My eyes adjusted to the moonlight and I realized I had the wrong bag. Catherine's backpack was the type the nerdiest kids at school had: L.L.Bean, covered in zippers and compartments. This one was a soft cloth. My palm ran against pilled suede at the bottom. It had to be Meg's. I should have put it back but my hands moved faster than my mind. I agreed with Sydney—I wanted to know more. I opened the main compartment and found a notebook. I pulled it out—a window into her life, another piece of treasure to bring to Sarah, or, if I was being honest, to look into myself, my curiosity piquing—and crawled back into the tent. I tucked Meg's journal into my sleeping bag, then leaned over Catherine and put the bag back where I found it. I moved my hand to the left and hit Catherine's bag, the sleek nylon against my fingers. I had seen her put her compass in the side pocket, the one meant for a water bottle. I slid my hand down and something crunched. Catherine's weird leaf collection, probably. I tried the pocket on the other side and my fingers hit a cold, smooth circle. The compass. I wrapped my hand around it and pulled slowly, trying to be as quiet as possible. The moment was almost too much, my lips pursed tightly to keep a gasp of excitement from escaping. I tucked myself back into my sleeping bag, kicking the journal and the compass to the very bottom, a secret storage space no one would ever think to search. Not only had I gotten the compass, but I had gotten something from Meg, this weird, mysterious object of interest for us all.

Sarah would be so proud.

May 13, 2014

[Blocked Number]

Adam, hey! It's Amanda
Brooks . . . Been a while

> Wow, Amanda. Hi!

> Yeah, it's been a while. How are you?

> You got a new number?

Long story

And I'm good

I'm in school in the city actually

> No way

> Where are you living?

Downtown

I was thinking about you the other day

I miss you

If you'd be game, we should catch up
sometime soon?

                                        Yeah, that would be fun

It's actually great timing because I
have my last final on Thursday

                                              Oh! Perfect

My friend Reggie is having a
party on Friday

                                        Is Reggie a boyfriend?

No . . .

You should come

                                  Where's it at? Maybe I'll stop by

                                        If that's cool, I mean

Ya I'd love that

We're doing dinner first but
then we'll be at Gatsby's

Prob around 11

Can't wait to see you

7

NOW

• • •

We're back at Catalpa, where wild greens snake up the poles holding up the entrance sign. It's somehow still there, smaller than I remember. The entire place is covered in overgrown weeds, their leaves bursting through dirtied windows and chipping wood. We wander in silence, eventually winding our way to the water. A few parts of the H dock are sunk, the water covering it like a tease of what's to come: obsolescence. I have put so much distance between Catalpa and myself, it's surreal to be here again. It does feel haunted, like I'm sleepwalking through a scene from my own dystopian nightmare. Yet I also feel nostalgia in the backward way that comes with most childhood memories. It's like rediscovering a movie you watched over and over when you were five, its plot and characters deeply ingrained in your brain. You can't remember the specifics, but you never forget how it made you feel. The rapid deterioration of Catalpa is almost tragic. It's amazing how quickly the earth reclaims places we once thought of as permanent until it's like they never existed. I feel a slight ache for

Catalpa, for Laura and Meg. This was Laura's home. It could have been Meg's future. And we destroyed it.

While we're walking, Meg explains that after everything happened, Laura sold the camp to an ambitious fiftysomething teacher from Philly. She didn't have a choice and he seemed like the best option. He planned to revamp and reopen the place, but then the financial crisis happened and the plans were put on hold. She points to a half-built addition behind the Great Hall. It's depressing to see big ideas in such disarray. We trudge across the soccer field, now brittle and unkempt. The rhododendron bushes lining the dirt trails have grown like us, big and bold and unruly. The mess hall has several broken windows, their glass covered in a thin layer of age and dirt. Fireflies begin to flicker in the evening air. One floats near my ear and I swat it, accidentally whacking its body with the back of my hand, laughing to myself when I do. I'm still a little tipsy, I realize. We walk along the stones that hug the shoreline of the lake, winding our way to Int Row. The massive rocks circling the bonfire pit are still in place, taunting us to jump into the circle's center and set it on fire. Meg has my blanket in her hand. I didn't even notice, transfixed by my fading buzz and old memories of Catalpa. She throws it in the circle, then tosses in a chip. I recognize it as one from AA. It must have been her dad's, a token of his brief sobriety and perhaps the only thing Meg thought was worth keeping.

"Are you ready?" Meg asks Catherine. Catherine pulls out my phone from her pocket.

"What the fuck?" I say, realizing she's had it this whole time. "What is going on?" I ask, reaching for my phone but missing as Catherine dodges to the side.

"I'm erasing us," Catherine says, tapping on the screen. "Meg and I already deleted all our emails to each other and to you. And now I'm deleting yours. It's not all the evidence, but it's a start."

I grab again for my phone. "Catherine, stop—" I say.

"You may not have a plan, Amanda, but we do," Catherine says, not looking up. "This is what you wanted, isn't it? It's what we all want. To be erased from each other's lives. This is where it starts." She's right, so I do nothing, standing stupidly as she gets to work. Meg gives me a half-hearted shrug, an obvious signal that she knew Catherine would do this, that they discussed it before we met. The manipulation doesn't bother me, though, as I watch Catherine's face glow from the screen, clouds overhead starting to obscure the sun. I hate that glow. That phone. It reminds me of the beginning of the end with Jackson, blue bubbles and late-night calls glaring at me in the dark. *Kill the evidence,* I think. *Kill it all.*

I got the first bad text in late April. Actually, it wasn't long after I accepted Catherine's friend request, like the mere act of letting her back into my life could throw things into chaos. It was late, almost two A.M. late, and I was cramming for a Risk Perception final. Frost coated the windows of the library, the heat inside teasing the chill on the other side. I knew Jackson had been out: a postwork happy hour with colleagues always seemed to morph into an endless series of drinks.

Where u at

I was almost done, only needed ten more minutes with the text I was reading. I felt the rings of exhaustion rounding my eyes, the lack of sleep weighing on my skin. I ignored his text in the moment; I'd answer it in a few.

I started reading about risk-taking and its related cost-benefit analyses when my phone buzzed again. A nerdy-looking undergrad glared from across the table. I picked up my phone, the shine of the screen piercing the library's soft nighttime light.

Who r u with

I stared, confused. What was he talking about? I scrolled up, reviewing our conversation. I had told him earlier that day I'd be at the library studying.

I'm at the library. Final is due Monday, remember?

I hit send, put my phone back down. Weird.

I looked back at my textbook, when my phone started buzzing, again and again. "Can you turn off your phone, or leave?" the kid across the table asked, his voice nasal. I mouthed "Sorry" and ran toward the bathroom, sneaking inside to answer the call.

"Hello?" I whispered. Jackson was breathing heavily on the other end.

"Where are you?" he asked, low and growling. "I'm home and you're not. Where the fuck are you?" Jackson sounded angry, a tone unlike anything I had heard from him before.

I felt myself getting annoyed. "I'm at the library, for the millionth time," I said, my voice hissing. "I'm studying."

"Sure you are." I couldn't place his anger. It was floating all around, seeping through my cell's microphone.

I pulled the phone away from my face, staring at the screen. "What are you talking about, Jackson?"

"Why don't you love me?" He was almost wailing, roadkill bleeding on the side of the highway.

"What are you talking about?" I asked again, wondering if he thought he was talking to someone else. "Jackson, I'm coming home. I'll be there in, like, twenty minutes."

"Don't even bother," he grumbled, hanging up right after.

I remember thinking how bizarre the entire conversation was, how it didn't feel real. I was sleep deprived and confused, in a dreamlike state, during my cab ride home. When I opened our apartment door, Jackson was facedown on the couch, passed out and snoring, an open hand drooping off the side of the sofa, his phone on the floor underneath. I tossed and turned in our bed, my racing confusion chasing away real sleep. At about six A.M., Jackson crawled in. His hair was tousled, part of it matted to his face. I turned to face him. "Hey," he whispered, his eyes sleepy. I could smell the previous night's vodka on his breath and winced.

"What happened last night?"

He scooted close to me, wrapping his arms around my waist and pulling me toward him. "What are you talking about?"

"Your weird texts and call."

"They weren't that weird," he said, his tone defensive. "I just wanted to see you."

"You seemed mad," I said, trying to push.

"No, I wasn't. I was fucked up, fine—but that's it. You're reading into it. Get out of your own head," he said, laughing like I was a silly girl overthinking things. "I gotta shower. Still on for dinner later tonight or do you have to study?"

And like that, we moved on. I pushed the moment into the back of my head, wondering if I had misinterpreted everything, blown it out of proportion.

Not long after, while watching TV, Jackson turned to me and asked, randomly, "Do you still talk to Adam?" He stood up as he asked, grabbing a beer from the fridge, his entire vibe casual.

"Adam Rhodes? Like, my ex Adam?" We had talked about our exes in the early days, our prying minds wanting to understand who we were dating, what they were like, who they had been, who they could be. That's when he first told me about Kelsey and Alexis. But that was it; none of our exes' names had come up since. "No." I shook my head. "I don't at all. I mean, I don't even have his number anymore. And he doesn't even have social media. I wouldn't do that to you," I added for good measure.

"Okay, cool," Jackson said. "Just checking."

He cracked the tab of his beer, the crisp shush making me jump. As he walked back to the couch, he smiled at me, then picked up the remote and turned the TV to ESPN. I stared at him for a moment longer, the profile of his face suddenly seeming foreign. I didn't like the growing number of questions; they filled me with fear. Fear for the end of our relationship, but also fear toward him, the uncanny feeling that something was off. A fear I had hoped would never visit me again.

We're sitting around the fire, my blanket charred beneath a Duraflame Meg lugged in her bag. She wasn't wrong to say we're having a funeral. It *is* a goodbye to the past, our memories released and swirling in gray circles above the small bonfire. "I started to notice things when my mom died," Meg says, looking directly at the flames. Catherine puts a hand on her shoulder, but Meg shrugs it off like she knows she has to tell this story alone.

"She had cancer. I don't know if you guys knew, but that's how she died. I was nine when she told me. She took me to Rita's, like it was a normal day. I even remember what we ordered, because it's what we always ordered. Mango ice with vanilla custard for me and chocolate ice with chocolate custard for Mom. She was cheery and totally fine, so I didn't think anything was up. But when we got home, my dad was there. He worked at a distribution center for some office supplies company in the area and, like, helped handle their warehouse logistics—so he was always on call. Even at that age, I knew it was weird he was home. His eyes were all red, you know, like a sad puppy. And then everything is sort of a blur." Meg pauses, rubbing her eyes. Her mascara, soft from the humidity and heat, smears a bit. She's not crying, exactly, but seems on the verge. Catherine and I don't say anything. We're enraptured, hanging on her every word. "They talked like doctors, using all these insane medical terms I didn't understand. But one stuck: *cancer*. I don't think I fully got what that meant at the time. I knew this girl Carly Ruffino from school, and her mom had a big tumor so she got all these surgeries and she was fine. So I thought, *Okay, we'll fix this. No big deal.* Because as a kid you don't ever imagine you can't fix something, like it's all rainbows and miracles and shit."

She clears her throat as her eyes start to well. "The thing is, my mom had melanoma and it had metastasized. It was stage three when they found it. And, like—" Meg's voice cracks. "Like, you know the rest. She died about three years later." Her mom was whittled away to nothing by the end, she says, my mind envisioning a parasite squirming through her blood and clinging on to all her vital organs, insatiably sucking. I shake the image out of my brain.

"So what did your dad do the whole time?" I ask, wanting to know more about him, how he really hurt Meg. My question is selfish; I know Jackson is bad, that I should leave. I want to leave. But there's a part of me that doesn't, that thinks we can maybe work this out. The longer I'm with Meg and Catherine, the evidence now gone, the more I find myself fantasizing about returning to my relationship with Jackson as if nothing happened. He can cut back on drinking; I can drop out of my program, get a more traditional nine-to-five so I'm around more. Maybe I can fix us.

"He just sat there. Like a fucking robot. I was so nervous when my mom told me all this, I puked orange ice everywhere. She came over and started rubbing my back and telling me everything would be okay. And my dad still just sat there, not saying a fucking thing." Catherine is oddly quiet through all this, nodding her head. She has heard this before, I realize. Maybe even more than once.

I'm impatient, wanting to know exactly what Meg's dad did.

I have always thought his death was justified. Her bruises and her diary entries had seemed solid enough evidence. But I don't think Jackson deserves the same outcome. I don't even know if he deserves my leaving. He needs help, support—and I can give him that. I'm staring at Meg, my eyes pressuring her to share more, to get to the good part—the part that will confirm her dad was much worse. That will make me realize I don't need to be scared. I don't need to leave Jackson. That I can convince him to calm down, that it will all be okay. "No, I mean, did he, like, regularly hurt you? Or what actually happened that led to the night we were all together with him?" I don't say what actually happened: "the night I killed him." None of us want to say those words out loud. We remember what happened. They understand we don't talk about the thing itself. And after this mess with Jackson, I don't plan to ever discuss it again.

"My dad sort of lost it when my mom died. Like, he became this shell of a person. For as long as I could remember, he had never had a sip of alcohol. And then at the reception after the funeral, I saw him drinking something brown. Aunt Laura saw, too. She gave me a look when he walked by and stumbled a little. I didn't know what it meant at the time, but obviously I now realize she was worried. And, like, my dad started getting super angry after that. It was like he blamed me for her death," she said, her voice quaking. "And it wasn't fair, you know? Because I was sad, too. So fucking sad. And instead of being able to focus on moving forward, he kept us in the past."

I don't understand what she means. "Why was he so angry?" I know my questions are prying, but I need more information.

"Tell her about hospice, Meg." Catherine urges Meg, getting her to refocus. Meg sniffles and Catherine hands her a tissue from the small pack of Kleenex she had in her knapsack. "It's okay," Catherine says. "She should know."

Meg wipes under her lower lash line. "So at the end my mom

was in hospice," she says. "My dad had to quit his job to be home with her. Whenever he went out and I was home, I was in charge. It was hard, you know? I mean, I was fucking twelve. Near the end she didn't want to be alive. She legit asked me to give her too much medicine so she would overdose." She shakes her head, remembering the scene. "And when she actually died, like took her last breath, I was home with her alone. My dad was just at the pharmacy. It was—" She pauses, then stops, keeping the story for herself. "My dad seemed to always be pissed at me after that. Like I had somehow caused her death?"

"Did you?" I ask.

"Are you serious?" Catherine interrupts, speaking up for the first time. "Is that what you told Jackson? God," she starts. Her frustration is directed at me, not Meg. In fact, she seems protective of Meg, as if I'm some sort of threat.

I put up both my hands, two white flags waving for forgiveness. "What? No. What are you talking about?"

"No," Meg interrupts, looking at Catherine, then me. "I didn't kill my own mom, for fuck's sake." She stares back at the fire, her voice starting to quiver. "It's so fucking unfair, you know? She was the good one." Catherine scoots closer to Meg and puts her arm around her, pulling Meg into her side. The movement is clunky, unrehearsed and a tad uncomfortable, two people familiar with one another's stories but not bodies. Still, I tense at the earnestness of the motion. It has never been more clear that I am the outsider. I should leave; I got what I needed: the promise of their silence and an erased paper trail. But it's not really all that I want, I realize. Meg relaxes, collecting her composure again. I lean closer, my face inches from the fire, its flames dancing between me and them. *More,* I almost say. *Tell me more.*

After the funeral, Meg's dad started drinking, she says. Quietly at first, sneaking bottles and cans into the house in crinkled brown bags. Then blatantly, each gleaming container a giant fuck-you to the world, to his wife's fate, and, in Meg's telling, to her. Her dad's volatile moods didn't scare her. Not yet, at least. They worried her—his pacing, his cursing at the TV screen, the dishes piled in the sink, the empty cans next to unopened mail—so she called her aunt, his sister: Laura. When they got foreclosure notices shortly after, the hospital bills too much, they moved to the campground outside of Catalpa. She was thirteen.

"It was only supposed to be for the summer," she says. "So he could clean up his act." She doesn't add the *but* that should caboose that sentence: he didn't make it past that summer. Instead, he snuck around behind Laura's back, which was easy to do since she was so busy watching all the campers. "Usually he only yelled, never touched me," she says. "Like I was always in his way. I was an annoyance, a troublemaker, an ass kisser, a bitch. It didn't matter what I did. It was always wrong. And everything sort of came to a head when I got my period. Because of course I had to get my period for the first time that summer." Meg rolls her eyes, karma her least favorite atmospheric influence. "And Laura was prepping the seniors for their big canoe trip. So I had to ask my dad to help out."

"Why didn't you ask one of us, or the nurse?" I say, thinking how obvious that solution seems.

"I didn't want you guys all knowing." When you're that age, avoiding embarrassment trumps everything. Her dad didn't know how to handle her request, awkwardly laughing. He told her to ask people in the park. Plenty of bleeding bitches here, he'd said.

"Ew," Catherine and I say in unison, the idea of those words coming out of either of our dads' mouths unfathomable.

"Yeah. When he said that, I knew he was in a fucked-up place. Looking back, he was probably even high . . ." Meg starts to trail off, looking at the woods beyond the fire as she finishes her story. "So he says he'll find me something, and he disappears for, like, hours. I'm not kidding. I think I stuffed my underwear with an entire roll of toilet paper before I finally started looking for him." She circled campfires, knocked on RV doors. Most of the people at the site were friendly, families and groups of friends passing through to take in Pennsylvania's Appalachia; they seemed worried she was alone. When it started getting dark, she heard her dad's voice in a trailer not too far from theirs. He was grunting, guttural and heaving. "I opened the front and he was sitting at a table, next to this loser woman, snorting some shit. So I screamed." When Meg screamed, her dad looked up at the door. The woman started yelling and all Meg remembers is the campsite whirring past her as she ran back to their RV. Her dad followed her, yelling as she sprinted. In the RV, she ran into the bedroom—his room— and shut the door. He kicked it in, his eyes nearly glazed over when he burst through the mess. I shiver. He grabbed Meg by the arm, but his hand slipped. She tried to push him away with her legs, but he caught one and dragged her off the bed. She twisted as she fell, her hip bone whacking against the floor, leaving a bruise—the one I saw during our overnight. "For a split second, I thought that was the first time I had ever been scared of him. Like truly, pants-shittingly scared. But when I was on the floor, my side aching, I remembered more." Her mom's broken fingers when she was really little, bandages covering her fingers in pictures. How her mom had a limp for about a week when she was five. They always joked that she was clumsy, that she had two left feet. But seeing her dad's angry stare made her realize it was all a lie. And then Meg remembered the time, the next year, she had walked into her parents' room and seen her dad leaning over her mom, strangling her on their bed. Meg had been confused, her presence enough for him to let go, to quit drinking, to be a better person. She had been so young, she had forgotten. How had she forgotten? That's why she had carried that chip. Not because she worried about addiction and the way it can course through families for generations. She carried the chip to remember that most addicts are good people, are worthy of being saved. But her dad? Alcohol wasn't his problem. He was already rotten—and drinking gave him an excuse to unleash his inner monster.

"I froze when it all came rushing back. He was sweaty and bloated and so gross, still holding on to my leg. And then it was like a switch went off," she said. Her dad collapsed to the floor crying, begging Meg to forgive him, saying how sorry he was, saying he loved her. He wept into her thigh, resting his head against her stomach. "It made me sick," she says. "In that moment I didn't fully understand how manipulative he was. I thought he was totally batshit. And I decided I was going to get away from him, whatever it took."

Whatever it took. The words ring in my ears. *Whatever it takes.*

There had been small warnings in the weeks leading up to the moment I reached out to Meg and Catherine. That time Jackson told me he liked my hair better straight than curly, and when I came home from class one day, he had bought me a new straightener. "You're hotter with straight hair," he explained, giving me a pat on the butt.

When he squeezed one of my love handles, a smidge of fat spilling over the edge of my pants. I'd gained a bit of weight after I first moved in, the combination of class and cooking and coupley laziness adding up my calories. "You want to go for a run tomorrow?" he said, giving my back another playful grab. "You love running. You should get back into it."

The weird block list I found on my Facebook, a bunch of random guys, some of whom I'd forgotten I was even friends with. I changed my password when I discovered it, assuming someone had broken into my laptop at the library. Jackson would never do something so insane, I convinced myself. It was just a weird bug.

The fact that we only went out with his friends, always, only pursuing plans he made. All things Rachel had mentioned, that I'd convinced myself she was wrong about, thrust into a new light. I never had a say, had become a shell of myself to please him. And I was alone. Totally alone.

Everything changed in late May. We went out to an open bar for Reggie's birthday, hosted by one of their friends from college who moonlighted as a DJ. The bar was packed, strobe lights bouncing off the mirrored walls. I felt trapped in a bro-y funhouse, the clownish colors making everyone look exactly the same.

Jackson was on the dance floor, high on something besides vodka, when I slipped away to grab a drink at the bar. I felt a hand on my lower back. When I turned, I saw a tall and teddy-bear-esque guy in a plaid button-down and did a double take. "Adam!" I screamed over the music. "What are you doing here?" I gave him an ass-out, one-armed hug. He lingered, his hand still on my lower back. He smelled the same, Old Spice and dryer sheets. I glanced at the bartender, who paused for a split second, looking impatient. "I'll have three shots of tequila," I said, Jackson's request. "And two vodka sodas."

"You know why I'm here." Adam smirked. He was drunk. Definitely drunk. But so was I, so I couldn't judge. I'd forgotten how cute he was, the boyish charm of a hardworking Midwesterner.

"You know Reggie?" I said, nodding toward the dance floor.

"No," he said, looking confused. "I thought you—"

The bartender slid the drinks across the bar. The vodka soda's condensation soaked my arm, shocking my overheated body. "Ooh!" I said, slithering away from Adam's touch. I threw back one of the shots, grimacing as I swallowed. "Well, it was fun seeing you," I said, giving Adam a polite smile before turning toward the dance floor, the drinks teetering like stacked stones between my fingers.

"Amanda!" he said, lightly touching my forearm. It disarmed the perfect balance required to hold all the drinks and I dropped all four, glass shattering everywhere. It wasn't that loud, but a flurry of barbacks swarmed, drawing attention. I looked up and Jackson was charging over.

Adam's back was to him. Jackson gave him a shove, nothing major but enough to loosen Adam's grip.

"Babe," he said, looking at me. "You okay?"

"Yeah, I'm fine." I was suddenly nervous, hoping Jackson didn't recognize Adam. Praying we could all move on.

But Adam, never one to forget his manners, turned around, facing Jackson. "Hey, man," he said, sticking out his hand. "I'm Adam." He shouted his name over the blasting EDM music. "You know Amanda?"

Immediately, I watched the recognition click. "What the fuck are you doing here?" Jackson's pupils were huge, his irises near-hidden. "What the fuck is he doing here?" I raised my shoulders, mouthing "I don't know," repeatedly. Because I genuinely didn't.

Jackson swatted his hand away, then pointed directly at Adam's face. "I know who you are. I'm only asking one more time. What the fuck are you doing here?" His slight twang thickened when he was mad, no amount of Southern charm able to help him regain his composure. Reggie walked up behind Jackson, putting his hand on his shoulder.

"We have a problem here?" He stepped forward, his huge frame looming over Adam. "Can we help you, man? This is an invite-only party."

Adam looked at me, his face sheathed in confusion. He looked back at Reggie, then Jackson, and nodded, throwing his hands up in front of his chest as he backed away. "No, I guess not. I thought I was invited," Adam said, looking at me for an explanation, then back to Reggie. "But I was wrong. Obviously. No problems here." He took another step back, hands still up as he turned toward the exit. As he walked away, he turned around once, his expression still completely lost. Why had he thought I invited him? Adam wasn't a liar; that had always been our issue, how pure he was. He was too kind, too straightforward, too good.

Jackson grabbed my wrist and pulled me away from the bar, to an empty corner on the other side of the dance floor where we were surrounded by people thrashing around with their eyes closed. We were right by the DJ booth, the bass thumping through my skin. Jackson put his hands over my shoulders, leaning against the wall.

"So you want to be a whore tonight, huh?" he asked, screaming into my ear over the music. The last shot I'd taken churned my stomach acid. I turned my head away from Jackson and closed my eyes, not wanting to look at him. He traced the insides of my thighs with his fingers, trailing up past my skirt's hemline to my underwear, pushing through and into me. I was paralyzed, unable to move. "You want someone else to do this to you?" he asked, pushing harder. No one around us noticed, everyone too engrossed by the music or their dance partner or the E they were rolling on.

I looked at Jackson, straight in the eyes. His pupils were big, two black holes sucking out all the light in our relationship. "No," I said calmly, trying to fight back tears. "Only you." He pressed even harder, so hard I thought he might rip my underwear.

"That's what I thought," he said, biting the side of my neck like a dog marking its territory.

I ran to the bathroom shortly after and puked, my fraught emotions making it near impossible to keep anything down. Wiping my mouth, I leaned against the grungy stall door, the wall in front of me softened by my tears. I struggled to breathe, my body shaking as I tried to catch the air.

The taxi ride home was silent, the cracked window and late-spring air the only thing keeping me from puking again. We trudged up our apartment building's front steps and rode the elevator not saying a word, but the second the door was shut, Jackson started yelling.

"You wanna tell me why Adam was there tonight?" He took a step closer to me, my back against the door.

"I told you, I don't know," I said, nearly sober at this point. "I honestly have no idea. It was weird. And now I'm really tired and don't feel like dealing with this." I ducked under his arm, which was against the door over my left shoulder. "With you." My rage was stronger than my fear at that point. Jackson was being ridiculous; I started walking toward our bedroom and he stormed after me, springing in front. He whipped his arm across my path, punching a hole in the temporary wall we'd gotten installed to convert our studio into a one-bedroom. The motion swept my hair, the wings of its anger lifting the strands and spilling them across my face. My heart seemed to stop for a moment. So did my body. Everything inside me screamed, *Careful*.

"I'm not done talking," he snarled, blocking the hallway with his arm. His face was distorted, warped into someone I didn't recognize. His nose was an inch from mine, his hot cheeks radiating.

"Jackson, stop," I said, ducking under his arm. "I'll talk to you in the morning." I walked to the bedroom, my back to him.

"You're *not* done with me," he yelled, nearly shouted, punching the wall again. I stood still, frozen in place. Fear. It coursed through my veins, taking me back to hiding outside of Meg's trailer, watching as I wondered if this person so much bigger than her, someone who was supposed to love her, would actually hurt her. I needed to get out. I wanted safe, not dangerous. Still, my feet wouldn't move, scared to make the tiniest disruption. Jackson walked toward me again, his eyes marbled with rage. His hand was covered in plaster and a few streaks of blood. "I could ruin you, you know?" he hissed. "I know your secret. One call, that's all it takes."

I didn't know what he meant, who, exactly, he planned to call. The police department that closed the case years ago? His dad

and his powerful network? What would they do? I didn't want
to know, so I didn't ask.

He took another step toward me, so close I flinched. "Why am
I not enough for you? Why?" His tone changed, suddenly softer,
desperate. "You love me. You won't leave, just like I would never
leave you. Don't do that to me." His spit sprayed my nose as he
spoke. My heart was racing, every muscle in my body tense.

"Okay," I whispered, so quietly I almost didn't hear myself.
"Okay," I said louder. "Okay," I repeated, the shock still gripping
my brain. I started to tear up, the emotion overwhelming. Jackson pulled me toward his chest. I melted, not sure what else to do.
He held my head, stroking my hair.

"I'm sorry," he whispered back, his breath hot on my ear. "I
love you. I don't want to lose you." I was trembling, the danger of
this situation still raw.

Because I didn't know how else to move on from the scene, we
had sex that night, slow and emotional and passionate, at least
on Jackson's end. I didn't sleep, afraid to shut my eyes. I had just
read about a girl who was abused over and over again when she
was only fifteen, who finally fought back and killed the man who
trafficked her. She was sentenced to over twenty years in prison.
There were so many instances of this, of women and girls de-
fending themselves against real-life demons, of battling to survive, of telling their truth, yet the man's version was always the
one believed. Most of the time, they were told they were wrong,
that their recollection couldn't have been correct, that they were
being crazy, that they would have been better off sucking it up
and staying quiet. The stories were all over the internet, outrageous reactions littering my timelines, but nothing changed. It
never did. I was trapped, petrified of the power he held over me. I
stared at the ceiling, wondering if I should tell my parents, or Rachel. She'd predicted this. Well, the Jackson-being-a-total-psycho
part. But neither my parents nor Rachel really knew what had

happened at camp that summer, just that I had witnessed something no twelve-year-old should. I could lie, tell them Jackson made it all up, that he was using this story to keep me in his grip. But what if Jackson did call the police force by Camp Catalpa? What if he gave them a thread to tug at, to yank and yank until everything unraveled? I had only shared the secret once, had only opened the door because I loved Jackson—and thought he loved me. He had betrayed that love, the trust of letting someone know your darkest parts. Worse, he had turned it into ammunition. Even if I cried self-defense and somehow won, the association of it all would ruin everything I'd worked toward, my perfect résumé smeared by a simple Google search.

The next day, Jackson acted as if nothing had happened, pointing at the huge hole in the wall and laughing. "Man, I was fucked up last night." He turned and wrapped me in his arms. I winced at his touch, at his avoidance of everything he had done the night before. "You wanna grab brunch?"

"Seriously?" I said, dipping out of his grasp. "Shouldn't we, like, talk about what happened last night?"

"We just did. I was fucked up. Don't make me being an idiot into something bigger, Amanda." He walked to the kitchen counter and poured himself some coffee. "You know I hate drama."

I nodded, pretending he was right, trying to hide the deeply unsettling bubbling I felt in my stomach, the hole in the wall still gaping.

On Monday, Jackson left early for work and I woke up around eleven, my mood an eternal hangover, my schedule empty before my internship started. I roamed the apartment, cell in one hand and laptop open on our coffee table. There was a cheap bottle of red wine next to our fridge, unopened and calling me. I screwed off the top and poured myself a glass, sitting and staring at the wall and thinking. I wanted to Google the case, to see what was online about it. The police could trace that sort of search, though. At some point, I looked down and my glass was empty. I walked back to the bottle and placed it on the coffee table. I filled my glass again, almost to the brim, each sip an escape, a way to smooth the jagged edges of my life. I started to pace, half of me wanting to call my mom and tell her everything, to cry and plead for her to fix it all. The other itched to revisit the past, Catherine and Meg's faces running through my head, Meg's dad's eyes glowing in the background. I sat on the couch cross-legged with my laptop perched on my knees. Typing, as if on autopilot, I logged into my old AOL account. The screen glowed against my glass, which I was emptying in record time. I squinted as I typed "Catherine Wagner" in the search bar. Her emails were still there. So were Meg's. They had sent a few shortly after we left camp, just checking in. Meg's shared updates about Laura, about the camp closing. Catherine's were usually bulleted, like a to-do list of questions or commentary about her day-to-day she felt she should share. I had never responded, eventually leaving them unread. About a year after the first email, I stopped receiving them. I had no idea if they still checked those email accounts, but I sent a message. "Hello from your past," I wrote in the subject line. "Do you guys still check these?"

Both replied within twenty-four hours. I responded to their emails while at the library, somewhere Jackson would never be. I typed fast, instinct taking over.

I told my boyfriend our secret. I told him everything. I shouldn't have. We should meet asap.

And to my surprise, they wanted to meet, too.

"The universe works in mysterious ways, don't you think?" Catherine asks. "Memories hide themselves, only to return at the most crucial of times." She's talking to Meg, who is nodding. "You needed that memory to create a safe future. I don't see the seeds you planted as wrong. It's not black and white. It was about survival."

"Yeah," Meg starts. "I mean, when my dad stopped taking his pills—"

"Stop, Meg," Catherine says, glancing at me in her peripheral vision. "It's not about that," she says. What does Meg mean? Does their scheming run deeper? I'm about to press when Catherine turns to face me. "Let's talk about you, Amanda." She's direct, clear voiced, like she's a manager about to give me an assignment.

"Me?" I ask. We talked about me all morning. What else is there to say?

"Yes, you. What are you going to do about Jackson?"

She says it like a statement, the underlying assumption that Jackson must be dealt with. I figured we would get to Jackson eventually, map out a step-by-step plan, a way to make sure no one ends up hurt—something that would require thought. Time. But this? This is happening much faster than I expected, Catherine's eyes demanding a list of action items. "W-Well," I stammer, still a little woozy from my afternoon cocktails. "I guess—I guess I'll move out?" I say it as a question, wanting them to tell me what to do. I worry I can't do it alone. That moving back in with my parents will feel like failure, an inability to grow up, move on, make a future worth living in. That he'll convince me to stay. That leaving Jackson isn't enough. I want them to tell me it will be.

"Tonight," Catherine says, brushing the dirt off her butt as she stands up. "I'm ready to be done with this."

"We could all sleep at my place tonight. I told you, Cat, I have to work tomorrow morning," Meg starts. The sun is low, twilight twinkling above. "I thought we were gonna go tomorrow afternoon."

I'm about to agree, in hopes of getting a good night's sleep so I'm not dizzy on the road, but pause a moment when I realize they've both already talked about coming to New York.

"No, tonight. He's not there this weekend," Catherine says. "Correct, Amanda? So it needs to happen tonight."

Meg pulls out her phone, her lips tight. "Okay, I need to get someone to cover my shift." She's texting, her fingers moving at light speed. "I can't fucking lose this job," she mumbles, but Catherine gives a look that shuts Meg up, and I can't get the image of Catherine as a puppeteer commanding her ventriloquist doll's every move out of my head.

"Amanda, you drive your car." Catherine's in action mode, her ability to articulate exactly what each of us needs to do as sharp as when we were twelve. "We'll follow in my car, to make sure you get there okay. We'll help you move." She walks over to me as she talks and puts out a hand, helping me up.

And like that, all three of us start to drive to New York.

— 8 —

THEN

. . .

"Where's my compass?" It was morning, the sun peeking over the horizon. The evening cool had disappeared with the darkness, replaced with the stifling heat that defined that entire summer. Catherine was frantic, her sleeping bag inside out and every item in her backpack strewn on the floor of our tent.

"Did you leave it by the fire?" I asked, packing up my own things and adjusting my sports bra. Catherine's compass was tucked inside, its smooth casing chill against my sweaty sternum. It was a chancier spot than the bottom of my sleeping bag, but I didn't want to risk a mix-up when we got back to camp; we all had the same puffy black and blue and green bags. Meg's notebook was in my backpack, my wrinkled outfit from the day before stuffed on top.

"What are you even talking about?" Meg rubbed her eyes, her morning breath lingering in the heat. It made me want to gag. I zipped my bag and started to crawl to the tent's opening. A hand grabbed my foot, pulling me back.

"No." I looked over my shoulder and Catherine was glaring at me. I was still on all fours, my butt near her face and my head near Meg's. "You're not leaving," she said. "What did you do with it?"

I shook her off my leg. "Let go, psycho. I didn't do anything." My heart rate sped up a touch.

"Girls in tent three, are you almost ready?" Betsy shouted from outside. She was pacing, going tent to tent to mobilize all the campers. We would be back in time for breakfast, a tradition everyone loved, campers who'd just done their overnight returning sweaty and triumphant, shouting over one another to talk about how cool it was, getting the next overnight crew amped for their experience. This was another one of camp's rites of passage earned with time and experience, an invisible badge we all couldn't wait to wear proudly. We had survived overnight, our muddied faces cheesing after we grilled dinner under the open sky, breathed in sync as we slept fearlessly in the thick of the woods, the threat of bears and skunks and coyotes nowhere in our minds. We would be like the older campers now, initiated into their club, the focus of mealtime conversation as we dished on every minute detail of the night.

"Yes!" I shouted, glaring back at Catherine. "You better pack," I said in a quieter voice. "You don't want to lose something else."

Meg sat all the way up, her face still soft from sleep. She ignored us both, pulling out a T-shirt and shimmying it over her tank top. I was halfway out of the entrance of the tent when I tumbled forward. "What the—"

It was Catherine, her puny arms pushing my butt with a force I didn't realize they contained. "Where is it?" She was shrieking, a banshee warning me to confess. My face was flat against the forest floor, a raw pebble scratching my cheek. Catherine crawled over my legs, pushed me onto my back, and straddled me. "Give it to me!"

Betsy ran over, pulling Catherine off and standing between us. I stared up at the sky, the clouds fluffy sheep against solid blue. I blinked slowly, not wanting to get mad, to draw more attention than Catherine already had. She was complaining to Betsy, her voice shrill. Sydney walked over and pulled me up. "What's going on?" she asked.

I rolled my eyes, not sharing the details. I needed to get the compass to Sarah, so no one could know I had it. Betsy put a hand on Catherine's shoulder and walked her over to me. "Amanda, Catherine thinks you may have something that's hers. Have you seen her compass?" She looked impatient, the other girls starting to abandon their tents, which we were all supposed to pack, and circle to see what was going on.

"I already told her no," I said, my eyes wide with innocence. "I don't have her stupid compass." I looked right at Catherine as I spoke, taunting her to make more of a scene. "What is your problem, Catherine? Why are you so obsessed with blaming me for everything that goes wrong in your life?" She looked ridiculous. My lips curled slightly, stifling the laugh I was worried would come, the nervous one I couldn't help because I knew I was winning.

Catherine's face turned a deep crimson, her fists in balls by her sides. She dodged Betsy's grasp and charged at me. Her hands hit the center of my chest and ricocheted me back into the tent. As I fell, my bra, which was already a little too big for my nonexistent chest, shifted and the compass came loose. It slid down my stomach and right out the bottom of my untucked shirt. Catherine looked down, the compass's metal catching light as it tumbled to the ground. She lunged, grabbing the silver circle, and pierced me with a glare. She let out a guttural scream, one so loud and gravelly it had to have been within her all summer, growing with each prank, each torment, until it barreled out of her mouth and smacked me in the face. She made her voice heard, her power known. It was both beautiful and scary, the way she flipped from aloof nerd to vicious savage in milliseconds.

"I'm. Going. To. Kill. You!" She panted, her face still red. I crab-crawled backward. Meg was still inside the tent, watching the scene unfurl with fascination. Catherine leaped toward me, but Betsy intervened.

"Enough!" she shouted, her body making an X in front of the tent. "That is enough! I'm sick and tired of this." She pulled Catherine to her side and stared into the entrance of the tent. "Something is seriously wrong with you two."

And you know what? Betsy wasn't wrong.

Our punishment was scraper duty for the week. No one wanted that. You spent all your meals in the kitchen, eating quickly with the Nancys, then fielding tray after tray of overflowing dirty dishes as each table's waitress—a different camper assigned to the duty every week—dropped off their finished meals. A spatula was used to scrape all the remaining food on each plate into a massive trash can. The result was a jumbo pile of half-chewed, vomit-colored leftovers. The only thing worse than seven days of scraping was having to do it next to Catherine. Up until that moment, she'd been Teflon despite all we'd done. Her anger, that primal cry from her gut, haunted me during our ride back to camp, the beastly way she looked at me when she charged, like she was out for blood. We were late to return because of the fight, so while everyone else scrambled back to the cabins to drop off their bags before breakfast, Betsy escorted me and Catherine straight to the kitchen. No one talked as we passed the tables of campers, a few whispering as they watched us trudge through the dining hall. The shame burned my eyes, tears of embarrassment welling. The Nancys nodded as we took our seats in the back corner, thighs chilled against two metal stools at a stainless-steel table. We were near the fridge and a lingering iciness soaked the air. I rubbed my arms, not sure what else to do.

Catherine and I were served breakfast first, before the rest of the campers, so our hands would be free by the time they all finished. I stared at my scrambled eggs, robotically chewing, avoiding looking at Catherine.

"Why'd you take it?" she asked me, her face blurry in my peripheral vision. I stuffed my mouth with a forkful of hash browns, looking straight ahead. "Why did you want my compass?" She flicked my arm with her fork, the vibration zinging my fingers. I turned for a moment, my eyes in line with hers, a silent standoff. I scooped another load of hash browns and looked forward again. "I pity you, Amanda. That's why your asinine bullying doesn't bother me. I see how desperate you are to make Sarah like you."

My cheeks started to burn. I didn't care if Catherine punched me, pulled my hair, scratched my arms. I could handle her violence. But calling me a follower, especially when there was a hint of truth—well, she might as well have stabbed my stomach with a knife and twisted it until I was completely gutted. I was not okay with this role reversal, with this surprisingly vicious side of Catherine. If I learned anything that summer, it's that we never know the multitudes we contain—good or bad—until they're tested. "Shut up," I mumbled, my fingers white as I gripped the fork harder.

"That's really why you did it? For Sarah?" Catherine let out a small laugh of triumph. "I knew it." She lowered her head so it was sideways, just below mine. She was quite literally in my face. "Do you not realize Sarah's an idiot? She's cool now, sure, but she's dumber than a jellyfish."

"A jellyfish?" I scooted my stool an inch back as I laughed, Catherine's insult lacking the bite she intended.

"Yes," she said, shuffling the eggs and potatoes on her plate into two clearly defined piles. "They don't have brains. They sting. But they really are dumb blobs that invade and destroy otherwise peaceful environments."

"You're so weird. You know that, right?"

"Of course," she said, tapping her fork against her braces. "You never let me forget."

I looked back at my food, unsure what to say. You never think you're a bully until it's impossible to ignore, the ugliness of your own behavior thrown back at you. I saw myself through her eyes, a weak, catty, desperate girl who got off on putting others down. I was repulsive, my abuse shameful. We didn't talk the rest of the morning and scraped in silence at lunch.

During Rest Hour, Sarah was in her bunk. She looked almost back to normal, only the slightest sheen of green under her eyes. Larry, Sydney, and I crawled up to smother her with hugs, peasants serving their queen. "Sarah!" Sydney said, resting her head on Sarah's lap. "You've arisen from the dead!" Larry bear-hugged Sarah from behind, loosely wrapping her arm around Sarah's neck. There wasn't room for me on the bed, their limbs sprawled all over. I balanced on the side of the bunk, my feet perched on one of the rungs, and reached a hand out to Sarah, who grabbed it like there was a gift in my palm. When she realized my hand was empty, her face turned. Before she could say anything, Betsy walked into the cabin.

"Girls! It's Rest Hour. Do I need to remind you every single day?" She was talking to me, the rule-breaker, the one already walking on eggshells. I slunk down the bunk and onto my bed, failure and regret gripping my every muscle. I curled up in the fetal position, facing the wall. I wanted to cry, though I wasn't even sure what about. It all felt so impossible. Impossible to please Sarah while getting along with Catherine, to just exist without causing some sort of issue. Sarah and Catherine were necessary opposites, Sarah's bossiness highlighting Catherine's innocence, Catherine's dorkiness amplifying Sarah's coolness. I didn't know how to please them both, how to not rock the boat without pissing off Sarah. I liked Catherine more than I realized, but not enough to want to spend all my time with her and Barrett. Sarah's friendship was like UV rays, all gorgeous glow until it turned into sunburn. I pulled my knees tighter. I missed home.

A piece of paper dropped down on my head, sliding through the crack between the wall and Sarah's bunk. *YOU LOSE* was written in her curly handwriting, both *O*s horribly drawn compasses. I crumpled the paper, throwing it under my bunk. I had done all of it for her—and now I was stuck doing stupid scraper duty. Did she not appreciate that? Did my effort, my loyalty, not count for anything? I stared at the scribbling on the walls, the names I had looked at so many times before. Former campers who had thought they'd be best friends forever, whose bonds seemed so simple and pure. I wanted that. I'd had it with Grace. Maybe I would never have it again. I decided I would write to Grace and set up a visit to California. We'd figure out the details later. I just needed a reminder of who I was, some way to escape who I'd become. Just thinking about it gave me a revived energy. I turned to my other side and unzipped my backpack, which was leaning against the base of my bed. As I pulled out my notebook, a flash of purple caught my eye. I had completely forgotten about Meg's journal. I swiveled my legs around and crouched over the bag, pulling the notebook out like it was illegal contraband. There was no signifier it belonged to Meg; the cover was bare, no name scrawled in thick permanent marker, no glittering stickers adhered to the corners. I was about to show Sarah, to slide it up through the slats between my bottom bunk and her top. Something made me pause, though, and I leaned back into my pillow, opening to the first page. It was dated August 19, 2000. Almost three years ago exactly. I started reading, skimming the record of Meg's life like it was mine to invade. We had objectified her with our interest, turned her into the target of our fascination and observation. It didn't even occur to me that I shouldn't read her diary, that she was a real person with a whole life beyond this camp. There were maybe twenty entries total, all short but packed with angst, information, tension. After watching her talk about Magda the night before, I knew she could weave a good story, but there were a few lines I couldn't shake, ones that circled in my head all afternoon:

> Mom has cancer . . . It's just on her skin right now. I am a little scared but I believe my mom. She's not a liar. It's gonna be ok.

> They left the coffin open. Mom looked too small and pale. I'm glad she's not in pain anymore though. She's happier, I think.

> Dad is always watching me. I don't like it. I miss Mom.

> Mom told me alcohol isn't for everyone, especially my dad. Last night he came home with a six-pack.

> I remembered Mom's broken fingers and the week she had a limp when I was five.

> He grabbed my arm and dragged me to the kitchen. I let my body go limp and squeezed my eyes shut.

I was so engrossed, I didn't even realize the gong had sounded, signaling the end of Rest Hour. "Amanda," Sarah said, standing over my bed. "Earth to Amanda." She waved her hand in front of my eyes. I jumped a bit, my body tense with unease.

"Huh?" I turned to Sarah, my eyes sore like they had been shocked by daylight after hours in the darkness. "Sorry," I mumbled, holding the journal in my hand. Sarah's eyes went to it, then darted back to me. Even in her post-stomach-bug fog, she was conniving.

"I forgive you," she said, her hands on her hips.

"For what?" I said, still inside my head.

"The compass, idiot. You failed, but it's fine. You're forgiven." Her face suddenly seemed sharper, less comforting than the one I'd stared at in the weeks before. "What's that?" She pointed at the notebook.

"Oh, nothing." I started to put the book in my tote as Sarah grabbed for it. "Stop!" I yanked back. "It's none of your business, okay?"

She let go. "Um, okay, crazy. Is it like your diary or something?"

I nodded, tucking it into my tote. I didn't trust leaving it alone, that Sarah would keep her hands off. I carried it with me, through every activity period that day, and even to dinnertime scraper duty.

When I arrived, Catherine was already there, globs of mashed potatoes lolling on her tongue. "Hi," she said, her acknowledgment a surprise.

"Hi," I said back, equally curt. Dinner was cornflake chicken, mashed potatoes, and green beans, a mess for scraping. "Ugh," I grunted, the grossness of what was to come too terrible to ignore.

"I know," Catherine said, her civility extending beyond the initial greeting. "This meal is particularly squishy." She made an expression of disgust. I sat down and picked up my silverware, then paused.

"I'm sorry." The words were barely audible, as unsure as what I was feeling. Alone at this table with her, I looked at Catherine in a new light. She was a person, one with hopes and interests and desires. Hers were completely different from mine, but they existed. Why did I hate her? I was tired of chasing the impossible, the goal of impressing Sarah like a sick funhouse. Just when I thought I'd done it, I'd figured it out, I'd run into a mirror. It was all a joke, an infuriating one that ate away at my patience. Sarah was no Grace. She wasn't even Rachel.

"It's okay," Catherine said, shrugging. She popped a piece of chicken in her mouth, washing it down with a guzzle of Sprite.

"That's it?" I asked, confused. Where was the blowup, the anger I would have unleashed? "You're not going to, like, punch me or something?"

"I already tried that and it proved a horrible decision." She motioned to the kitchen, flimsily lifting a scraper from the container holding them to our left. "My dad says my ability to compartmentalize will make me a great engineer. It's why all the comments don't bother me." She raked her fork through her mashed potatoes. "I'm not excessively emotional. That's why I'm great at solving problems and why I don't mind bullying. One day, I'm going to be more powerful than everyone who was ever mean to me."

"Oh," I said, her frankness a little freaky. "Well, that's—that makes sense, I guess." I twirled my fork in the potatoes. "Did you ever solve that problem, by the way? The one you were working on last night?" I rested my head against my palm, looking right at her, engaged.

"I did!" she said, her excitement picking up. "During Rest Hour, yes. I'll show you." *Great,* I thought. My olive branch had led to a math lesson. What happened next happened so quickly that I couldn't stop it, and it would change everything. Catherine leaned over, sticking her hand in one of the totes slumped on the floor. We all had the same standard Catalpa ones, each labeled with our name. She pulled out a notebook—Meg's—then realized the mistake. "Oops," she said, and started to put it back, then paused, her brow furrowed. "Wait," she said gripping the journal. "Isn't this the book Meg was writing in last night?"

Caught, I stammered, "N-No, it's mine. It's my diary."

"Please," Catherine said. "As we've established, I'm not the brainless one here. Why do you have this?"

I debated what to say next. I could defend myself, my natural reaction. But what I had read, it seemed more important than a petty fight. "I know, I shouldn't have taken it," I said, looking down. "But I did, so whatever, okay?" Catherine tried to interrupt me, but I grabbed her forearm. "Catherine, listen to me." I lowered my voice, digging my fingers into her skin. "You need to read it. It's—it's serious." She shook me off her arm, not saying anything as she put the book in her bag.

"Is there any level you won't stoop to?" Catherine asked. We scraped again in silence.

"You were right," Catherine whispered the next morning. We poured near-empty bowls of milk dotted with soggy Lucky Charms and Trix into a massive metal pot. The milk sometimes fought back, springing up and soaking our sleeves or spraying our faces.

"You read it?" I asked, wiping a hand against my forehead. It was even hotter today, the air as brittle as the dehydrated land.

Catherine nodded. "What's the plan?"

I was confused. What plan? I stared at her, my face twisted like the sun was in my eyes. "What plan?" I asked, this time out loud.

"I assumed there was a reason you shared the notebook with me. We have to help her, somehow. Was I wrong? I didn't show it to Barrett, but I can—"

"No, no," I said, pouring another bowl into the vat. I didn't have a plan, but that didn't mean I couldn't come up with one. Merely holding the notebook had felt intrusive. I was a voyeur peeking into private moments in Meg's life. What difference was it to intrude into her actual life? "We could go to Laura?" My answer's simplicity and lack of daring obviously bored Catherine.

"That would solve precisely nothing," she said. "Meg's dad is her brother. I highly doubt Laura would turn her brother in to the police?"

She had a point. "The police," I said. I hadn't thought about them. "Let's go to them? They can help, for sure."

Catherine put down the bowl in her hand and crossed her arms, looking up to her left. She was thinking. The pause made me jittery, anxious for whatever conclusion she'd come to. Even then, I hated uncertainty. Not knowing—or being able to control—the outcome of any given situation made me intensely uncomfortable. It made me a good peon: Always ready to act, but never the one to decide what, exactly, the act would be. Always the best friend, never the star. I had thought that approach was safer, a way to taste the fun without bingeing so much it made me sick. In Catherine, I found another person to follow. I wouldn't let her realize it, but I looked to her for answers. For our plan of action. "The police won't be able to do anything," she finally said. "We're not even positive her dad's abusive." She picked up another bowl, the two of us pouring to avoid the attention of the Nancys. "We'll spy," said Catherine, like the answer was obvious. Like it was the only option.

"How?" I asked. There was one bowl left and we both reached for it, our fingers overlapping as we grabbed. Catherine pulled hers back, instead placing her palms on the table, hands backward and elbows locked. She paused again, smiling at nothing in general.

"I'll figure it out."

At Rest Hour, I watched Catherine, waiting for some kind of signal, for any hint of guidance. When she got up to use the bathroom, I nearly followed her there. On her walk back, she dropped a folded piece of paper. Betsy noticed, but instead of attempting to confiscate it, she smiled at me, likely thinking her scraper-duty punishment had brought us together and we'd formed a new bond. *So sweet!* I could hear her saying. *Like, the cutest!* She was oblivious to the fact that we were coconspirators. I liked having a secret with Catherine; it made camp all the more vivid once again, everything slightly electric with anticipation. It was a different high than with Sarah, one grounded in good. I smiled back at Betsy, a sweet girlish one full of innocence, then unfolded Catherine's note.

We're going tonight. I'll wake you. Wear black. Now tear this note up.

My heartbeat quickened. I had so many questions, so much to worry about. But what was the worst that could happen? Real danger was nothing more than a concept, an intangible I had only ever seen on TV or read about in books. I thought the ultimate punishment would be another week of scraper duty, which seemed worth the price to make sure Meg was okay. I held the top of the paper with each hand, my pointer fingers pressing against my thumbs, and I pulled. The tear was a clean cut right down the middle, smooth and easy, a surgeon's cut. I ripped again. And again. And again. It was satisfying, hiding the evidence.

"What was in that note Catherine gave you? So weird," Sarah asked after Rest Hour. We were about to dive into the water, toes dangling over the edge of the H dock, its metal cooled by the water.

"Just some of her survival crap. I don't know why she was asking me." I adjusted my swim cap, looking straight ahead. The rest of the juniors were still filing out, all of us lining the water and ready to dive.

"You're lying," she said, taking a sidestep closer to me. She turned her head, her voice wet against my ear. "Why are you lying?"

"Lying about what?" Sydney asked. She was on the other side of Sarah, craning her body to join the conversation.

"Nothing," I said, reaching out and flicking Sydney's head. Two days earlier, I would have loved this focused attention from Sarah. Finally, she was as obsessed with me as I had been with her, but I'd already moved on. I was over her. Now it was all about saving Meg. "Sarah's being crazy." I made the loco hand motion next to my ear, crossing my eyes as I did it.

"I'll find out," Sarah said, ignoring my attempt to shut her down. I pretended I didn't hear her, looking straight ahead. Julie, the swim counselor, blew her whistle and I jumped right in.

When our cabin lights were turned off and the nightly taps played on the loudspeaker across camp, I tried to keep my eyes open. Junior Row bedtime was nine thirty P.M., not so late we might get a crazy second wind, but not so early we couldn't fall asleep, our bodies exhausted from hours and hours of activity. My eyelids drooped within a few minutes, the crickets chirping outside blurring into a singsong melody. Before I knew it, I was being shaken awake, Catherine's face millimeters from mine. "Shh," she hissed, too loud at first, then quieter. My eyes adjusted to the darkness and I slid my feet around to the side of my bunk, slipping them into the plastic Adidas sandals I'd left on the floor. Catherine motioned toward the door to the bathrooms, one that wouldn't raise questions if it was opened at night. She walked quietly, crouching with each step. I followed her lead, my chest tight with fear. Betsy was a heavy sleeper, her snores as loudly perfunctory as her way of speaking. The other girls were passed out, too, the drinks and snacks from Milk Line heavy in their stomachs. Catherine and I both wore black pajamas, mine a silk button-down and hers a generic tank top and sweatpants. We tip-toed out of our cabin, Meg's notebook in Catherine's hand, and we blended with the dark as we followed the path from Junior Row to the woods. Breaking the rules was exhilarating, our mission seeming like the only thing that mattered in the world. With one-track minds, we barreled toward danger without hesitation, or at least I did. I always struggled to see the big picture. Our feet grinding against the dirty gravel as we dodged the occasional spotlight was all I cared about; the adventure of it all made me feel alive.

We used the moonlight as our guide until we were about fifty feet into the woods, clicking our flashlights on and waving them against the forest of trees. The mess of weeds and overgrown plants covering the floor scratched my ankles, tickled my toes. A few pebbles lodged between my shoe sole and my foot. Neither of us spoke, listening to dry leaves crunching beneath our shoes and for out-of-place sounds—from animals or humans, the tale of Magda still creeping both of us out. We weren't really scared of Meg's dad. We were just going to watch, to do some reconnaissance. Every crack, sticks snapping beneath our feet, moved us unknowingly closer to danger.

"Do you know which RV is hers?" I asked Catherine when the few lights still on at Catalpa were nothing more than specks in the dark and the campground was in view. It was surrounded by a high metal fence, another warning we should turn around, race back to our cabin, and dive under our covers where life was warm and safe.

"No," Catherine said. "But I recall when I drove by the campground on my way to Catalpa that it's not a huge park. We'll find her." When we got to the fence, Catherine grabbed it with both hands and placed her foot in one of the diamonds, ready to climb. Meg wasn't always at camp with her dad; sometimes she roamed on her own. There had to be a vulnerable area in the fence, one she climbed under or through. I traced the perimeter, the fence singing against my moving hand. "What are you doing?" Catherine asked, now a foot or so off the ground.

"I'm not climbing that," I said, nodding to her. My foot caught a part of the fence that was sticking out. "Bingo," I said, getting on my knees and pulling the loose area up. I crawled under, my legs itchy from the dried grass under the fence line. Catherine hopped off and did the same. She looked at her digital watch, its blue glow showing the time: 12:37 A.M. She put a hand over her mouth, miming *Shh* again, and started walking. Most of the RVs were dark, though a few people gathered around a small fire at the center of the campsite, their sunken tailgate chairs and foldable beach loungers cradling their lazy bodies, a few holding a beer or a red Solo cup. Some song about a crazy game of poker played, the volume loud enough to mask our steps but not so loud it kept the entire campsite awake. There was a girl lounging on a boy's lap, her arms draped around him like they belonged there, their bond so natural. I stared, wondering what that would be like, to be in love one day, to adore and be adored. She threw her head back and laughed after he whispered something in her ear.

"Amanda!" Catherine broke my fantasy, the reality of why we were there coming back into focus. Everything was new, an energy pulsating from the scene. The couple in love. The trees shimmering in the moonlight, their leaves dancing with the slight breeze. Catherine grabbing my hand, dragging me to an RV to our right out of view. It was rectangular with faded orange and brown streaks; a light was still on inside. She pointed to the sign next to the door: PERKINS.

I followed Catherine up to its side, my pulse racing and adrenaline powering my feet. She pulled over a trash can and flipped it, the two of us climbing up and balancing on our knees. We heard loud eighties-style music as we pressed our noses to the window. I first saw Meg's dad. He was wearing an oversized T-shirt and trucker hat, swaying in a trance. His eyes were closed and his face was scrunched in pain, or maybe joy. It was transcendent, whatever was coursing through his body. There was also a woman inside, her hair short and dyed some outlandish reddish purple.

She had cracked fluorescent-blue fake nails, which were spread against a bed covered with a rusty, sun-washed comforter. I began to process what we were actually seeing, something we'd all heard about but didn't fully understand. The woman was bent over, shirt and bra on the floor, shorts and underwear scrunched at her ankles. Her boobs seemed to flap, not jiggle, two sagging pancakes resigned to gravity, brushing the comforter every time Meg's dad thrusted. My eyes wide and face hot, I buried my nose into the crook of Catherine's neck. "Oh my god," I whispered, a touch too loudly. Her hand was over her open mouth, eyes as wide as mine. Together, we ducked down and fell off the trash can, trying to stifle our giggles as we rolled into a hysterical pile together.

"We did not just see what I think we saw," Catherine whispered once we had both calmed.

"That was . . ." I tried to find the right word. *Embarrassing. Unexpected. Disgusting.* "I mean, oh my god." There was no better way to summarize our incomprehensible feeling, one of muddled emotions and surprise and discomfort, than with those three simple words: *Oh. My. God.* I giggled nervously again, looping my arm through Catherine's like I had done so many times with Sarah or Sydney or Rachel or Grace. It was only after our limbs were twisted that I realized my mistake, how this wasn't a move Catherine was used to. I felt her arm stiffen, a millisecond of discomfort, before it relaxed again. She yawned, using her free hand to cover her mouth, and leaned her head against the RV, her body melting into the siding. I did the same, the night sky hazy as my lids drooped and my neck grew weak, my head too heavy. It rolled onto Catherine's shoulder and we sat in silence, tired and at our most vulnerable, tweens stuck between youth and adulthood, what we knew and what we had yet to learn. I yearned for the next phase, to be seen as an adult, to have the ability to make my own choices, to not have adults telling me what to do. But there was something serene about childhood, so much of it make-believe and safe. You couldn't get hurt if it wasn't real.

The RV door suddenly opened toward us, nearly hitting me and jolting us out of our daze. The woman who had been with Meg's dad barreled down the makeshift stairs, her stature compact and troll-like. She grunted a goodbye and more lights inside the trailer turned on. I held my breath, hoping she wouldn't notice us. She stumbled after the last step, her ankle turning on a rock. "Fuck," she muttered, wobbling as she adjusted the elastic band of her shorts, and walked in the direction of the campfire. The door was still slightly ajar, warm light spilling out. I crawled to the other side of the steps, near the opening, and motioned for Catherine to do the same. A few inches smaller than me, Catherine squatted in front, placing her fingertips against the wall of the RV for balance. Meg was talking, her throat groggy with sleep.

"What the hell, Dad." I saw a sliver of her legs; she was on a couch, a ratty blanket balled by her feet. We had heard her dad was in some kind of financial trouble and Laura paid for his spot at the campground. *Meg isn't allowed to stay in a cabin because our parents all pay and, like, it's not fair for her to get a free ride,* Sarah had said at the time. This, though, seemed wrong, the difference between my life and Meg's never starker. She had a roof over her head, sure, but the entire setup was as big as my bedroom in New York, my mattress fluffy and full and covered in a crisp comforter, hers thin and colored by faded pastels. Meg stood up from her bed, stretching her arms above her head. It sounded like her dad was searching the fridge, the scene confirmed when we heard the cold crack of a carbonated can. "She was gross. Seriously, I could hear everything."

He took a gulp, the guzzling sound loud and thirsty. "Nah." He spoke slowly, his thoughts muddy from booze. "Deb's a good girl. Your mom would've liked her."

Meg laughed with a bite. "You're joking, right? Mom wouldn't have even liked you." She took a step back, like she knew she was entering rocky waters but she couldn't help it.

"Watch your mouth, you little cunt," her dad hissed.

Catherine and I locked eyes. "What's a cunt?" she whispered, grabbing my arm. I brought my finger up to my lips, my awareness heightened. This was bad. He threw an unopened beer can at her, an extra one he must have grabbed from the fridge. Meg dodged it, her body nimble like she knew some sort of assault was coming. The can rolled away from the couch, creeping toward the opening of the door.

"Fuck you," she said under her breath. "I wish it was you who died," she muttered as she crawled back onto the couch, pulling the blanket over her legs.

"What'd you just say?" Her dad was thundering, his steps heavy as he got closer to the couch. Meg stood up, yelling in his face.

"I wish you were the one who died, you piece of shit!" He slapped Meg, the fleshy contact so loud and jarring it made my stomach turn. Catherine let out a small gasp, the two of us watching the unthinkable unfold. This sort of violence, from a parent no less, felt dreamlike, the reality too unimaginable for either of us to process. He wrapped his fingers around Meg's upper arm, pulling her from the couch and throwing her on the ground. Her raw skin against the floor screeched, like basketball shoes mid-pivot. She was crying, her whimpers full of *I'm sorry*s and *please don't*s. My blood got hotter and hotter, all the wrongs that had led to this moment stirring inside. Who were any of these people, thinking they had the right to tell us what to do, who to be? I thought of every shitty thing that had happened to me over the past year, ever since Grace left. All the stupid social orders I had to follow, the rules imposed by teachers and parents, the many times I'd been told how I was supposed to behave, react, love. The bullshit Sarah made me do to be her friend—the bullshit that never seemed to end. I was tired of it all, and angry. So angry. Screw Grace's parents for moving. Screw my parents for sending me to this stupid fucking camp. Screw Sarah for making me feel I had to prove my worth to her, like friendship was something you had to earn. Screw Laura for not realizing her brother was a monster, for leaving her niece alone with him in this godforsaken middle-of-nowhere campsite. I deserved better—and so did Meg.

Before I knew what I was doing, I ran up the stairs of the RV, pulled open the door, and picked up the beer can. My body was floating, my muscles possessed with a tingling energy as I wound up and chucked the can at the back of Meg's dad's head. Meg was scuffling away from him on the ground when the can hit, the sound juicy. He stopped cold, turning around. "Who the fuck are you?" he asked, taking a step forward. I ran toward the front of the RV, the kitchenette to my right, trapped like a mouse in a maze. I almost froze, Meg's dad's grip nearing as my chest caught. A six-pack sat on the counter inches from my hand, the green cans shimmering like Oz under the fluorescent lights. I grabbed the entire thing, the cans strangled together with plastic, and whipped it at Meg's dad, my throw so forceful I let out a deep grunt. As it left my hands, the release was immediate: the rage I had toward Sarah, my parents, all the people trying to tell me what to do, telling any of us what to do, shot forward in full force. I was sick of the rules, the judgments, the pageantry of keeping everyone pleased. They could all go to hell, starting with Meg's monster of a father. His reflexes were too slow and the six-pack whacked the side of his neck, an artery pulsing as he took another step forward. "You little bitch," he said, turning to Meg. "This one of your frie—" he started to say, his eyes wicked with rage, but suddenly stopped, his face warping. He tried to speak, but only gibberish came out.

Meg hopped on her feet. "Dad?" She put a hand on his shoulder and he started to convulse, his arms flailing and his eyes rolling into his head. Catherine ran up the stairs, dropping Meg's notebook just as he fell, his knees buckling. The singular moment seemed to go on forever, this zombielike dance in the air, as gravity pulled at him. We heard his head crack against the sharp corner of the fridge, the placement of his fall a heartless karmic joke. The fridge housed his true love, his liquid courage, his way of coping with the world. He crashed to the ground; his body continued to spasm, slower and slower until it nearly stopped, the occasional twitch all it mustered.

Meg stood on one side of his body, her hand over her open mouth. Catherine and I were on the other. I quickly squeezed Catherine's hand, which was trembling. I walked closer, unsure whether he was still alive. His eyes looked up, not blinking, just staring. I stared back, until I saw the edges of my sandals, blood seeping into the rubber soles. What had we done?

February 5, 2011, 1:29 A.M.

megaraspellz89: yo what u up to?

clwagner314159: @ the library

exams start tomorrow so it's going to be a long night

megaraspellz89: lol sux so glad i didnt go 2 college

clwagner314159: why are you up? It's so late

megaraspellz89: can't sleep

been thinking about that summer again

you realize its almost been 8 years

2:01 A.M.

megaraspellz89: cat u still there?

clwagner314159: yeah . . .

don't think about it, not worth revisiting

megaraspellz89: then why do you still talk to me?

clwagner314159: don't do that, meg. we're friends now, we've been friends for years

megaraspellz89: then why won't you visit me here? I haven't seen you irl since then

clwagner314159: it's complicated, you know that

megaraspellz89: maybe you just want to keep an eye on me

clwagner314159: are you drunk?

stop being a buffoon

megaraspellz89: you know it wusnt amandas fault

clwagner314159: what?

megaraspellz89: my dad dying

it wusnt her fault

he took pills for his seizures and when he started drinkin agn and being rough n stuff he would sometimes forget 2 take em

clwagner314159: okay

we already knew that why are you bringing this up now

megaraspellz89: well bc i didnt remind him to take them u kno?

n i hated him so much i just wanted him gone

clwagner314159: meg stop I'm logging off

megaraspellz89: so i started throwing them out when he forgot

i don't think he noticed

clwagner314159: WTF

clwagner314159 signed off

9

NOW

• • •

We make it to the Lincoln Tunnel before ten, jaundiced light filling its hollowed core. I open my window and take a breath of New York's stale air, raw from the summer rain that finally broke the heat spell during my drive. It's not welcoming or threatening. It's just there—heavy smog I've grown used to over time that usually reminds me of home but now, compared to the fresh winds of the woods, seems subpar. It simply means we're close. My stomach does a small somersault.

We park in a garage close to my building, Meg sliding her beat-up Jetta into the spot next to mine. "Sixty bucks for a night? Are you fucking kidding me?" she says as she gets out of the car, tossing her bag over her shoulder and rolling her eyes. "This is why I will never be a city person." Catherine adjusts her backpack on her shoulders. The three of us emerge from the bowels of the garage onto the slick New York sidewalks. The world feels new. Clean. I can do this, I realize. Especially with Meg and Catherine by my side. The fact that we're together after all these years is already a feat.

I give my doorman a wave as we walk into our apartment building. "Hey, Hal," I say.

"Who are these gorgeous ladies?" he asks, his Eastern European accent thick.

"Ah," I say, never one to be rude, "Hal, meet Catherine Wagner and Meg Perkins. We're friends from camp," I say, leaning both elbows on the high reception desk. "Um, Hal." I pause, unsure how he'll react. "I know it's against the weekend rules, but can we use the service elevator tomorrow morning?" I bat my eyelashes and give my pearliest smile. Hal has seen me walk in countless times too drunk with red eyes, Jackson storming a few feet ahead. If he understands what the request means, he never lets on, New York's finest at my service. He nods, giving me a wink.

"You got it, Ms. Amanda. The earlier the better, okay?"

Catherine and Meg are wandering the lobby, taking in its glossy interior, the latest renovation less than ten years old. There are mirrors everywhere, plus minimalist furniture and edgy artwork with Dalí vibes. Its sparkle distracted me when we first moved in, but I see it through their eyes now: an ostentatious attempt to build on top of the rat-filled foundation. It's all replaceable: the artwork, the flashy amenities, Jackson.

When I walk into my apartment, flipping on the lights with Meg and Catherine behind me, my throat tightens. There is the gray West Elm couch Jackson and I bought together, a floor sample we got at 25 percent off and our first purchase for the new apartment. The picture frames on the wall are filled with photos of us draped on each other and smiling: upstate at a vineyard; toasting with champagne at a café in the West Village; sun-kissed in the Hamptons, the dark ocean in the background. We look so happy. There is the bottle of Veuve sitting on our kitchen counter, wedged in the corner next to the fridge; we were saving it to celebrate the end of my summer research program, which we hoped would lead to a job offer for next summer. I run my fingers against the thin entry table we pushed behind the back of our couch, a pile of unopened mail on it. Some pieces are addressed to me and some to Jackson; one is to both of us, a postcard from Reggie, when he was at Yacht Week earlier that month and thought it was retro-chic to send postcards rather than texts, on-brand with his love of eighties-era neon windbreakers and Chubbies. Will I miss this, sharing my space and life with Jackson? Things were good before they were bad. Who says we couldn't get back there?

"Guys," I say, so quiet I almost don't hear myself. "I'm not sure I can do this." The postcard from Reggie is shaking in my hand. "He's not so horrible. Maybe I was overreacting. I was sort of drunk back at camp."

"No," Catherine says. "You need to separate yourself from him. None of us are safe until you do."

"What do you mean none of us are safe? I'm the only one he cares about."

"That case cannot be reopened, Amanda." Catherine doesn't give me an explanation and this time Meg keeps her lips pursed together. "Go get your bags and we'll start packing. It's time to finish this."

On a deeper level, I know she's right. Things with Jackson will only get worse. Being with him feels like choking, his hands growing stronger and more possessive each day, slowly suffocating my will to fight back. I walk into our bedroom, its exposed brick wall no longer exciting me the way it did when we first looked at the place. The duffel bags I used to move in are stuffed under the bed. I pull them out, laying them on the floor next to my closet.

"I'm so hangry right now," Meg says from the living room. "You guys want some pizza?" I pop my head out the door. She's curled on the couch, already making herself at home. Catherine's pacing, her eyes wandering around the room, soaking it all in. The pictures throughout are all of me and Jackson. Until now, it never occurred to me that this might be weird. No pictures of our families, our friends. My cheeks warm as I make eye contact with Catherine, then look away, embarrassed by what she sees.

"Um, yeah," I say. "Patsy's? You can use my Seamless account. My laptop's over there," I say, pointing to the bar-sized table in the corner of our kitchen. Jackson would lose it if he knew I was about to stuff my face with gooey carbs. I smile to myself.

"On it," Catherine says, her change in attitude surprising. "What's your password?"

"You're not gonna hack in this time?" I joke. She sticks her tongue out at me as I walk over and type it in.

"When does Jackson get back?" Meg asks, running her fingers through the top of her hair, her legs now outstretched. "Because, honestly, I don't feel like packing you up tonight. I am wrecked." She throws her head on the couch's angular armrest, her hair spilling over and nearly touching the floor.

"Tomorrow night," I say, joining her on the couch. "I think his train gets in at, like, six or something." An exhausted silence catches our tongues, both our faces drooping. We sit and sigh, the gravity of everything we did today weighing on the room. We all know we're about to start a new chapter in our lives. We're on the cusp of the change, its closeness teasing our moods—and also freezing us in this moment, likely the last we'll all spend together. All I need to do is leave, to pack up my things and get the hell out of this horrible relationship. It may not be the full solution, but it's a start; who would believe a scorned ex anyway? I could paint him as a liar, a crazy former boyfriend willing to do anything to bring me down. With Meg and Catherine backing me up, Jackson would be another psycho making pathetic claims to get back at an ex. I daydream about it all, my imagination running as I think of all the ways I can discredit Jackson, until I feel my stomach rumble. It's almost eleven, the city outside dark but still full of life.

"Catherine, did you order the pizza yet?" I ask over my shoulder. She's typing away, the click-clack of the keys almost melodic.

She doesn't answer, so I turn around. The light from my laptop screen glows against her face, her eyes glued to the screen, her brow creased in concentration. "Catherine? What are you doing?"

She looks up, realizing we're both staring. "Done," she says, her frantic energy suddenly gone. "One pepperoni, one white pizza, and one veggie. Are you amenable to that?" She snaps the laptop shut and walks past us on the couch, to the wide window overlooking the city. She stares out, placing a hand on the frame. "It's funny to think, after all this time, here we are, together in New York City. Coconspirators once again."

Meg stiffens, sitting upright. "I wouldn't call us that. Is it too far-fetched to say we're friends?" The sentiment makes me smile. I hope it isn't, too. Catherine's still looking out the window, her arms now crossed. She seems calmer, no longer pressuring me to speed-pack or get out of the apartment immediately. Finally, for the first time all day, we are on the same page. I hop up from the couch, moving toward a mini-speaker and hooking up my phone. Dolly Parton's gentle lyrics fill the room. "Wildflowers." It was our year's song, a reminder of Catalpa and the girls we once were.

"Oh my god," Meg says. "I forgot how obsessed you all were with this song. This takes me back!" Meg cranks up the volume. I sway over to Catherine, placing my hands on her shoulders and turning her around, my hips swiveling to the beat, one arm waving in the air with the music. She's awkward, her face stern for a flash, but then she smiles. It's tight at first, until she looks in my eyes and starts laughing. It builds and builds until it's almost maniacal, her body bouncing awkwardly. Alanis is next, and suddenly we're all jumping, time-traveling back to the early 2000s, our energy revived. We scream the lyrics to every song, *Say my names* and *Strongers* bouncing around the room, our voices the loudest during the camp classics—Dixie Chicks' "Ready to Run," John Denver's "Take Me Home, Country Roads," Pearl Jam's

"Last Kiss," Madonna's "Like a Prayer"—the music drowning out our off-key voices. We are joy. We are free.

We're almost delirious when the bell rings, a loud buzz heard over the music. It's nearly midnight now, all three of us ravenous, crowding around the coffee table and stuffing our faces, the only noise the sound of our chewing.

"God, I needed that," I say, wiping my hands on my dress when I finish. I rest my head back, looking up at the ceiling. *I'm moving out,* I think, repeating it to myself. And for the first time I don't feel scared. I feel excited, like the moment you send in your college applications, the possibility of bad news too far in the future to seem immediately stressful.

"Let's watch a movie," Meg says, her hands on her belly. "I don't think I can talk, let alone move, until I get out of this food coma."

"Would it be inappropriate to suggest *Parent Trap?*" Catherine says. She's perched against the table, jittery as her elbow props up her head above a single slice of pizza half-eaten. "The Lindsay Lohan version, of course."

We push the coffee table to the side and strip my bed, laying the comforter on the floor in front of the TV. It is perfect. Our stuffed stomachs. The movie. The three of us shoulder to shoulder on this makeshift bed, each half-asleep, our guards down, relaxed. It is a type of friendship I didn't realize existed, one of ease and calm and comfort, of old memories rooting us together no matter how we try to shake them. I feel at ease, like I'm a kid again, comfortable and safe. As the movie nears the end, I hear Catherine's signature snoring purr, unchanged since we were twelve. It makes me laugh to myself, my eyes tired and ready to close.

"Amanda," Meg whispers, turning to me. "Are you still up?"

"Yeah," I mumble, my lips almost paralyzed with sleep.

"You deserve to be happy. You realize that, right?" *I don't* is my immediate thought. I have become a person who doesn't think she's allowed to feel true joy, to have healthy relationships, to be loved. Years of internalizing a singular trauma led me, in my deep-est depths, to hate myself and who I've become. To get wrapped up in a cycle of destruction, reacting to one mistake with more, over and over, until I felt redemption was out of reach. There were blar-ing signs that Jackson wasn't good for me, yet some deep part of me thought, *I deserve this, I deserve him. Anyone better would never, could never, love me.* So I shrank myself, melting into who he wanted me to be, isolated and obedient and always there. Perfect for him, until even my best efforts didn't seem enough. My eyes well, Meg's question opening doors to my long-locked-away emotions.

"You can drive yourself crazy thinking about the past, about what could have been different, or punishing yourself over and over again for a single mistake. Don't do that." She grabs my hands, squeezing. "Seriously, don't fucking do it. Sometimes things don't seem fair. How they go down and all that sort of shit. But you can't blame yourself for it all." Had I indulged in a fan-tasy all these years, one that made me both aggressor and victim? It had trapped me in a limbo of sorts, where I pushed the right people out and let the wrong people in.

"My dad, he wasn't a good guy, you know? He was an addict, fine, but it's like what I said earlier today: that's not what made him bad. He had this darkness. A need for control. He resented who he was and his lot in life. And, now that I'm older, I think maybe he hated women, too, because I can't make sense of why else he would hurt my mom. Alcohol flared that up, but it wasn't the reason he acted that way." She pauses, looking away at noth-ing really. "It's not bad to not feel bad he's dead. At least I hope not. My life is better without him in it. Can you imagine where I'd be if he were still alive?" I'm quiet, unsure how to answer. "I guess what I'm trying to say is it's okay to not regret how things went down. It's okay to have complicated feelings about it all. It's natural to replay those final moments in our heads and wonder if the outcome could have been different."

"It still scares me that I killed him," I say, my anxiety unsettled. "It scares me that I'm capable of something like that."

"What are you talking about? He died of a seizure," Meg says, putting a hand on my head. "You didn't kill him, okay? I know that for a fact." I look at her, the glow of the TV illuminating her face. She looks so sure. "It wasn't your fault. My dad had a few seizures that year. It's not like that was his first. I figured you knew that."

I shake my head. I didn't get many details of the aftermath, my parents wanting me to move on from the drama as quickly and cleanly as possible. It wasn't until I started acting out in high school that my mom even mentioned that summer again, and even then it was in the context of what I had seen, not what I had done. "It wasn't?" I ask.

"No!" she says, grabbing my cheeks. "If anyone deserves the blame, it's me." She pauses, propping her head up with her arm. "Catherine will lose her mind if she knows I told you, but it only seems fair." She looks at Catherine, whose snores are a sure sign she's not waking any time soon. "So, my dad took seizure medicine daily. When he got all fucked again and into drugs, he'd forget. At first, I reminded him. I was like his fucking mom, chasing him around to take his meds." A little joyless laugh escapes, then she continues. "And after a while, when I remembered a lot of the bad stuff, I stopped. When he left pills out on the counter, I threw them out. Not intentionally, really. Like, as I was cleaning up. I'm not a fucking murderer, I mean." She pauses, waiting for a response from me. It's late, the entire confession like a dream. I don't even know what to say. "I didn't realize you thought it all was your fault all these years. I mean, we hadn't heard from you in, like, a decade. We didn't know what you knew, so Cat honestly thought you had told Jackson about the pills. And then—" She stops again, another confession bubbling. "So, don't get mad, and I swear to fucking god I wasn't involved at all, but

Cat, like, catfished or trolled—or whatever you wanna call it—
Jackson. She only told me about it after you emailed us, because
she felt all this guilt and then started spiraling and making all
these strategy charts on how she could fix it. I told her she was
being nuts. There was no way you could even know about the
pills. I mean, I hadn't even told her until a few years ago. But she
was convinced somehow it came out in all your parents' convos
with the lawyers."

I start to speak, the words slow to come out. "Wait, wait," I
say, grasping for the right question. "So, I didn't kill your dad?"
Meg shakes her head, her brows angled in concern, like I might
punch her. "And what do you mean Cat catfished Jackson?" The
past few months start to make more sense, Jackson's increasingly
unhinged questions, his obsession with my texts and Adam. Had
that all been Catherine?

"I don't know the full details. She sort of word-vomited it all to
me. Basically, she sent some creepy *Pretty Little Liars*–style texts
as a prank, like a small little revenge plot to get back at you for
the dumb shit you did to her at camp." Meg takes a deep breath,
her frustration with Catherine's plotting still raw. "I told her to
get the fuck over it. You guys were twelve. But, like, too late, you
know? She couldn't have predicted he would react like he did."

My body begins to shake, the emotion uncontainable. I am not
a murderer. There's an explanation for Jackson's behavior. He
was provoked, pushed to a limit he otherwise never would have
hit. "Oh god." I roll onto my back. "This is insane!"

"Yeah, I know. It's all so messed up." She turns on her back,
looking up at the ceiling, too. I wipe my eyes, the knots bunched
in my stomach loosening. "I'm sorry I didn't tell you earlier. Cat's
real protective about that shit and had this whole plan to sort of
protect me, and her, hence the whole deleting ceremony. But it's
unfair to you." She takes a deep breath. "I guess what I'm trying
to say is Jackson has nothing on you. And tomorrow morning,

even if we have to drag you out of this stupid little apartment, you're getting the fuck out of here."

I still remember the noise the beer cans made as they hit his body, the guilt that lurks because I don't feel bad that he's no longer in Meg's life—and who else but a murderer could feel that way? But here she is, telling me I am wrong. I am not a killer. I can't even be mad at her; the relief of this news is so overwhelming it makes me giddy. I start laughing, a delirious giggle that snowballs into a full-on maniacal cackle.

"Amanda!" Meg punches my arm, which only makes me laugh harder. Catherine rolls in her sleep, her snores skipping with a snort. "Amanda!" Meg says again, punching me harder. My hand over my mouth, I take breaths until I'm calm again. "Alls I'm saying," Meg says, "is that Jackson's a piece of shit, just like my dad. And pieces of shit don't deserve people like us," turning back to face the TV. "Fuck 'em."

"Mm-hmm," I say, facing the TV, too. *But he's not so bad,* I think. He had a motive for all his craziness, was poked and prodded by Catherine until he burst. Suddenly, a move seems too extreme. A conversation—yeah, that's all we need. Some time to explain everything, to clear the air. I'll go to my parents for a day or two, until Jackson and I have a chance to get back to a good place. Meg's arm is against mine, her skin warm and soothing, like my mom's circling hand on my back, helping me get to sleep. I pull out my phone and text my mom, knowing she'll be worried by the timestamp but unable to hide my longing to be back in the safety of my parents' apartment.

> Long story, but I'm coming home for a few days. I'll explain tomorrow. Love you ❤

"Good night," I whisper to Meg, who's already asleep. For the first time in years, my mind is quiet. I gently squeeze Meg's left hand, a reassurance to her—and myself—that tomorrow really is a new day.

The subtle glow of the TV shades the room blue, the movie long over and dawn peeking through the windows. There's a jingle outside, my sleeping mind not fully processing what it means. I rub my eyes, face inches from Meg, who's out cold. I turn and see Catherine's no longer next to me. That must be her outside, trying to get back in. I roll back over, nearly letting sleep take over again until it hits: Catherine doesn't have keys to my apartment. Only I do. And Jackson.

I jolt up like a caricature of the "Don't Wake Dad" game we all played as kids. "Meg." I shake her, whispering, before I start to panic. "Meg. Meg!" She looks confused, her deep REM cycle disrupted. I put my hand over my mouth and point at the door. The keys drop, wind chimes crashing on the ground.

"Fuck," he mumbles, his voice low and slow. He's drunk. Most definitely drunk and delirious, which makes sense. I pick up my phone: 4:07 A.M. He must have cabbed here from the Hamptons. There's a text from Jackson, in response to one I sent asking him to come back, a text I don't remember sending. None of it makes sense. My heart is racing, adrenaline coursing through my mind, kicking me into action. I motion at the bedroom, grabbing the comforter and pulling it with me as I jump in bed. I point at the closet, motioning for Meg to hide there. The lights are off, nothing more than the rising sun highlighting corners of the apartment. Where the fuck is Catherine? I look back at my phone and something starts to click, her distant reserve, the all-day jittering, her hovering over my computer a few hours earlier. She did this, she asked him to come back. Her plotting is still far from over. What has she done?

The lock on the door clicks and I push those thoughts out of my head as I hear it creak open, comforter pulled above my head and eyes squeezed shut, hoping, praying, Jackson will think I'm asleep.

"Amanda?" he shouts, the door slamming behind him. I hear a bag thud against the floor. Our neighbors already hate us; what's one more reason? "Amanda!" he says again, stomping toward the bedroom. I keep my eyes shut, until I feel his presence in the doorway, his silhouette hardly visible but there, a black hole sucking the courage out of me. "Amanda, what the fuck. I'm here!" he says, his voice deep and erratic, the way it always is right before he breaks. My hand trembles as I pull the comforter back and sit up, keeping the lights off.

"Jackson," I say, the surprise in my voice obvious. "I thought you were coming late tonight."

"I was," he says, taking a step forward. "Until you texted me. Are you okay?" He takes another step and stumbles, his foot caught on something. "What is this—" he says, and I see the vague outline of his body bent over. "Is this a suitcase? Are you— are you packing?" The pitch of his voice is high, incredulous. My hands are clammy, my tongue fat and immobile. I have to lie. It's the only way.

"No," I start, "I'm taking some things to Goodwill. Come to bed—"

I'm interrupted by the sound of the toilet flushing. The sun rises another inch, enough for me to see Jackson's head jerk toward the doorway. "What was that?" he asks, pressing his hands into the end of the bed. "Who's here?" He pivots toward the doorway and I leap out of bed, weaving around him and making myself an X against the door, my body the only thing between his rage and the bathroom door.

"Stop it, Jackson! It's not what you think!" I shout, desperate to explain everything, but his rage overpowers any capacity he has for rational conversation.

"It's Adam, isn't it?" He grabs my shoulder, the move so quick

I can't stop it, and pushes me to the side, my body flying and my head bobbling.

Everything is fast and slow all at once. Jackson moving past me, opening the door, the edge of our wardrobe coming closer, then making contact, hitting my eyebrow at the perfect angle to slice, the pain sudden and surprising, my eye quickly flooded with blood. I hold my hand up, gasping in shock, crying out for Catherine, telling her to run.

I hear Catherine's voice as a light switches on, my hands covered in red now, both pressing against my temple. It's throbbing, pulsing with my quick heartbeat.

"What did you do to her?" she asks, Jackson turning back to me when he realizes Adam is nowhere in this apartment and I'm on the floor. I'm crying, too, everything unleashed all at once. Meg walks out of the closet, both hands on my face. She's talking, screaming, but I can't process it all. The room is spotty, black dots clouding the edges of my view. I see Jackson walk back in, crouching down. Meg recoils, glaring at him as he talks to me. There's a spike of pain in my head, hammering at my brain. He's saying "I love you" and "I'm sorry," his face full of fear. He buries his face in my chest, the blood still dripping into my eye, onto the back of his neck. "Please, please. I'm sorry. I can't not be with you, Amanda," Jackson says, and pulls away, his face ugly with tears. I pause, looking into his eyes, all soggy and sad. I'm amazed by this brute man's delicate underbelly. He uses it to lure me, its tenderness a promise of partnership and kindness.

"Jackson," Catherine says, the room coming into focus once again. "Please step away from her." She's even-toned and calm. In control.

"Who the fuck are you?" His hand is still on me, but he's looking up at Catherine, his face strained like it's trying to solve an impossible proof. Meg backs away from me now, too, and stands next to Catherine, her face white.

"I am the person who knows about Kelsey Margraff," she says.

"Wait," I say, placing the name as Jackson's ex, the one from college. "What are you talking about?"

"And Alexis Fulton," Catherine adds, taking out her phone. Jackson ignores Catherine, putting all his focus on me.

"Babe," he says, whispering. "Are you okay? I love you, babe, love you." He mumbles it over and over, the words stirring until they're meaningless mush. He has never hurt me before, the copper stink of my blood stinging my nose, waking me like smelling salts after a long bout of illness. Meg was right: fuck 'em.

I gently push him away. "Jackson, stop." I say it softly, the words caught in my throat. I thought they would come out with more force, all my pent-up aggression toward him unleashed. Instead, they're weak, like me. I place a hand over the cut again, and the pressure on the wound gives me a little relief. "Catherine, what about them?"

"You're hurt," he says. "You're not thinking straight. It was an accident, I'm sorry." His hand moves toward my brow. "Let's not focus on them."

I swat it away. "Don't fucking touch me." I try to get up but stumble, the blood coming out faster than I realized. I'm woozy, trying to get my balance. Catherine is talking again, almost shouting this time.

"Your dad has a pretty powerful boss, huh, Jackson. But it's not that hard to hack into your mom's desktop," she says. "She loves a good J.McLaughlin sale." I'm leaning against the bed as Catherine holds up her phone, a grainy white document with typewriter-style text glaring on the screen.

Jackson is standing next to me, holding my arm as I'm bent over the bed. His grip stiffens as he looks at Catherine's phone. "Let go of me," I say, so quiet I'm not sure he heard.

"Kelsey and Alexis both tried to file restraining orders against you. You know this. So do your parents and your lawyer." Catherine is pacing now, like an eccentric detective in an ensemble murder mystery.

"So what?" he says, his grip loosening. "Who cares? It was all bullshit. A misunderstanding. They were insane. Kel was, like, bipolar or some shit and Lexi was a pathological liar. It's not my fault they were both fucking crazy. That's why they never could file anything against me. Who would have believed them?" His tone is suddenly cocky, like Catherine's an idiot he can't wait to squash.

She tsks and shakes her head. "Oh, Jackson. You think I don't know your parents' deal with the girls? That each received a huge check for her silence?" She swipes her phone, a picture of a tiny girl with brown hair looking right into the lens, her eyes full and afraid. Her right eyelid is swollen, a hint of blue peeking through. She must be Alexis. Catherine swipes again. Kelsey. Rachel showed her to me on Facebook months ago. She looks younger here, her hair bleached blond and long. She's sideways, her shirt pulled up to reveal a massive bruise on her right side. Catherine swipes yet again, a photocopy of two checks, each six figures. She swipes to a picture of Jackson pushing me moments ago, my body a blur in the dim room as I fell. Meg is quiet, not saying a word, but her cheeks are splotched with fire, like a Rorschach of rosacea exploded.

Suddenly Jackson turns to me. "Did you plan this? Did you bring them here to get rid of me, so you could be with Adam?" His grip is tight again, his fingers digging into my upper arm.

"What? No, Adam has nothing to do with this. I've told you this so many times. Stop talking about him." I twist my arm; his hand gets tighter. "I said let fucking go of me!" I scream this time, taking my bloody hand and smashing it against his chest, the aggravating reality of everything that led up to this moment coming to a head inside me—and the realization that my anger, no matter how strong, is still not strong enough to get him to loosen his grip. As his body towers over me, his face getting redder, I worry that maybe Meg was right. Is he just like her dad? Would he intentionally hurt me? Suddenly, his body stiffens and his grip loosens.

He turns and I see Catherine by him, gently pressing the tip of a kitchen knife to his back. "I didn't want to have to use this, Jackson." Her voice quivers a touch. "Don't you ever come back to this apartment. Don't you ever touch, talk to, or even look at Amanda again. And keep our names out of your mouth."

"I don't even know who you are!" he says, hands up in surrender. "I'm not going to hurt anyone."

My head is pounding now, the blood still running. "Catherine, what the fuck?" I try to push myself up off the bed, but I'm still too weak. "What are you doing? Don't hurt him," I say, grabbing Jackson for support. He's staring at me, his eyes begging for answers, for me to make this all stop. I remember how much I love those eyes, their rings like a fire that lit me up, how I adored waking up to them, their intensity and the way they made me feel so loved.

"Are you fucking kidding, Amanda?" Catherine says, the knife now waving in her hand. "I'm tired of your bullshit. I don't give a shit about you. I haven't since we left Catalpa. You don't want to leave him? Fine. You two deserve each other. Two despicable people with a knack for ruining everything they touch."

I ignore Catherine, looking at Jackson. "This is all a misunderstanding, okay? We all need to calm down. We can talk."

"Amanda," Meg says as Catherine turns. "Let's go." She's holding out a shaking hand.

"Just leave," I say to Jackson, not acknowledging Meg. "Just for a little, till you sober up. We'll figure this out tomorrow."

"Wait a minute," Jackson says, his hands still up as he slowly turns to face Catherine, the knife still pointing toward him. "Wait a fucking minute. Catalpa? You guys are from camp, aren't you?

You're Amanda's fucked-up camp friends," he says with a laugh. Catherine, off her game for the slightest minute, turns to look at me. Jackson grabs her wrist, the knife falling from her hand and clanging against the floor. Catherine's head whips back around and Jackson's hand goes to her throat and his nails turn white as he pushes her against a wall. He reaches for the phone in her hand, his grip on her neck so hard her feet are barely touching the floor. I try to push him off, to intervene, but he elbows me away, my body again flying to the floor.

And then I hear a sound I will never forget for the rest of my life. Jackson's scream, high-pitched and inhuman, a bird shot midflight. His face kinks, eyes looking up and mouth agape. His grip loosens and he grabs for his side, spinning and looking at me. Catherine falls to the ground, her hands racing to her neck, little more than a cough escaping her throat. "What did she do?" he cries, crumpling and nearly falling on top of Catherine. As he goes down, he clutches our dresser, then melts off the side, puddling on the floor, his arm stretched toward me, his eyes full of worry. He tries to talk, to say something, but he can't, his fingers resting on the knife buried in and slashed several inches across his left thigh. I look above him and Meg's there, shock in her eyes, her hand shaking, her skirt covered with a splatter of dark red.

Jackson's leg is spurting blood all over the room. I run to him, putting my hand over part of his wound, the knife starting to slouch. I'm shouting his name, touching his cheek. This isn't what I wanted. I look at Meg, who's still standing, eyes glazed over. She's crying, mumbling about her mom. All I make out is "He won't hurt you anymore. He can't hurt you anymore," over and over again like she's in a trance.

"Call 911!" I shout at Catherine, my lips trembling. But she's not in the room anymore. I look back at Jackson, my entire chest hollow. Meg's still chanting to herself, now rolled up in a ball on the floor and rocking. There's more blood than I can hold, and

I feel the flow slowing. I know what that means, what's coming next. I turn to the side and puke.

"Hold it together, Amanda," Catherine says as she walks back in, her hands shaking as she snaps on a pair of rubber gloves she must have found under our sink. "Hold it to-fucking-gether!" She never shouts, never loses her cool.

"Is he dying? Is he dead?" I ask between sobs, still petting his hair.

"I think Meg hit an artery. Shit," Catherine says. "The knife was only supposed to be a threat. Shit. Shit. Shit." She reaches into Jackson's pocket, pulling out his cell phone and using his finger, which is twitching, to open it. She's deleting texts, presumably the ones she sent from my computer asking him to come home.

"What the hell are you doing? Call fucking 911!" I'm screaming, my vision blurred with tears. Meg is still rocking, useless in a corner. "Catherine, hello. Call 911!"

"Your phone," she says, ignoring me. "Where's your phone?"

"Call fucking 911!" I shout again. She reaches for my phone, a hairline fracture now sketched across the front. She opens it with ease, my password my birthday, and she deletes my end of the conversation.

"Done." She slides Jackson's phone back into his pocket. He's mumbling words, but none of them make sense. His lips are light, trembling from the blood loss.

Catherine picks up her own phone. A deep breath, then she dials. "Hello?" she says into the speaker, her voice uncharacteristically frantic. "Hi, um, yes, I'm freaking out. Our friend was attacked by her boyfriend and we fought back and now the guy is bleeding. I think he's dying."

"Calm down," I hear someone on the other side of the line say. "Where are you?"

As Catherine keeps talking, I look down at Jackson and, for the second time in my life, watch the light fade from a man's eyes.

10

THEN

. . .

I will never again run as fast as I did from that campground. The moment I realized Meg's dad was dead, the world went into slow motion. I looked down at my feet, the dark red pooling under my shoes, and just stood. I didn't yell or cry or vomit. I was still, my environment blurred and fuzzy, an old television set out of focus, the voices nondescript and faraway. His eyes stared up at me, dull marbles shining in the aggressive light of the RV. He was calm, his wrinkles and anger lines smooth, a perfectly constructed wax figure, his mouth slightly ajar, a hint of foam spilling out one side. This wasn't happening. I tried to calm myself. It felt like I was watching the situation from afar, disassociated and outside my-self.

"Amanda." Catherine grabbed my hand. "Amanda," she said again, pulling me toward her. I fumbled over my own feet, clumsy and forgetting how to walk. Nothing was the same anymore, color draining from my world as fast as it drained from my face. "Stay with me," she said, snapping her fingers in front of me. She pulled me close, hugging my body and rubbing my arms. The friction snapped me out of the shock I was feeling, at least enough to bring me back to the present. "Here, sit." She sat me on the couch, where Meg's blanket lay. Meg's head was on her dad's stomach, her body shaking with heavy cries. I thought this was what she wanted, him to be gone. To be dead. Wasn't that what she had said? But wishing for something and its coming true are two very different things. I took another deep breath, watching Catherine calmly go to work. She picked up the beer I had thrown at Meg's dad, popping the tab and pouring the liquid down the RV sink. She crushed the can, wiped it with a paper towel, and threw it on top of an overflowing waste bin under the sink. She then wiped the six-pack and put it back in the fridge. "Meg," Catherine said quietly. "Can you hear me? Can you look at me, please?"

Meg lifted her head, her eyes red and overwhelmed. "He, I just—" she said through gasps of air. "Is he dead?" Meg knew the answer but seemed to need confirmation. "Shut his eyes, please," she said, looking away. "Can you close his eyes?" Catherine leaned down and wiped her hand over his face, his lids dropping as she moved. She was robotic, every gesture like she was in survival mode, like she'd been trained for a situation of this nature. My hands were shaking, as was my whole body. I felt cold, rubbing my arms to keep my goose bumps in check.

"Meg, Amanda and I came here tonight because we thought you might be in trouble. Were you in trouble?" Catherine sounded like a parent speaking to their child. It was otherworldly, another layer to the entire fucked-upness of the situation. Meg looked back at Catherine and nodded, so slight I almost missed it.

"We," Catherine said, looking at me, "are going to get Laura, okay?"

"What are you going to tell her?" Meg said through sniffles. She was looking at me.

"Are we going to jail?" I asked suddenly, my own face turning into a pool of tears. "What have we done? This is all my fault. It's all my fault." The room started to fuzz again.

"Listen," Catherine snapped, a general in command. "It was no one's fault." Meg looked guilty, her eyes anywhere but on her dad. "Amanda, you and I came here to meet boys, because we heard Meg talking about them at camp. We heard a crash and that's when we found Meg and her dad, who had a seizure and tripped. Right, Meg?"

She hesitated, realizing Catherine was crafting an easy lie, one that was believable, that made sense. "No one can know the truth." Meg said it quietly, not looking at us again. I got up and walked to Meg, crouching down, and stuck out my pinky, almost resting my elbow on her dad's stomach. Catherine did the same. The three of us interlocked, shaking all at once, a simple bond, a secret tying us together, one we promised to leave in these woods forever. I didn't know then that truth is fluid, formed by perspective and experience and other secrets harbored.

And then Catherine and I ran, shoes in hand, so fast the woods whirred at our sides, our fears of bears and raccoons and Magda suddenly gone. We were the scary ones, the girls people should fear. We were the monsters haunting these woods.

We got to Laura's cabin, panting and doubled over, banging on her door until she answered. Her eyes were half-closed from sleep when she came to the door; she looked confused and irritated. I started, the words spilling sloppily; Catherine spoke at the same time, too, our jumbled story only confusing Laura more. Snuck out. Boys. Meg. Finally, she put up both hands. "Slow down," she said. "What happened? What about Meg?"

I told her Meg's dad was hurt, that he had a seizure and we needed to help him ASAP.

"How do you know this?" Laura asked, the fact that we had

actually been there—in the RV—slowly registering. "Shit," she suddenly said, repeating it over and over again as she raced away from the door. "Come in." She waved and pulled us inside. She called Liz, the head counselor, who bunked in one of the rooms in Laura's house. The top counselors and the Nancys all slept there, making them accessible but at a remove. By the time Liz had put on her shoes, the entire house was awake. When we heard the ignition of Laura's car and the telltale crunch of gravel, the car backing up, the clock above the kitchen sink read 2:17 A.M.

"Oh, girls," one of the Nancys said. "You're shaking." She made us a cup of hot chocolate, the steam tickling my nose as I held it close to my lips. "We'll talk later about why you two were there, okay?" She was kind, calm—a master of the crisis rule book. I could see she was scared, though, her eyes bigger than usual and her mouth twitchy.

It was funny to finally be in Laura's house, a spot any camper would have clamored to check out. It was a small cottage with old, soft floral furniture and rooms occupied by aging counselors, reminders of aged singledom—or freedom, depending on your take. One of the Nancys arrived with a few items from our beds—a blanket and sweatshirt for me, an oversized cardigan for Catherine. We were cross-legged on Laura's living room couch, not talking. Catherine looked pale, the color in her skin drained. Nancy draped my blanket over our shoulders and walked us to a bedroom. "Laura wants you two to stay here until she gets back. Try and get some sleep, okay?" A digital alarm clock read 2:43 A.M., the flashing red breaking up the darkness.

"Can I call my dad?" Catherine asked, then sniffled. "Please?"

"It's late, girls. We'll call them once Laura is back, okay?"

We nodded. The grown-ups would know what to do. We didn't know yet they were as clueless as us. Catherine crawled to the center of the rose-patterned comforter, curling into a ball like a doodlebug. I followed, spooning her on the outside. The room was warm, like a glass of heated milk lulling us to sleep.

When I woke up, Catherine was gone. The clock read 8:22 A.M. and my parents were sitting on either side of me, their hushed worry shooting back and forth inches above my face.

"Sweetie," my mom said as I came to, the world a blurry dream. "How are you? We've been so worried."

My dad stroked my forehead and hair, which was a wild dewy mess. "What happened, Mandy?" he asked, his voice gentle but urgent. "Can you tell us what happened in that RV? How you got there?" He was talking down to me slowly, like I was a baby learning to turn my babbles into words.

"I just want to go home," I said, sitting up and rubbing my eyes. My memories felt suddenly hazy, the unspooling of events mushed and meddled. I knew I had seen something I shouldn't have. Had I done something, too? And then it all rushed back: the thick clunk the beer can made when it hit his skin; the smell of his spit as it foamed from his mouth; the relief when Catherine wiped down the beer cans, putting the six-pack back in the fridge, erasing any obvious evidence; the nagging guilt. It ate away at my desire to share more information, to have my parents tell me it would all be okay. It wasn't okay, none of it. The second I saw his head hit the fridge, the blood pooling once he lay on the floor, I knew it wasn't okay. That things would be different. "Where are the police?" I asked, wondering what they knew.

My mom rubbed my shoulder. "Laura took care of that, don't worry."

"What do you mean she took care of it? Where's Catherine?" What did they know? Had they talked to Meg? I didn't want to seem panicked, but my voice turned shrill with each question.

"Catherine's with her dad, honey," my mom said, "and your friend Meg told the police her dad was prone to seizures when he drank and had one while the three of you were there."

A sliver of truth, it seemed, but not the entire thing. No mention of the catalyst. Of me. I was both relieved and terrified, the image of him staring up at the ceiling of the RV replaying over and over, an old movie haunting my mind. I never wanted to watch the life slowly drain from anyone's eyes again. It gave me a chill, the memory; it had sucked away some part of my soul, the hole gaping and drafty, a pathway to somewhere damp and dark and cold. My dad put his arm around me, his touch bringing me back to the present. I felt my lips, chapped and trembling.

Then they launched into a hurricane of questions: Where was my counselor? How often were Meg and her dad at camp? Did the counselors do bed checks every night? In the morning?

Their questions swirled, leaving me exhausted all over again. It was the beginning of a new drama, one created entirely by their fear. And that fear quickly turned into anger—an anger I had never seen in them before. It wasn't directed at me, but at someone else, something bigger. At Catalpa. At Laura, specifically. That type of combination tricks the mind into blocking out rationality and lucidity. It gives you tunnel vision—but what light is there really at the end? I was thankful for their anger, though; it distracted them from asking me more questions about the event itself, prying to find out every detail about what actually happened in that RV. They didn't actually care. They were madder about how I had gotten there in the first place.

Laura was in the kitchen, sitting at the dining table with Meg, Catherine, and Catherine's dad. They all turned to look at me and my parents as we walked down the stairs, each exploring our faces for answers, for a way to make this all go away, to erase what couldn't be erased. "Amanda, girls," my mom said, looking at Catherine and Meg, "why don't you go upstairs while we adults sort through some things." They nodded and followed me up the stairs, back to the room I had slept in. My blanket was still there, a lump of flannel piled at the center of the bed. I crawled up, burrowing my face in the blanket and wrapping it around my shoulders. Catherine and Meg were on either side of me and I stretched my arms, still holding the blanket, and pulled them into my grip.

"I wish this was like Harry Potter's invisibility cloak," I said, ducking under and enveloping us all in a fortress, the light soft red and hot underneath. "Then we could, like, disappear and run away all together." Catherine giggled, a nervous, tired sound. She rested her head against the bed, rolling into the fetal position just as she had hours earlier. Meg was quiet, stiff. "Are you okay, Meg?" I asked.

She licked her lips, dry from the summer sun. "I'm not upset he's gone," she said, so low the sentence sounded unearthly, like something was deep inside possessing her with its spirit. "Don't tell anyone I said that, please," she added, her eyes suddenly round and desperate. We were all a little feral, unpolished but innocent no more. "If you do, I'll tell them what you did. What you both did." She hissed as she spoke, the severity of her threat slipping off her lips like it was ready to sink its fangs in us. Before Meg's dad, the tiniest look or passing comment in a friendship meant everything—like the world could end at any minute if things didn't go perfectly. Now we saw how stupid those worries were. How this, this was what would end us. Not some girl thinking we were lame or some crush never returning our affections. We were the only thing that could ruin each other.

"Never," Catherine said. "We promised in the RV and I meant it."

"Same," I said, the air under the blanket feeling holy. Even then, at that age, I realized the three of us were bonded. We would never forget that summer, that night. It would forever scare, motivate, shape us. We heard shouting on the other side of the door, obscured but loud. It was my dad's voice. I pulled the blanket off and walked to the door, putting my ear against the unfinished wood. Lawyers. He was talking about lawyers. Meg and Catherine joined, the three of us silent with our ears pressed, like prisoners on death row awaiting our arraignment date. It wasn't until we heard footsteps climb the stairs that we spoke again.

"Remember," Meg said, "not a word to anyone."

My parents opened the door, grabbing my hand and pulling me down the stairs. I followed, ever the dutiful daughter. As we walked out of Laura's house, she stood awkwardly by the door. She started to speak, to fumble over her words, unsure how to wipe the aggrieved look off my parents' faces. By nature, she was a nurturer, always wanting to take care of people and make them smile. This situation wasn't in her comfort zone. It was new territory. My mom uncharacteristically raised her hand. Her flat palm inches from Laura's nose signaled "stop." My dad looked right past Laura and spoke to Catherine's dad. "Doug, we'll call you tomorrow." He nodded, uttering a thanks and giving a small wave as he headed up the stairs to get Catherine.

My parents marched me from Laura's house, past the lodge and Roost, all the way back to my cabin. No one was there, all the girls at the second activity period of the day, which was field. I sat on my bed, numb and motionless, as my parents scurried around the cabin, grabbing my shower caddy and clothes and throwing them into my trunk and a massive duffel bag. I leaned onto my pillow, once again curling up as I stared at the wall. As I put my hand under the pillow, I felt a piece of paper, the edges so sharp I gave myself a small cut. It was Sarah's stationery, her squirrelly writing, like she couldn't hide her inner ugliness when she expressed herself on paper, all over it in big caps: *LESBO*. She had drawn two stick figures holding hands, *Amanda* ❤*s Catherine* scribbled beneath. I crumpled the paper; my blood pumped with rage. Not at the word, or what she was implying, a stupid, pointless insult only a loser from small-town America would make. I was mad at how absolutely horrible she was, that I had let myself get so caught up with her. I left camp without saying goodbye to a single person, not even Sarah. It allowed for a clean break—I'm pretty sure I would have murdered Sarah, too, had I seen her that morning. There's a freedom that comes with going wild, letting your inner demon do exactly what it wants. But there's even more power in staying calm, in making a decision to move on and not acknowledge bad behavior. It diminishes it, cutting at the source of its strength.

Once I was in my parents' SUV, the cold air prickling my skin, I leaned against the headrest, closing my eyes as the forced air blasted against my sweaty face, then rested my head against my mom's lap, the sobs sudden, heaving and breathless. "I want to go home," I gasped. "Please, take me home." She petted my hair, her touch as magical as ever. And for only a second, it felt like maybe everything could be all right.

Tennis reminded me of life before that summer. Its rules weren't overly complicated or strict. Just enough to keep things orderly. I craved its normalcy, the escape that came with the focus required: the ball flying toward me, the positioning of my feet and shoulders, the sweeping of my racket, the contact, the follow-through. I loved the control of it all, knowing with enough training I could determine the outcome. It's why, when we got home, I didn't up-end life too much, why I clung to my social scene with Rachel and the popular girls. I didn't share a single detail of what happened with my friends in New York. My parents were embarrassed that they'd put their daughter in such a predicament and asked me to keep the events to myself, said that it wasn't appropriate to share this story, not even with Rachel. When she asked why I was home early from camp, I just said, "Something weird happened." She nodded, then started telling me all about Drew's pool party and who kissed whom.

She was like tennis, the predictable repetition of a singular neon ball sailing over the net. Back and forth, consistent thwacks and bounces interrupted only by the occasional sneaker squeak or player grunt. There's a cleanliness to the sport. A simplicity. Same with Rachel. I knew what I was getting with her: a queen bee too interested in herself to pry unless it benefited her. She was simple, a puzzle I could figure out in minutes. She was misunderstood, a girl I wanted to impress but who also wanted to impress me, deeply insecure, a by-product of absentee parents and an overachieving brother whose accolades she could never live up to. I needed simplicity, stability—especially once the lawsuit started—and so did she.

Catherine and her dad visited a few times that fall, her dad meeting with the lawyers my parents had hired. We kids were never part of the discussions, relegated instead to my bedroom, where Catherine and I sat on my bed listening to Backstreet Boys or playing Crash Bandicoot or helping each other with school projects (me taking on the creative elements and her the technical ones). We spent a good amount of time together, sometimes tiptoeing outside of my bedroom to try to hear what our parents and the lawyers were discussing. There was occasionally exasperated shouting, more from my parents than Catherine's dad. We'd look at each other, curious but never saying a thing, and turn up the volume of whatever was on.

Only once did Catherine bring up that day. It was early winter, a light dusting of white sweeping the city streets. Cool, cloudy light filled my room, the bright, moody kind that makes you feel like you're at the center of a snow globe, all peace and quiet and calm. "What do you think happened to Meg?" she asked. We were gluing balsa wood sticks together to make a small hut for my science class. I played with the Elmer's glue on my fingertips; it had hardened into clear crumbly chunks on the tips. I wondered what Meg was doing, too. All the time. Was she with Laura? Was she in a foster home? Were our parents robbing her of a stable future? Were we? Had she told anyone what really happened? I didn't say any of this, though. Better to avoid the details, to never wonder what might happen. Because what good was that, worrying about yet another thing? My guilt was still messy then, consuming my quietest moments and eating away at my conscience. I hoped that if I didn't talk about it, if I bottled it up and tucked it away, it would disappear. Life would go back to normal. I shrugged in response to Catherine's question. "I dunno," I said, pretending I didn't really care. She handed me a new batch of balsa sticks and we kept gluing.

"Do you think she broke our pact?" she asked.

I looked up from the wood. "Shh," I said, my face stern. "Are you kidding me? Shut up, Catherine."

"What?" she said. "It's just us here. No one can hear us."

"You have nothing to get in trouble about. I do. Are you trying to ruin my life?"

She looked down, taking the glue and lining one of the sticks with it. "We were all there," she said under her breath. "If we hadn't gone inside . . . ," she started to say, trailing off. "You weren't the only one involved is what I'm trying to say."

We didn't talk about it again. That's why, when Catherine sent the first email a year later, I ignored it. She probably thought we were friends. And we had sort of become close, spending weekends together while our parents hashed out the lawsuit. But I didn't want it to stick. The longer I was in New York, the more I wanted to pretend none of it ever happened, that I'd never even met Catherine or Meg. I had done my best to ignore the memories, the images of Meg's dad forever in my head, and they'd started to fade. If I ignored Catherine and Meg, maybe they would fade, too.

The lawsuit was settled in late spring, only a few months before the next session of camp was supposed to start. We hadn't gotten much, but that wasn't the point, my parents explained. It was to set an example. To make sure this didn't happen to someone else's child in the future. That seemed like stupid logic to me; the series of events that led us to Meg's dad was so particular, the path a set of unique dominoes, each more disastrous than the previous. But what did I know. I was a kid, my parents and the lawyer kept reminding me; even though I shouldn't have snuck out, even though I shouldn't have been in that RV, I should have never had to witness what I did.

I read online that camp closed two summers later after rumors of how Laura's brother died, of the lawsuit, made their way from campers to campers' parents. No one reached out to me—not Larry or Sydney or Sarah—until we all went on Facebook friending sprees in the late '00s, but I assumed my name was sometimes whispered among them that next year. Maybe even now. "Remember that New York girl who ruined camp?," they probably say to one another. Sometimes I stalked old campers on Facebook, never sending a request but watching from afar. They all looked the same, just taller with straighter hair and whiter teeth and curlier lashes. Girls full of promise. I probably looked like one, too. No one knew the truth, the darkness I expertly hid.

Eventually, life became pretty standard. School, tennis, parties, college. Adam. Yet part of me—a part bigger than I liked to admit—missed the drama that came with messiness. Predictability provided no thrill. Stability left me with very little to look forward to. Maybe it's why I gravitated toward Jackson. I wanted to play outside my self-contained court, even if I knew it was against the rules. Running from what happened that summer was about guilt, not about repentance. When enough time passes between you and the thing you feel guilty about, you get complacent. You forget why you created your boundaries. You miss fire and start playing with a flame, just to remember the rush it brings you.

But the flame is hard to contain. The more you want it, need it, encourage it, intentional or not, the more it grows. And if you don't stop it before it gets out of control, it will burn you.

11

NOW

. . .

"Amanda," Dr. Neuhaus says, "it's good to see you." It has been about six months since Jackson died, a week since we finalized a deal with the Huxleys, and six days since I read Catherine's letter. I'm back in the chair across from my therapist.

Do I start by telling her about that night? The sadness I felt as the police stuffed me into the back of a car, sandwiched between Meg and Catherine. But also the relief. I was still processing what had happened, that Jackson was dead, that Meg had done it, that Catherine had, in a way, plotted it all. Watching her coldly go through his phone, sifting through his messages like she knew exactly what to look for, made me see firsthand the extent of Catherine's calculation. It made her good at her job, at separating numbers and codes from reality to see both the trees and the forest. It turned out it could also make her a borderline sociopath. And in her quest to protect Meg, to mess with me, she killed someone. Not Meg. I would never fault Meg. In the back of the car, I scooted away from Catherine, afraid I would catch whatever psychotic disease was eating at her brain. Meg stared straight ahead, her eyes still glossy. We didn't talk about what we were going to say to the police. We didn't have to. We already knew there was a way to tell the truth without telling the whole truth. I hardly got through my interview, gasping every few seconds for breath and tissues, the reality starting to set in. Jackson was gone. Dead. Not coming back. In the moment, I felt shock, the most intense loss I had ever felt, like he had scooped out a part of me and taken it with him to his grave. I don't know what, exactly, Catherine said to them, but her story seemed to match mine: We were friends from camp, we reunited because I needed help leaving Jackson, and they came into the city to help me move out. He showed up, attacked me, Catherine grabbed a knife, he went for her, and then Meg picked it up and stuck it in him. It was self-defense, we claimed. The history of Jackson's texts and calls, the cut above my brow, and the fingerprints on Catherine's neck were all obvious evidence. Hal even backed up the narrative, sharing anecdotes about the nights we came home drunk, Jackson storming ahead, me trailing behind crying; having to ask the super to fix a hole in the wall; the neighbors' complaints of noise. The Huxleys moved so quickly, making calls from their columned home in Georgia. They didn't want their son's (i.e., their or the Warners') name in the paper. And so it all moved fast, from the initial arrests to closing the case—with a few conditions, but no charges pressed.

Do I tell Dr. Neuhaus about calling my mom? How I fell into her arms when she walked inside the jail? I could hardly speak, my exhaustion and relief crashing into a manic rush of emotion. Catherine was sitting on a chair, giving a statement to the police. She looked nervous, on edge. We all were, I guess. I walked past her and we made eye contact, the last we ever would. Catherine was released that night and neither Meg nor I had heard from her since—until last week. The warmth of my mom's arms around me, like a promise that everything would be okay, pulled me out of Catherine's icy glare. It gave me hope. Meg was held at the police station that night, the outcome of her confession—that she wielded the knife—still a question mark, until the Huxleys paid her bail. Both my parents took off work that week, smothering me with reminders that I wasn't alone, that they would love me no matter what. So I told them the truth. About Meg's dad, I mean. That I had thought all this time I had killed him and I couldn't lie anymore. It was damaging everything I touched. And then I told them about Jackson and all the little aggressions that led to the biggest, an ice pack pressed against my brow, a gushy blue reminder of what his vitriol could do. My parents ended up hiring a lawyer for Meg, letting her crash at our place whenever she needed to meet with her, a friend of theirs from college who worked at a fancy midtown firm. They paid for the lawyer because they wanted Meg to have the best, but also because Meg's having a good defense meant I wouldn't get dragged back into the mess. The Huxleys ultimately said they wouldn't press charges if we all remained silent, each of us signing an NDA about the events of that night and the abuse that led to it. And Meg's lawyer required that she go to therapy, paid for by the Huxleys.

Do I talk about Rachel and how she came to visit me the day after Jackson died, not saying anything, not calling me out for my horrible judgment or for the horrible things I said to her? Jackson had convinced me that Rachel was nothing more than a Sarah, a vapid mean girl who used me for her twisted plots. That was unfair to Rachel, who was real and funny and loyal— and had been for over a decade. I had been the bad friend, not her. She stayed with me the next few days, sleeping next to me in bed and rubbing my back when I woke up screaming, Jackson's blood haunting my dreams. We watched Bravo nonstop, zoning out and laughing at the mindless drama of the women's lives. It was what I needed, this easy, low-stakes escape.

Or should I start by telling Dr. Neuhaus about last week, the day after Meg was exonerated when we met at a diner near my parents' place? It had classic New York City vibes with silver paneling on the walls, big windows steaming against the frigid temperatures outside, and cheap Christmas decorations—snowflakes, shiny balls, plastic pine—draped on the edges of the booths. Across from me in a booth, Meg smiled. She reached her hand across the table and placed it on mine. "In many ways, this is your fault for dating such a prick." She laughed, then got serious. "But seriously, thank you. I am forever indebted to you and your family." She paused, adding, "I know you needed to get out, but I am sorry it happened that way." I gave a weak smile. Part of me was happy Meg had done what she had done, but another part of me still missed Jackson. He had been a huge part of my life, the person I thought I was going to spend my future with. If Meg hadn't done what she had, would I still be with him? Would he be the one across from me instead of her?

"How's the therapy going?" I asked. Before things were sorted with the Huxleys, Meg's lawyer suggested she get a psych assessment for PTSD, in case it helped her defense. Turns out not processing what had happened with her dad had also worn on Meg, causing a sort of psychosis in highly stressful situations. She started seeing a teletherapist shortly after. She hardly remembered stabbing Jackson, said it was more like a fever dream than anything. We all process life in our own ways, I've realized. No matter what you've been through, it's fucking hard. But we both made it out alive—at least for now. So we have something to celebrate.

"It's been helpful, yeah," she said, looking off. "I call her every Wednesday. It's good, you know? Talking about shit I stuffed down for so long. Even stuff when my dad was alive. I'm remembering a lot more. My therapist says they're repressed memories. Very deep in my feelings and all that crap." She laughed. As we were chatting, a random skater kid, the flat brim of his hat wide and his pants saggy, came up to our table. He couldn't have been more than thirteen. He dropped a scrap of paper on the table. "This is from her," he said, nodding out the window. We both looked up but only saw the back of a black puffy coat, hood pulled up.

"Who?" I asked him again, but he was already walking away.

"Dunno, but she gave me this!" he said, flashing a twenty-dollar bill.

The scrap read, *Check your phones*. I looked at Meg.

"It can't be Catherine," she said. "She's back in Boston."

We unlocked our phones at the same time. There was a new icon on the home page, something called Whispr. I'd seen journalists talking about it on Twitter. It let you send encrypted messages that disappeared seconds after they were read. It was near impossible to track. "Should we open it together?" I asked. We both pressed on the icon and then started reading.

Amanda, I've never really liked you. Sure, we had our moments, but we both know a friendship was never in the cards for us. When I ran into you in NYC a few months ago, it reignited an anger I hadn't felt since I was twelve. I wanted to mess with you a bit, like the way you messed with me at camp. I wanted Jackson to think you were cheating on him and break up with you. A little pain for all the pain you caused me so many years ago.

I know Meg told you what I did. I swear all I wanted was to make a small mess in your life. When you accepted my Facebook request, it gave me everything I needed: Jackson, pictures of you and Adam, party invitations, your whereabouts. I sent a few texts to Jackson and it all seemed innocent enough, until you emailed me and Meg out of the blue.

That's when I realized I had messed up. I never thought you would be so stupid as to break our pact, but you were. And I assumed you had told Jackson about Meg and the pills, not realizing you knew nothing about it. The assumptions, in the end, were what put me in a tailspin. Still, in the beginning, how was I to know my texts and meddling would trigger not just jealousy but actual danger? It wasn't until you reached out to us and I dug a little deeper into Jackson's past that I realized what I had awoken. And by then, it was too late.

Part of me wanted to ignore it all. To let you suffer. But I had no choice. Reopening the case would hurt Meg, and maybe even me. And if anything happened to you, Amanda, it would be my fault. I just couldn't let any of that happen.

I'm sorry I caused you both more trauma. I'm sorry we had to go through this. I'm no good for you. For either of you.

Once again, we find ourselves with a shared secret. But it ends here. This is my goodbye. And just know, if either of you share what really happened, I will find out. After all, you've seen what I can do.

Goodbye.

When I reached the end of the message, the words turned into pixels scattered across the screen, like ash blowing in the wind after a bonfire. I looked across the table at Meg, whose finger was still on the screen. She looked up with an absent expression, like I'd interrupted a daydream. "Does this mean it's finally over?" she said, her tone little more than a breath.

The message made it clear that I didn't know Catherine. Looking across the table, I realized I hardly even knew Meg. We each knew a slice of one another, perhaps the darkest part. I was tired of this drama, of the secret after secret that seemed to emerge, of always being mad or scared or traumatized. I turned my phone to Meg and held my finger over the Whispr app until it vibrated, clicking the X in the top corner. "Deleted," I said. She looked up again, surprised. She took her phone and did the same.

"Goodbye might not be such a bad thing, right?" She smiled.

When we finished our meal, the check paid, Meg said, "That summer at Catalpa, you guys saved me." She cowered a bit, a shyness in her I had never seen. "I guess this past summer, it was my turn to save you." She gave me a hug, one that she meant. "Stay in touch, okay?"

We both knew we wouldn't—but that it was okay. It was time to move on. The thing is, Meg and Catherine are now my past. Two parts of my very unlucky, damaged, baggage-filled past. I am allowed to move forward. I am allowed a fresh start.

I take a deep breath and look at Dr. Neuhaus. I'm twelve again, countless paths at my feet. "It all started when my best friend Grace moved to California . . ."

This time, I promise myself, I'll choose right.

ACKNOWLEDGMENTS

My brilliant agent, Michelle Brower, was the first person to make this dream of mine feel like it could be reality; she held my hand as I killed darlings and twisted plotlines and sent spastic emails with too many exclamation points. Thank you, Michelle, for believing so wholeheartedly in this story and all the others I throw your way—and for being a generally wonderful person. Danya Kukafka, Michelle's partner-in-crime: you have the sharpest eye and the gentlest tone, the perfect combination. I feel beyond lucky to have you both in my corner.

Sarah Stein: you have been the ideal collaborator while working on this book. Your enthusiasm, vision, smart edits, actionable mom-hacks, and lol-worthy texts have made this entire process a true joy and I'm so happy to now have you in my life. Endless thanks as well to the entire Harper team— Katherine Beitner, Robin Bilardello, Katie O'Callaghan, Hayley Salmon, and more—for your creativity and support, and to Alice Lawson at Gersh for your passion for this book.

The road to publishing a debut has been winding and bumpy and full of pit stops—and there are a zillion people and places to thank for offering inspiration and encouragement when I most needed it: Camp Oneka, for providing five of the best summers of my life and introducing me to the loveliest, spunkiest girls in the world; Stephanie Mehta, my mentor and friend who has long championed my career (and with that given me the confidence to keep writing); my entire *Marie Claire* family—in particular Anne Fulenwider and Riza Cruz for their kind leadership and teaching me the art of a tight edit (though you both know I'm still partial to a flowery sentence)—and Jen Ortiz, Kayla Webley Adler, and Megan DiTrolio for making life at *MC* a total delight and overflowing with laughs, as well as Jenny Hollander, Danielle McNally, and Rachel Epstein for their continued collaboration; Julie Buntin for organizing Catapult's 2018 Don't Write Alone program and Gabe Habash for leading the critically helpful workshop I joined there; and, of course, Heather Lazare and Chelsea Lindman for creating the Northern California Writers' Retreat, which gave me the time and space in 2018 to finish the first draft of what would eventually become *The Wild One* and introduced me to a truly incredible group of women writers. Speaking of . . .

Lina Patton! My work wife, my literary soulmate, my earliest and most diligent reader. Thank you for tirelessly dissecting draft after draft, for personifying a sparkling glass of bubbly, and for bringing together the most supportive unyoung writing group imaginable: Sheila Yasmin Marikar, Avery Carpenter Forrey, Liz Riggs, and Brittany Kerfoot—you are all so talented and hilarious and FUN, I can't imagine working on book two while publishing book one without you. My many early readers—Kristin Zimmerman (my fellow former wild one and ultimate cheerleader); Stacy Lee Niemiec; Caro Claire Burke; Catie and Will McKee; Emily Isayeff; Carl Kelsch; Kristin van Ogtrop; Emily Demchyk; Ariel Pechter; and Megan Abbott, Jo Piazza, and Caitlin Mullen—thank you for giving me and my novel your time.

My sisters, Kelly and Jen: thanks for believing in me and this book since its infancy, letting me dig through your childhood memory boxes, fact-checking all my camp references, and being my best friends. The McKeegans: Kevin, for being my excuse to talk to your brother; Mary, for reading and loving *The Wild One* throughout its phases; and Beth and Pat, for inviting me to Lake Wallenpaupack that first summer, embracing me as your own, and watching our two tornado-ish children whenever I need to chase my goals. My parents, Alan and Kathy Leahey: none of this would be possible without you pushing me outside my comfort zone as a kid, your insistence on educational excellence, and your unconditional support. I have always believed I can achieve whatever I set my mind to because you never let me think otherwise, and for that—and your top-notch grandparenting skills—I am forever grateful.

Patrick George and Ronan Alan: you keep my heart full and my feet grounded with your silly stories and adorable coos and snotty noses and warm hugs; being your mom is my favorite job of all. (So, so, so many thanks to Jade, Laura, Tarika, Jailene, Alyssa, Melissa, Morenique, Sashana, Jhamoy, Namiah, Grace, Sakile, Pashanna, and all the teachers who have cared for my boys over these past few years.) And Pat, my husband: this has been a long process, yet you've never wavered, consistently sharing your Eagle Scout knowledge, helping me laugh off the moodiness that comes with writing tense scenes, keeping the kids entertained on weekend afternoons when I need to put more words on the page, and shaking up two dirty martinis to toast the moments worth celebrating. I love you, and couldn't do any of this without you three.

ABOUT THE AUTHOR

Colleen McKeegan is a writer and editor who's held roles at *Marie Claire*, where her work was nominated for a National Magazine Award, Bloomberg, and *Fortune*, among others. A native of Allentown, Pennsylvania, and a graduate of Georgetown University, Colleen now lives with her family in New York. As a child, she spent five summers at an all-girls sleepaway camp in the Poconos. *The Wild One* is Colleen's debut novel.